Sparrow in a Tin Can

Sparrow in a Tin Can

C.K. Turner

NEW YORK   LOS ANGELES

Jacket design by C.K. Turner
Jacket Copyright 2023 by Winding Road Stories
Interior book design by A Raven Design
ISBN#: 978-1-960724-08-3 (pbk)
ISBN#: 978-1-960724-09-0 (ebook)

Published by Winding Road Stories
www.windingroadstories.com

for katherine. who took me to vermont first.

"Whatever way you cross the border. Something about the foliage. It's so not real, it's so not real. It's so distinct. It just is. You see a sign 'Entering Vermont.' Click. It's the trees, it's the variety. Dense. Colorful. It's a haunting kinda … that's a weak word, but …"

WALTER RAYMOND HUNTER JR.

OPENING

January, Vermont. Chartered 1762. Essex County, Northeast Kingdom. Population 3. Missing 1987. January, Vermont is a ghost town. But don't confuse January, Vermont with a few abandoned buildings outside old logging camps and discarded mines. Because January, Vermont went ghost the way people go ghost. Missing, never found, now haunting the Vermont woods. Felt by some but never seen. Late October nights, heard on old winds revisiting the forests. But once upon a time January, Vermont was an ordinary small town. A small town never destined to be a poster-child for small towns. January, Vermont did have a white clapboard church and a covered bridge, but the leaves didn't quite touch over the streets, there was no army of uniformed milkmen greeting the day, the mailman did his rounds with a cigarette hanging off his lip and if there had been, once upon a time, a white picket fence anywhere in town there was no evidence it had ever been there. But if you had walked down Church Street in early October of 1987 you'd have seen Pastor Phillips polishing the sign of the town church, Mr. Fitzroy and his boy stocking shelves in the gas station across the street. If you'd followed Main Street out of town you'd have passed Boucher's Dairy Farm, where a man could set his watch by the hour and minute the cows got milked—every 12 hours, on the hour. And if you'd doubled back down the road you would have likely seen Sam Samuel, Vietnam vet and armchair mechanic, in the house on the edge of town, rocking on his porch, or perhaps poking under the hood of one of the dead cars in his yard while his son laid out in the grass daydreaming and picking shapes out of the clouds. This is not just a Sunday drive through the country. This is the story of a little town Vermont lost. A place you can no longer get to by any road. Because you won't find January, Vermont on any map. You won't drive through it on accident or on purpose. Vermonters won't be able to give you directions. There are no covered bridges that spit it out. And only three people in the world know where it once was. Because one week in late October of 1987 the little town of January, Vermont started losing its grip on the world. Roads stopped turning there. Trees started growing. Road signs went missing. People got forgetful. And one by one the little black dot—*January*—fell from every map, past present or future. Swept off the face of the earth. This is a story from the dustbin of America, about a town no one remembers existed, and the three people who still call it 'home.' Somewhere up ahead we're looking for a little lost town. And somewhere up the road, we'll find something else.

PART 1

ORANGE

ONE

THE CRACK of the church's spine woke Angus.

Above the gas station, the boy's bedroom walls danced with a jack-o'-lantern glow. A burnt smell clogging his nostrils.

The boy out of bed, at his window.

Flames swung at the stars. Night air warmed to summer heat, July on his face, a small sun risen in the middle of the night, across the street ... clapboard wilting, shutters falling, windows dripping like water, flakes of the old hymnals scattering in the wind. Layer by layer, fire peeling the church like an onion. The boy's nose on a journey of years. The top layers, the last five, ten, twenty years, new and plastic-y—the full flame scent of varnish, paint, floor lacquer. And deeper still the old layers, fifty, one fifty, two hundred impossible years deep in the bones of the church—wood and stone —searing his lungs with an old world incense cast off pews of oak or cherrywood, maple altar or cross, cedar beams or siding. The boy coughed. The church so far gone, Angus unsure who he'd call? His father, at least, but his voice tarred to his throat. The boy watched from his bedroom window. Warm, but getting hot, relieved to be across the street, wishing he was further ...

A black silhouette below, printed on the flames.

Pastor Phillips.

Watching his church burn.

Standing over scattered gas cans, like pews. His open hand reaching for the flames. Like he was preaching.

"*Three,*" a voice said, Angus looked to his bedroom door, shut, but dripping voice like a faucet in the night.

"*Three . . .*"

Dad's voice, awake now, moving down the hall, speaking to itself.

"*Three . . .*"

Angus heard the door to Dad's reading room whine back on its hinges. Tall footsteps cross the continental dark. The click of lamp. The rustle of pages.

"*Three . . .*"

In the next room, Vern Fitzroy, father to Angus, stood at his open window watching the church blow away like autumn leaves. He licked his lips. Tasted something like ... cigarettes ... in the air.

Flames *flickered. Popped.*

Slid.

Crinkled.

Why, he'd never noticed it before, but that sound ...

ruffle

rustle

wrinkle

The flames swung a right hook.

whisper

whisk. Threw a left jab.

Flit. Shh.

Two drunken fists thrown wide.

Flip-flick-shhh.

... was the sound of paper. *All* the sounds of paper. Bound paper. Loose paper. Bible paper, book paper. Magazines, newspaper. Picture, print. High gloss, low gloss. Smooth as ice, pulpy as Vermont Northern Hardwood ...

The ceiling fan stirred the room softly.

Mr. Fitzroy's eyes turned to a magazine on the end table.

His thumb peeled back the cover.

slide. crinkle.

The church split in two, like campfire logs.

TWO

Somewhere, across town, in a small house surrounded by a litter of dead cars, a man stirred in his sleep.

One bloodshot eye took the glow of the clock.

3:33

The room heard his heart working. A man in harmony with a clock.

tick.
  tick.
    tick.
beat.
  beat.
    beat.

Well-timed as Bach.

Mr. Samuel sat on the edge of his bed wondering why he was awake. Feeling rustled, stirred, jostled from sleep; *shaken* awake.

"Henry . . . ?" He looked around the room.

He was alone.

His mouth dry.

"You . . . *all* right . . . Henry?"

He looked to his bedroom door. It was shut. No light on in the hall behind. No sign his son had been up. Body heat fading from his sheets, bed cooling to winter beneath him. He sniffed. Was something burning in the house? He limped across the floorboards, his hand stopped on the doorknob.

He did not twist the knob.

He did not turn the handle.

Strangely, he stood still. Sensing something behind him.

Sam Samuel turned.

Glow at the window. He pulled the blinds. No. Not in the house. Some kinda pocket-sun crashed off in town. Glowing low and soft. Orange Northern Lights, come to Vermont. Something burning deep in town.

tick.
  tick.
    tick.
beat.
  beat.
    beat.

His face, dirty with guilt for watching.
His hand, itching for a cigarette.

THREE

IN THE HALLWAY of the small house surrounded by a litter of dead cars stood a barefoot boy.

Henry Samuel.

Unsure why he was awake. Mistaken it for a midnight piss. Now realizing, he didn't have to go.

The boy stood in the hallway.

Wind blowing the warmth of his footsteps out of the hardwood. Feet caught in the flow of a river. Cold air coming from beneath dad's bedroom door.

October air.

Outside air.

Bitter on his toes.

Dad had opened a window. Let Vermont *inside*.

Vermont's newest stream ran down the hallway of the Samuel house. Whistling, like a ghost.

The boy sniffed.

Was someone burning leaves? At this hour?

The boy shivered.

The door—at the deep end of the hall tall, lean and dark.

"*Three,*" Dad's voice, half-aloud on the other side. "*Three in the morning ...*"

Henry let out a breath. It was warm as August on his teeth.

FOUR

IN THE MASTER bedroom of the small house surrounded by a litter of dead cars, Mr. Samuel was cold. His skin brittle like thin ice. His stomach groaning like rust. His mouth tasted like night damps.

Yet he could not turn from his bedroom window.

Far off something flickering in town ...

The church, going under.

Perhaps the flames said something.

Perhaps they spoke in Morse code.

I'll go there, thought Sam Samuel, *I won't go there.*

I like it, he thought, *I don't like it.*

A moment later the bedroom window slammed.

Mr. Samuel sat on the edge of his bed. Wrapped in a blanket. Trying to warm up. Needing a smoke to do the job.

"Three o' clock . . ."

Henry, deep under the covers of his own bed, three pairs of socks on each foot, heard Dad's voice, awake now, moving down the hall, speaking to itself.

"Three . . ."
Dad's footsteps creaking wood.
"Three . . ."

In the kitchen Mr. Samuel put a kettle on. Reached for a box of tissues. Tried to blow the church out of his nose.
He drank three cups of tea,
hot as he could take them.
Anything but a cigarette.

FIVE

Henry lay in bed. Feet frigid.

Heard dad put the kettle on again.

Four cups.

Five.

Coffee? Tea? Hot milk?

Outside,

the sky glowed orange. The boy could smell the road-tar scent of fire. Something bigger than leaves burning ...

But what?

Then it told him.

The organ was last to go.

Like a toddler smashing keys,

the church organ began to play random, sour notes

a million miles away.

Covering the town like a blanket.

Then one long blast,

like a ship calling for help.

Sinking underwater.

SIX

MORNING THEN, had come to the little town of January, Vermont. The sun peeking over the hills like a nosey neighbor at a fence. The sun did this every day, and every day saw the same thing. Pastor Phillips, in some way, tending to his house of God. Vern Fitzroy and his boy, in some way, tending to their house of gas. Mr. Boucher, out in his barn, tending to his cows. Sam Samuel, in the house on the edge of town next to the covered bridge, tending to nothing in particular; here and there ministering to a dead car in the yard. January, Vermont was a forgettable small town. Even the sun knew that. Maybe that's why she liked it. But when the sun came to the fence the morning of October 30th, 1987, she dropped her cup of coffee. Worry fret her eyes. Down there, in the little town of January, Vermont, something was dangerously missing. The town had lost its church, somewhere back there, last night. In the long miles between sundown and sun up. Morning then, and the worried sun combing the town with golden fingers, looking for the church. Realizing it was lost. A knot in the pit of her stomach.

SEVEN

Daylight come morning, and two boys across town sitting up in bed like mirror images of each other. Henry Samuel. Angus Fitzroy. The frosty Vermont morning sluggish with sun. Grey and glum at the windows. And then two boys stepping into their own respective hallways, no dads in sight. Shut up in their rooms. Sleeping from the long night. Hallways frozen over from windows left open or reopened, air thick with the scent of smoke. Boys feeding themselves breakfast. Leaving for school, without saying goodbye.

Except Angus Fitzroy didn't go to school that day.

Stepping out the front door of his gas-station home, he was punched in the face by the sight of the church *not* being there. A few last, black timbers rising up like the burnt ribcage of some impossibly-inland beached whale. The church lost somewhere back there, last night, three deep in the morning. The woods around the town silent. As if they were about to say something, but didn't. Angus Fitzroy felt his heart pound one special time. Suddenly he was sneaking back inside, quietly climbing the side of his gas-station house so not to wake dad, to his second-floor bedroom

17

where he sat perched in his room, like a bird in a nest, watching the tarred black hole across the street.

Wondering ...

Who would come to say goodbye?

EIGHT

THEY HAD TAKEN the pastor away.

He had not hidden. He did not care that he was caught.

Like God had told him to do it.

Henry Samuel stood looking at the burnt field in front of him. This strange version of a farmer's fall burn. The school day was over. The day was getting Vermont dark. A state that manufactured its own brand of dark. Held onto dark by waving away street lights like cigarettes. Turned down interstates like whiskey. Vermont was a state that liked it dark. Was, for fourteen years, its own country Henry had learned in school and now he was on the cusp of fourteen himself, almost understanding how Vermont felt because he could measure its sovereign nation fling against his own turn on the carousel.

He looked down the road; it looked like a lot of roads in Vermont.

They all looked the same.

It went somewhere. So why did he feel like all Vermont roads went nowhere? Suddenly he felt the loneliness of the only state that was once its own country and still acted like one... that country where nature was always lighting leaves on fire. The old country where the hills are leaves and the rivers are men's best pissed away thoughts, whose folks stay in nights, and if they must go out, know they are guests. Where high noon is a stranger and midnights collect. That country made up of covered bridges, old highways, the north faces of trees, shadows from beneath barns and the silence of a country that's having a lover's quarrel with the sun.

Henry left the lot.

Crossed the street and turned the corner behind the gas station.

The red light of a cigarette smoldered. A voice husked through the smoke, "Henry Samuel."

It didn't sound like Mr. Fitzroy.

Henry looked at the cherry held between two fingers. Did not recognize the hand. "Who's there?"

The cigarette simmered. Rose to a pair of lips. Lit a face.

"Angus?"

The smoker took a drag. "Where's your butt buddy?"

"What?"

"Not sure I ever seen you without Ethan Chambers. Figured you two must be Siamese twins or lovers. Or both."

Henry didn't respond.

"Hopefully he's not dating someone else," Angus goaded.

"Like Cindy Barker?"

"Shut your fucking mouth." Angus stood like he was ready to come at Henry.

Henry, ready to run.

Five seconds passed.

Angus took a drag instead.

"Since when did you smoke?" Henry asked.

The red light blinked on and off.

"I was born to smoke."

Angus had the kind of name that put him in Limbo. Some kind of bastard in-between name that would map out the rest of his life.

A name too rough for a boy to shoulder, too foreign for future fellow-adults to swear by. Dave was the name of a man you'd trust with your bank account. Harold was a name of a man you'd someday count on to do you taxes. Grown-up names a boy would grow into. Then there were names that insured a boy would stay a boy forever, Connor, Donny, Benjamin, Ryder. Billy could grow into William, Mikey into Michael, but Luke was stuck, no matter what the Bible said, Luke was a kid who would grow old but never up. A prisoner never be able to escape his own name. He would fumble through shit-rate jobs in a world that hadn't figured out how to monetize being a boy. But at least a boy like that would have had his childhood. Kids named Conrad or Colton or Chase would never fit into adult country with their kid's-stuff names. Boys named Cornelius or Xavier or Thaddeus would never fit into kid country, with the way they worried about being home on time, or saving their allowance. But at least both groups had a place, once upon a time, yesterday or tomorrow.

Angus Fitzroy had no place in this binary world of kids and adults. Give a kid a name like that and it's the same as not baptizing them. And, by the way, Angus hadn't been baptized. His parents had given him one of the few names that ensured he would never belong anywhere. Peter, James and John went on. Brody, Riley and Andy stayed behind. Angus was the name of Limbo. A name too old for a boy. A name too young for an adult. A sound both tribes raised eyebrows over. Angus was the kind of name that made a boy start smoking cigarettes at sixteen. Angus Fitzroy was a full two years older than Henry, which to a boy of almost-fourteen is a continental distance, a cultural difference, the language barrier between almost-fourteen and sixteen is troublesome, even if you ignored the names. It was easier to get by on English in the Frenchiest parts of Quebec City.

"I didn't know you smoked," Henry said.

Angus shrugged. "Smoking's good for you."

"It is?"

"Sure. You ever sit by a campfire in the woods?"

Henry nodded.

"All the memories around that, Dutch-oven cooking, dad on guitar, maybe a ghost story or two, smores ... campfires are the bricks of truth, justice and the American way."

"Ok," Henry said.

"And a cigarette's all that wrapped in paper. A portable campfire."

"My dad says smoking's bad for you," Henry said.

"Your dad smokes," Angus pointed out.

"Doesn't that mean he would know?"

"If it was bad for you, he'd quit."

"He's hasn't smoked in forty-three weeks and six days," Henry announced proudly.

Angus stopped smoking. The cigarette hung low in the dark behind the gas station. "You sure?"

"Positive."

"How positive?"

"100%"

Angus tapped ash. "If you say so."

Vermont was very quiet.

"How do you even get them?" Henry asked.

"My old man."

"He gives them to you?!"

"Fuck no. He comes out to smoke, but sometimes he doesn't get to finish before someone shows to gas up, so he puts it out and sets it up here to save for later." Angus pointed between two bricks.

"You steal them?"

"I *borrow*."

"But you don't give them back."

"Sure I do." Angus took the last drag. Put the stub-filter up between two bricks. Fished another cigarette from the wall. He sparked his lighter. Dragged. "See?"

"You borrow something and don't tell nobody they call that stealing."

"Who?"

"Pastor Phillips."

"Funny, you burn down the town church and don't ask nobody they call that arson." Angus's eyes narrowed.

Henry didn't have a response.

The state waited patiently for either boy to talk.

"You won't go somewhere else?" Angus asked.

"Maybe we'll drive the twelve miles to Whitechapel."

"Seems like a waste of gas."

"Says the guy whose dad sells gas."

"Doesn't mean you should waste it."

Angus took a drag, waved his free hand like he was pushing the conversation away.

The boys had too many years between them. And the problem of names.

They had nothing left to talk about.

"It's getting dark," Henry said.

"Uh-huh."

"I guess I should be getting home."

"Yeah, sure, I get it, you're afraid of the dark."

"No, my dad gets mad if I'm late for dinner," Henry defended.

"Right. Cya around," Angus said in a tone that said goodbye.

Henry watched the older boy thresh his lungs once. Home was a half a mile off. Walking distance. He took a step.

"Why do you think he did it?" Angus called after him.

"Huh?" Henry turned.

"The pastor."

"Whaddya mean?" Henry asked.

"Burnt down the church. I saw you standing across the street. Why d'ya think he did it?"

"I dunno, why do *you* think he did it?"

"I asked first."

Angus sparked his lighter randomly, dragged his cigarette casually.

Henry bit his lip. "Maybe God told him to do it."

Angus snorted, "Or maybe someone else told him to do it."

"Who?"

"*Le Diable.*"

"I don't speak French."

"Satan."

Henry felt the Vermont chill suddenly. He'd remember hearing a group of kids had played with a Ouija board last summer, that some ghost or departed spirit had told Scott Leslie, through the board, it had pot. *Scott I got pot.* And everyone said it was Angus Fitzroy who actually owned the Ouija board. So here Henry was, behind a gas station, in a very dark corner, in a very dark state, with a boy who smoked cigarettes and owned a Ouija board, talking about The Devil, and a pastor who burnt down his own church.

"Doesn't make much sense, you know?" Angus explained. "That's how Pastor Phillips makes his money. Would be like my old man burning down his gas station. Then what? Or Mr. Boucher shooting all his cows."

Henry stood silent.

"It's strange. Don't you think it's strange?"

Angus blew smoke.

Henry stood still.

"And no one seems to care. You're the only one I've seen cross the street."

"What do you mean?" Henry mumbled.

"The fire department came and said it was too far gone, nothing worth saving, just hung out in case it leapt to the trees, but it didn't so they just let it burn, that's why there's nothing left. Didn't even get out their hoses. And the whole day, in this piss-little town where nothing happens, you'd think that old ladies and men would wander over and give a shit. They were all born, blessed, baptized, married and buried there. Not to mention all those Sundays. But no one has. Hell, at the very least you'd think folks would shuffle over to play Sherlock Holmes—look at the pile of ash, see what was underneath all these years. It's like no one cares, or ..."

"Or what?"

"Eh, nevermind." Angus dragged his cigarette.

"Nevermind what?" Henry asked.

"Forget it."

"No, say it."

Angus watched smoke rise off his cigarette.

"It's just like ... well, I was watching all day, and people both pretended nothing was wrong, *or* crossed over to the other side of the street like they were ..." Up with the cigarette.

"Like they were what?"

Down with the cigarette.

"Afraid."

Angus stamped out the butt. Fished a new one out of the bricks. Sparked his lighter. Dragged and spat smoke to the first bashful star in the sky. "You're the only one. Not the firemen. Not the police. Not the choir director. Not old lady Brogan coming from next door for a quart of milk. No one crossed the street to take a look except you. Got a whole town built around a church and it's torched to shit by its very own pastor and no one shows up to the funeral except you Henry Samuel, and I'm sitting here smoking, wondering why that is?"

Henry did not have an answer.

But there Henry stood, and there Angus sat, the only two at this sad funeral for a church in a town full of prime clucking folk, the only two who had noticed, really *noticed*, the murder of their church ... and one of them didn't even go to church on Sundays.

"Have you ever even been inside?" Henry asked.

Angus spat smoke.

"So why do you care?" Henry whispered.

Angus put his cigarette to his lips. "Because no one else does." His voice filtered through the grit of his cigarette. He sanded thirty seconds off his life.

"Everyone in town shows up there on Sunday—"

"Everyone but you and your dad," Henry added.

"Lemme finish, kid."

"Sorry."

"Everyone shows up on Sunday, but no one shows up for the

funeral. No one but you. And I'm sitting across the street asking why. And the funny thing about asking *'why'* is you do it enough, and sometimes you get an answer that smacks you in the face. Why is Henry Samuel the only one who came to the church's funeral? And isn't it obvious. Who would be most likely to show up for any funeral? Henry Samuel, the deadest boy in town! The only boy who's been there and back! The boy who shouldn't be alive! How long was he dead? No one knows, but they found him in the swimming hole, bloated, eye-opened dead!"

"Shut up!" Henry started walking away.

"Don't pull your panties up your ass-crack, kid. I didn't mean nothing by it, it's just ..." Angus's voice trailed off.

There was something uncooked in it.

Raw.

Henry stood ten feet off, his back to the boy who smoked cigarettes.

"It's just what?" Henry asked.

The gas station light around the corner buzzed.

The air still smelled like fire and leaves.

"That church. It's just ..." Angus's voice got mixed up with smoke. "You don't know what it looks like."

"Whaddya mean?" Henry asked.

"The church, when it's full of people on Sunday. From the outside."

"You mean what *did* it look like?"

Angus nodded.

"It looked ... pleased." Angus's face bent. "Nah, that's not it. More like ... ... smug."

"Smug?" Henry repeated.

Angus nodded. Conferred with his cigarette. "Smug."

Henry could smell the cigarette mixing with the raw musk of Vermont's annual death scene. They smelled like very different ways to die. One was permanent, the other temporary. Like Jesus. Somewhere between dead and sleeping.

Henry watched the cigarette blink in and out like a radio tower.

"When God sets stuff on fire, it comes back," he said.

"Whaddya mean?" Angus asked.

"Like leaves. He sets the whole state on fire every year, and they comes back. But when man sets something on fire ..."

"So we'll see if God told him to do it," Angus said.

"I guess."

Everywhere, a priggish breeze was blowing, coming from the north. The gas station sat quiet in the growing dark.

"You don't think the church is coming back," Angus said.

Henry shook his head.

Angus burnt his lungs.

"You don't think God burnt that church, working through his little shepherd?"

Henry shook his head.

Angus played with fire.

"He stood over it," Angus said, "watching it burn, huffing the fumes, like it was the world's worst cigarette. Maybe the preacher—"

"Pastor."

"Whatever. Maybe he just wanted to smoke." Angus took a drag. "*Wanted to smoke* ..., but cigarettes weren't *bad* enough."

The boys met eyes.

Henry bit his lip, continued the thought, "... ya, because a cigarette only kills you, maybe your kids, because there's all that talk of second hand smoke, and think about it, if it's a sin to cut down some plants and dry them out and roll them in paper and light it on fire and take it in your lungs, if *that* is a sin, what do you think it is to take a gas can to a church, slice a match on the steps and stand there two nights before Halloween and take a whole burnt religion into your lungs? And then there's all the town folk. Because life is like being in an ocean, waiting for Jesus to come save you, and church is the lifeboat, the way you keep from drowning until you find dry land, which is Heaven, but Jesus put this guy in charge of the life boat, and he sinks it, knowing all these people were gonna drown."

Angus watched ghost stories rise off his cigarette.

"There was only one church in town," he said quietly.

The boys met eyes.

"You saying he drown the whole town?" Angus asked.

"Maybe." Henry whispered.

Angus Fitzroy ran smoke between his teeth. "God, they teach some weird shit in there."

"*Taught*." Henry corrected.

"Yeah," Angus nodded. "*Taught*."

Henry looked across the street. Sunset went quick this time of year, in this part of the country. And somehow the charred hole across the street was blacker still.

"Are you afraid?" Henry asked.

"Afraid of what?"

"God."

"No. I'm afraid of what he's been collecting in there," Angus said.

"Huh?"

"You don't know what that building was, do you?"

"Whaddya mean?" Henry asked.

"What it *actually* was. You believers can't see it. But I see it. People go in, people come out. And something's different. Past the smiles. Used to sit on my bed and watch Sundays and try to figure out what it was that goes on in there, then I realized I'd seen that look before—my dad's face, the drive home from the dump. We drop off an old sofa and a broken washing machine and suddenly my dad's got the same look on his goddamn face. Well, think about people. What do they do with the bad, garbage parts of themselves? Everything to the left of good? The parts that make politicians lie, the parts that make men hire prostitutes, the parts that make them knife other men, the parts that make them touch other men's wives, the parts that make fathers take belts to their kids, the parts that makes kids light cats on fire, the parts of you that felt sad when you hit the bird with your wrist rocket, where do you take them?"

"The church," Henry said quietly.

Angus took a drag.

"You're saying a church is like a dump," Henry said. "For all the bad parts of people?"

"Lot of people dropped off the worst parts of themselves in there. Over a lot of years. The church is really old," Angus explained.

"*Was* really old."

Both boys looked across the street.

"Well, God takes the sin," Henry explained.

"Takes it where?"

"To Heaven, I guess."

"You think sin can get into Heaven? If people smuggling sin in their bones can't get in, how could *raw* sin get in?" Angus asked.

"I dunno."

"No. That sin ain't gone nowhere. It's sitting right across the street."

"*Was*."

"Huh?"

"You said *it is*, but you meant *was*. The church burnt down."

"Right ..." Up with the cigarette.

"You think that sin's still there?" Henry asked.

Angus burnt a hole in his Levi's. "You tell me church boy. If the fires of Hell can't burn up your sins, how could the fires of man?"

"What do you mean?"

"Hell's got the hottest fires in creation, right? Hotter than anything we can stoke in a furnace. So Johnny Sinner lives a bad life, and doesn't shuck his sins off to Jesus before he dies, the weight of his sins plunge him down to Hell, where he's burning for all eternity or whatever. But if sin could be burnt away by fire, then soon as the devil's put the iron to Johnny's feet, there goes his sin. Poof! No sin, no weight, wouldn't Johnny float back up to Heaven? If sin were vulnerable to fire, then why's Hell full of fire? They in the business of getting rid of sins down there? Correct me if I'm wrong, but that's God's business, or so he says. God scrubs sin, Satan collects sin. And you ever know a collector who destroys their collection? Doesn't make any sense. So, if sin were flammable Hell wouldn't be full of fire, now would it ... which means all that sin God collected for 200 years across the street wasn't affected by Preacher Phillip's little campfire."

"Pastor."

"Whatever."

Angus took a drag on his cigarette.

Henry stood uneasy behind the gas station.

Vermont is quiet country. The silence tends to beat the shit out of you, unless you keep talking. The boys felt the coming blows. Henry spoke first.

"Have you done it?"

"Done what?"

"Crossed the street."

Angus shrugged. "Bit of a walk."

"Crossing the street? That's a bit of a walk?"

"Yeah." Angus tried to sound convinced.

"Are you afraid?" Henry asked.

"Fuck no."

Henry looked at the boy.

"I'm not afraid to cross the fucking street," Angus said with a fist.

But Henry wasn't convinced. He didn't know a boy two years older than himself could feel fear. A boy named after Limbo. A boy who looked normal smoking a cigarette. Angus drifted still white cinema from his fingers. Henry had never known a smoker that was afraid. It didn't make sense. Everyone knew smoking killed you. Even smokers. And they still smoked, which meant they weren't afraid to die, were not afraid of Death. Sat daily shaking hands with their killer. And here sat this boy, full of two-year-older, sixteen-year-old grit, riveted at the seams with a name plucked straight out of Limbo, steeled by the sexiness & hilariousness & the famousness of smoking in lonely America, carrying the weapon that had fired the smile that had killed every American rebel and put them to dust, sitting here in the footprint of a gas station across the street from the murder scene of a church admitting by staying put that he was afraid *to cross the street*.

Angus dragged his cigarette. "I'm a smoker. They just sit around, you should know that better than anyone."

"He's quitting."

"He bought a pack of Cattlemans this morning from my old man."

Even in the growing dark Angus saw Henry's face go white and slack jawed. "Sorry you had to hear it from me, kid. But hey, one is less than two, you think anyone ever quit cold turkey? People claim they do, but that's bullshit, trust me, we sell the cigarettes. People taper out, you know? Slowly. He'll hide it for a while. Smoke one or two here or there, it's just the way it goes."

"It's just ..." Henry's voice got lost somewhere in Vermont.

"It's just what?" Angus asked.

"*This* morning."

Henry's eyes went to the crime scene across the street.

Angus looked too, at this late-late afternoon Americana, gritty, grainy movie. The burnt center of town that had turned into something so lonely. The church had left a shadow. A big black shadow. Burnt it into the ground. Pounded into the dirt by the bullfists of fire. And now this sad corner of this sermonized state slouched without its fine, firm chapel. Over there, behind the missing church, the trees rose like the hands of drowning men. A plastic sack ran through the burnt field like a lost sheep.

"He hadn't bought any for over forty-three weeks," Henry said in a hushed tone.

"How do you know?" Angus's scuffed voice was suddenly serious.

"I know where he hides them. We kept a calendar. Have you sold him any recently, I mean before today?"

"No. But my old man might have, I'll ask."

"No," Henry said, "I don't think you need to."

Angus sat quiet.

Cigarette waiting to be tapped. Humming softly between the boy's fingers.

He took a drag.

"I got a feeling, Henry..." Angus's voice got stuck in the tar.

Henry saw it in Angus's eyes. The dewy glisten that waters up during horror films. The eyes trying to protect the brain. Obscure vision. Water down the images, the scene, the awfulness taken straight. The quarrel among body parts—the lids refusing to shut, the eyes forced to watch not wanting to see, calling water, to cleanse, block, water-down, wash away, baptize.

The cigarette rose to the boy's lips again.

Smoke did not make him brave.

Lighting things on fire did not work this time, for this boy.

"... your dad won't even try to hide it."

The boys broke staring at the church that wasn't there.

It was time to go home.

The gas station light hummed around the corner. The pump stood motionless beneath the car port. One boy took a drag to warm himself before stepping into the night.

"You going trick or treating tomorrow night?" Henry asked.

"I'm not a kid." Angus put out the end of his cigarette, hid the rest between two bricks. "I'm goin' to Cindy's party."

"Oh, right." Henry kicked himself for sounding stupid. "She invited you?"

"She didn't tell me to stay away."

NINE

Vermont swallowed Henry whole.

Behind his gas station home, Angus stood to walk inside, but he got stuck turning the corner.

The church.

The sight of it *not* being there.

A hole in the town.

Black-trunked trees surrounded it. The church had been tall. But the trees were taller. Sideshow men towering over a burnt match. The boy drifted to the sidewalk in front of the gas station. Stayed on his side of Church Street. Looking across the black river of asphalt. Testing the temperature of the road with his foot. It felt cold. Sneaker be damned, it felt cold. Wind rattled the thinning trees. Branches threw-away leaves like movie stubs. They pelted the boy. He was stuck in that moment, shoe in hand, spider on the wall, willing himself to do what he needed to do. Move! Swat! Move! Swat! Trying to pull-start his own engine, except this time he was wearing his shoes and the spider was crossing the street.

Angus Fitzroy didn't move.

Footsteps came down the marble sidewalk of Church Street. Big, meaty, boot-wearing footsteps, 237 concrete pounds of a man.

Nearby a spider web trembled. Broke. Red flannel. Blue overalls. Brown boots. Rounded beer gut. A John Deere hat. Mr. Boucher's face tucked up underneath in a blackboard slate of shadows.

"Hey, Mr. Boucher."

"Angus." The man tipped his hat. "You all closed up for the night?" He fiddled his teeth with a toothpick ... no, ... his teeth fiddled the toothpick. Mr. Boucher was chewing it.

Angus stared.

He'd never seen a man chew wood like bubblegum.

The hat and clothes and toothpick that was Mr. Boucher didn't seem to notice.

"Huh?"

"Oh," Angus looked over at his service station home.

All the lights were out on the main floor.

"Yeah," Angus licked his lips, "guess my dad closed early."

The man was all hat & shadows. Only the toothpick stood out far enough past the brim of his hat to catch the service station lights. It wiggled and bobbed. Angus could hear the man's jaw grinding.

"I can sell ya something," Angus said over his shoulder opening the door, hitting the lights, stepping behind the counter. "Whaddya need anyways?" Mr. Boucher's heavy hand on the counter. A box of toothpicks. 1000.

"Came out just for toothpicks?"

Mr. Boucher didn't answer.

Chin rolling, teeth chewing, toothpick splintering.

"Hey, won't you get slivers in your mouth?"

"How much?"

"Oh, uh, lemme see." Angus punched on the calculator. "With tax that'll be 87 cents."

A dollar on the counter.

"Hey, don't you want your change?"

The bell rang. Mr. Boucher out the door. His jaw ground. Wood snapped. He spat. The man fished a new toothpick from the box.

Planted it on his lips like a cigarette. But instead of a drag, he took a bite.

And then off down the street.

Angus stepped outside to watch him go. And soon Mr. Boucher was gone. Barely noticed boy. Hadn't noticed church. Angus looked across the street. Something was missing. Not just bricks and mortar. Wood and pipes. Hymnals and Bibles. A chunk of the world had been cut out. The space where the Church had been.

The boy steeled himself again.

He just had to cross the street.

Angus Fitzroy stood on the sidewalk. Breathing quietly. Eyes fixed on the leafy darkness on the other side of Church Street. The space where the church *used* to be. The wind ran through it. Happy the bull building was no longer in its way. Cold Canadian wind crossed the street, hit him in the face, refit his clothes, parted his hair; like a boy might for Sunday service.

He just had to cross the street.

Stand in the burnt lot.

There was nothing to be afraid of.

Nothing.

Old wood. Burnt Bibles.

He looked up the street. The yellow lines ran off into the hills.

Down the street. Trees ran away into the country.

All he needed to do was cross the street.

Step on the marble sidewalk. Foot the grass. Stand in the church.

Go. He thought.

No. He said.

It's just there. Across the street. Just one minute there. Back. Nothing to be afraid of.

He glanced up the street.

He glanced down the street.

The black river of asphalt that'd kept the church away. Once flowing currents of cars. Frozen over now. He could cross. See what it was like, now that the church was ... he tried to think of the word.

Now that the church was ... He knew what word he wanted to say. He could not say it.

Wind shucked the trees.

Passed through the missing church. Like autumn branches. The wind gets stuck on bright green summer leaves, but come autumn the wind gets revenge. Come November, the wind laughs through the skinny-naked boughs. The church had blown away like an autumn leaf. The town was left with winter. This cold thing you survive in Vermont. Another gust from Canada passed through the missing church, hit the boy in the face, carrying the burnt religion, echoes of last night's hissing church, the crack of its spine, two hundred years of pack-ratted sin broiling so hot dogs'd feathered their ears.

He just had to cross the street.

He told himself to step.

He did not step.

He told himself to walk.

He did not walk.

His mind touched towards the street, his foot trembled inside his shoe.

There was less to see, across the street, so why did his eyes feel tired? So much more tired than swallowing the church whole, whitewash, clapboard and all.

He looked up the frozen black river.

Down the frozen black river.

He just had to cross ...

The wind blew. He sniffed.

No ...

No. He didn't.

The church was going to cross the street. Already had. Carried by the wind. Unrooted by the fire. Angus looked back at his home. The second floor of the gas station. Dad's reading room. A light on.

TEN

C-R-A-S-H!!

Angus whirled around. The noise came from old lady Brogan's house next door. Machinery squealing inside.

"Mrs. Brogan?" He called out.

Angus at the window looking in. He didn't see her.

Angus on the porch. Knocking. Ringing the bell. Going inside.

An electric hand mixer thrashed around the kitchen floor like a loose pig. Cake batter splattering walls, ceiling, linoleum floor. Piggish machinery squealing, knocking about, scraping floor, biting cabinet. It bucked up against the table legs. Metal beaters on metal leg howled down the boy's spine.

He unplugged it from the wall.

The pig simmered.

Softened.

Slept.

The T.V. idled in the front room. *"President Reagan's nomination of Judge Douglas G. Ginsburg to the Supreme Court was met with criticism from several Senate Democrats who called the nominee too controversial."*

"Mrs. Brogan?" Angus called out.

No answer.
Big city voices blathered behind him.

ELEVEN

ANGUS STOOD in the doorway of dad's reading room.

The faux-wood paneling. The piles of magazines. Shelves of books. Windows filling up with night. The ceiling fan sleeping silently above. In the deep end of the room, caught under the high-tilt of a crooked lampshade, was dad's chair. Facing away ... when did he move it? All Angus could see was the high back of the chair and Dad's hand.

It turned a magazine page.

flit

"Dad, you know where Mrs. Brogan is?"

Another magazine page fell.

flick

"She left her hand mixer on. It made a real mess in her kitchen."

Tall fingers pulled at a corner.

whisper

"She wasn't anywhere in the house. It's not like her to leave after dark."

The hand turned the page.

whisk

"It was like a handheld one, so she must a left it running propped up on something, I guess."

The hand stopped turning pages.

A voice with as much gravity as the moon came from the chair.

"What did I say about my reading room?"

"But she's seriously missing—"

The thumb on Mr. Fitzroy's hand began cracking knuckles.

Index. *crack*

Middle. *crack*

Ring. *crack*

Angus was gone before the fourth crack.

Because four led to five. The number needed to make a fist.

TWELVE

HENRY SMELLED cigarette smoke from outside his house.

Dad hadn't tried to hide it.

Henry opened the door slowly.

Dad sat in his chair, lost in the folds, blasted by the television, performing the same motion over and over—

Up.

Deep breath.

Down.

Up.

Thresh the lungs.

Down.

Henry walked in the room. Dad didn't notice. Didn't stop smoking. The ashtray was overflowing. A Killington kind of mountain of ash. How many cigarettes had he smoked? Henry could not tell. Dad would not say.

"Hi." Henry said. The house was missing the smell of food. The kitchen was cold. "What's for dinner?"

Up. Down.

Deep breath.

Thresh the lungs. Again, and again.

"Dad?"

Dad clicked channels. Hunting the shut-in country inside the box wired to the pulse of middle America.

"Sources say—"

"Heather, would you just—"

"Order! Order in the—"

"Sometimes, it's the little—"

"Damage to the building is said—"

"Damn you, J.R., Damn you to Hell." The Magnavox spat back a buck.

Dad put down the remote.

Lifted his cigarette.

Why this channel? Dad never watched *Dallas*. *"You think I'm some kind of nickel and dime whore? Well you can burn in Hell!"*

It was the swearing.

Henry knew.

Cigarettes and swearing went hand in hand. Lines that ignited each other.

"Dad?"

Dad jolted, like Henry had just woke him up. His eyes fled to the fool thing burning in his hand. He moved to stamp it in the ashtray, but crashed the cigarette into the little mountain of ash, blowing the top off this little miniature Mount Saint Helen's. Ash rained over the side table, over the floor. Dad didn't know how many cigarettes he'd smoked. How many *packs*.

"You shouldn't go around scaring people," Dad chastised.

"I didn't mean—"

"Where have you been?" Dad tapped at this watch.

"I, er ... it's only 5:30."

Dad stood. "Where?"

"I was talking to Angus."

"The Fitzroy boy?"

Henry nodded.

"I don't want you hanging out with him."

"What's wrong with Angus?"

"He's a smoker."

"You're a smoker."

Henry hadn't caught himself in time. His heart had tapped it on his bones, and his bones had breezed it through his teeth.

"What did you say?!" Dad rose like a puppet hanging off the rising moon.

"Nothing." Henry shuddered.

"I think you have something to say, don't you Henry?"

"I don't."

"Say it." Dad said.

Henry tried to shrink. Dad rummaged through the wreckage of his day for a cigarette and a lighter. He lit himself on fire. Blew a cloud of smoke on the boy.

"Say it."

"No," Henry whispered.

"Say it." Dad hollered, "Say it!" Dad hollered again. "SAY IT!"

"YOU'RE A SMOKER!" Henry yelled. And then was leaking water, trying not to cry, knowing he was on the edge of crying, but knowing there was a difference between leaking water out of his eyes and crying; sobbing like a baby, and dad didn't raise babies, only men.

"Angus said you bought cigarettes this morning."

"That boy doesn't know when to stop running his mouth and mind his own business. I don't want you hanging out with that boy." Dad had a finger halfway through Henry's sternum. "Ever. You hear me? You see that boy you cross the street, you hear his voice you plug your ears, understand?"

"This isn't Angus's fault, you're the one—"

"Did I not make myself clear?" Dad's finger's tapped Henry's chest, a three finger sermon of obedience.

Henry nodded. Tried to nod without jarring loose tears.

"I didn't hear you."

"*Yes sir.*" Henry whispered.

"You sound like a faggot."

"Yes Sir!" Henry barked, knocking tears out of his eyes, sending two rivers down his cheeks.

"Go to your room."

"*... what about dinner?*"

"No dinner."

Henry looked back as he walked down the hall. Dad sunk in his chair. Lifted his cigarette.

Up.

Deep breath.

Down.

Up.

Thresh the lungs.

Down.

"*... no dinner ...*" Dad muttered to himself.

He picked up the remote.

Lifted the cigarette.

The T.V. threw light on the smoke.

Some film noir. The greatest cigarette smoking movies of all time.

THIRTEEN

T H E R E   W A S a tap at the window. Henry wiped at his tears. Peeked behind the curtains.

It was Ethan Chambers.

Henry mopped his eyes with his sleeve. Looked at his clock. 10:33 p.m. Looked to his bedroom door. The blue light from Dad's T.V. pulsed at the foot of it.

He drew the curtains, opened the window.

"Just out for an evening stroll and—" Ethan blinked. "You've been crying?"

"I, uh, thought I got them." Henry pawed at his face again.

"It's your eyes, they're all red." Ethan hopped into the room. "What's wrong?"

"It's my ..." Henry looked to his bedroom door. The light blinking beneath it. "... dad."

"What about him?"

Henry sat on his bed. Wiped at his eyes. "He's acting strange."

"Strange?"

"What about your parents?" Henry asked.

"What about them?"

"Are they acting strange?"

Ethan shrugged. "They're always strange. They're parents."

"No, I mean, different. Are they acting different?"

"Different how?"

"I dunno, anything different?"

Ethan thought. "Nope, just as boring as ever."

"You sure?"

"Sure I'm sure. Wait, I guess my mom said an extra long prayer over dinner tonight. That or it felt really long because I was hungry. But it did feel long. You know how prayers change when you got an audience? Like the prayer you whisper at the foot of your bed tired at night is different from the one someone says in front of the congregation? It was a prayer like that. Said a congregation prayer over dinner. Used 'thee' and 'thou.' That was different, I mean, at home, praying over dinner that way. That count?"

"Hmmmm. Maybe not."

"Well, like I said, parents are strange."

"My dad's acting *stranger*." Henry said.

"Whaddya mean '*stranger*?'" Ethan asked.

"Got really upset with me for talking to Angus. Sent me to bed without dinner."

"What's wrong with Angus?"

"That's what I said."

"I mean aside from the fact that he smokes and drinks and has a collection of girls' panties from school, and tries to stick his fingers in every girl's bra strap, and steals stuff from Revelli's store, and his dad won't let him get a driver's license because even he knows the boy's not to be trusted operating machinery, and he got caught trying to look up Ms. Hewett's dress or was it down her blouse I can't remember, and he listens to Satan's music, and he plays with Ouija boards, shot the Barker's cat with a cherry from his wrist rocket, wears eye liner, has a lot to say, punches kids at school, might have set The Whistling Hermit on fire, certainly set the town scarecrow on fire, has a 'reserved' seat in detention, kicked over a headstone in the graveyard, has a collection of Playboys he brags about, thinks denim vests with patches go with everything, actually come to think of it, Henry, I don't want you talking to Angus either." Ethan winked.

Henry laughed a little. "Yeah, he is a bad kid."

"Eh, he just belongs in the city."

"Huh?"

"You go to Pittsburgh, Boston, New York, he'd fit right in. They're all like that there."

"That so?"

"I've been there," Ethan said.

"Do you think it's true? About him and Cindy Barker?" Henry asked.

"Let's hope not, for Cindy's sake." Ethan laughed.

Henry's stomach grumbled.

"No dinner, huh?" Ethan asked.

"Dad was mad at me."

"Alright, hang on, I'll be back. Can't be out too much later or Mom will know, but I'll drop something off. Know you're not a biggest fan of Mama Chambers's green bean casserole, but desperate times. You'll have to eat it cold, so he doesn't smell it."

Then Ethan was gone, out the window.

And Henry was left wondering if dad could smell anything through the heavy curtain of cigarette smoke.

FOURTEEN

ANGUS SAT on his crummy little twin bed.

Surrounded by faux wood paneling.

Old fist marks in the walls.

Metallica posters the only decorations. The boy halfway between the *Hell On Earth* Tour and the *Ride The Lighting* Tour. An Avon paperback collection of Sherlock Holmes stories one of two books on his shelves. A single September 1975 Playboy collecting dust under his bed. And a drawing, spread over four different sheets of paper, lying unfinished, paperweighted on his squatty desk by the combined gravity of his Faber-Castell #2 and Pink Pearl. Last night, after the church blew away in the wind, he hadn't gone back to bed. He'd gotten out his pencil and paper and started drawing the town as it was *before* the church was gone. Like January, Vermont had become a loose thought the boy was afraid of dropping. Written down like a note to one's self in the middle of the night.

The drawing sat on his desk, waiting to be to finished.

In just a few days, it'd be the last map of January, Vermont in the whole world.

But the boy didn't know that, yet.

His fingers fiddling an old cigarette burn on his Levi's.

Behind him was a window with a view once monopolized by the town church.

Now, he had the view he always wanted.

He was afraid to look.

FIFTEEN

Long after midnight the lights were still on in old lady Brogan's house.

The utility meter ticking away pennies.

The T.V. glowing quietly.

Making small-talk, keeping itself company.

The house waiting for her to come home.

A man's voice piped into the room. *"Ladies and gentlemen, this concludes our programming for today. We welcomes any comments you may have regarding our programming. WNEK-TV telecasts from Channel 5, with the power of 105,000 watts video, and 21,000 watts audio as authorized by the Federal Communications Commission. WNEK-TV is an affiliate of CBS, the Columbia Broadcasting System, and is owned and operated by Central Communications Corporation. WNEK-TV is located at 672 Nightingale Ave, Montpelier. With our transmitter atop Burke Mountain. Northeast Kingdom TV is a subscriber to, and member in good standing of, the National Television Code. We proudly display this seal, your assurance of quality viewing. Some of today's programming has been mechanically reproduced. WNEK-TV wishes you a pleasant goodnight and good morning. And now, our national anthem."*

The American flag flapped on screen.

The best continental wilds shown off.

The Star Spangled Banner fanfared out.

The T.V. went to static.

Idling in the empty room like a chainsaw.

Waiting for Mrs. Brogan to shut it off, or the broadcast to come back.

Whichever happened first.

SIXTEEN

In the middle of the night, in the middle of town, sat the Leblanc house.

Front door hanging open,
swinging back and forth in the wind.
a dusty, dark saloon vignette.
T.V. blowing static into Vermont.
Lamps glowing low.
Beds empty.
In the deep end of the kitchen hot metal coiled like a sunning orange snake.

The teapot *wheezed* like an old woman.
Whistled like a young girl.
Screamed like a newborn.
Trying to get attention.
Call someone home.

SEVENTEEN

THE SETTING SUN warmed Angus's back as he stood on the Sindell's porch. Pumpkins keeping him company as he waited. He peered past the paper skeleton hanging in the window. The house looked empty.

Fred had disappeared after math class.

Hadn't been at the flagpole after school.

And Fred had slipped Angus a note during class. *"Need to talk. ASAP. Overhead Rose Foquette tell Katherine Leblanc that Cindy told her she still loves you."*

The house sat powered up.

The radio chatting.

Angus rang the bell again.

ding dong

He waited with the smell of pumpkins on the porch.

The house did not shift.

Did not stir.

He looked in the driveway. The family car was there. Mr. Sindell's work truck was there.

He raised his hand. Knocked. The door whined back on its hinges.

The front room presented itself.

A radio narrated the scene.

"Stock prices found more footing again as Wall Street, buoyed by the stability of the dollar and recovering stock prices abroad, continued to push back the effects of the market's midmonth collapse."

"Hello?" Angus called in.

No response.

The radio went on.

"Canadian media bristles at 'patient zero' assertions implied in San Francisco Chronicle reporter Randy Shilt's novel 'And the Band Played On' which frames Gaëtan Dugas, a Canadian flight attendant who died of AIDS in 1984, as playing a key role in spreading the virus from one end of the United States to the other."

"Anybody home?"

The boy stepped inside.

"An airline consumer protection bill that also requires testing for drugs and alcohol—"

click

Angus's hand left the radio dial.

"Fred?" He called out.

But there was only the sound of his own voice, lonely in the house.

"Mr. Sindell?"

Angus sniffed. Something was burning.

He crossed into the kitchen.

"Mrs. Sindell?"

An ironing board was out. A job half-done. Burning the shit out of a dress shirt. He lifted the iron. A big black mark on the shirt. The shape of the iron; peaked at the top. Like the shape of the church.

He turned off the iron.
It clicked and cooled.
The cat clock on the wall looked from side to side.
tick. tick. tick.

EIGHTEEN

"Do you think a church can have a ghost?"

Henry was looking at the burnt hole in town.

"Whaddya mean?" Ethan took a bite of his candy bar, swung his legs, dangling off the gas station porch. Ethan was Henry's best friend. To be honest, his only friend. Less best friend to any one boy, and more best friend to the whole citizenry of boys. Ethan Chambers was the kind of boy who fell out of a tree and laughed on the way down. A fine boy who raced ahead of every other boy and then, realizing other boys a mile back, stumbled and fell, waiting for them to catch up and letting them get one stride ahead. The kind of boy that'd pass the ball when he wanted to shoot. A boy that liked to get into mischief, but never enough to ruin his soul for Sunday service. And it was said the day Ethan Chambers was born, even Vermont smiled. Dawn, lying in bed, Henry heard a bird peck at the window? Ethan Chambers. Summer nights a cricket at the window? Ethan again. The first fall of snow, Ethan catching it on his tongue. The first flower to push its head past the dirt, Ethan Chambers there holding back other boys from accidentally trampling it while simultaneously encouraging it out. In summer, his face always burned with sun. In autumn, he smelled of leaves. The kind of boy who raked piles just to jump in. At all times, his eyes flashing Morse code signals to be translated by the nearest boy. Ethan, a cuckoo for the world, first to realize the hour, every hour. First boy to announce it was spring. First boy to realize it was summer. First boy to point out it was fall. And now ... today, sensing a change in the winds, mistaking it for growing up ...

"Remember? It used to be there." Henry squinted the sunset outta his eyes.

"Yeah," Ethan said vaguely. "Burnt down three days ago?"

"Two."

"Hmm. You sure?"

"I'm sure."

"Why you askin'?" Ethan asked.

Henry looked at the trunks of trees he'd never seen because a church had been in the way. They were sooted from the fire. "They say Pastor Phillips did it."

"Did what?" Ethan asked.

"Burnt down the church."

"Why would a pastor do that?"

"I don't know. They arrested him. So, they must have had evidence."

"Maybe they just want to question him? About old wiring, or something?"

It was Halloween and the boys sat next to the stack of pumpkins for sale at the far end of the porch of Fitzroy's gas station. Orphan pumpkins still dreaming of being taken home and carved into jack-o'-lantern. Fitzroy's gas station was the place kids came for their cheap candy. The feeding corral adult came to for their pet cars. Somewhere inside three plastics masks (He-Man, Robocop, Hulk Hogan), pressed thin as razor blades (and just as sharp at every edge), hung on metal hooks impaling their vacant eye slots. Somewhere inside a homeless collection of paper skeletons and orange and black crepe paper and witches brooms and mummy wrap were still for sale. But outside the day was through with death scenes. In this part of the country, this time of the year, everything was dying as fast as possible. The pageantry of leaves was done. The old state had given its last show for the season. It may have been Halloween to boys, but to Vermont it was merely the last day of the month. Vermont was tired and ready for November, a month it didn't have to try. Ready to sleep through a cold winter.

"Why you askin'?" Ethan said.

"People have ghosts," Henry Samuel said.

"Not proven."

"Yeah, but there's stories. What about all the stories?"

"People used to tell stories about moon Quakers and shit, said they met them, they were pleasant, liked tea."

"Don't say that," Henry said.

"Moon Quakers?"

"No."

"Shit?"

"Yeah."

"Oh, sorry."

Henry was looking at the burnt field. The space that *used* to collect the sins of the whole town.

"When did you start swearing anyways?"

Ethan shrugged. "I dunno."

"You didn't used to swear."

"I didn't used to have size 7 shoes either." Ethan held up a black footed Converse.

"Where did you get those?"

"My birthday. My uncle mailed them to me."

"Fourteen sounds weird." Henry said.

"Fourteen feels fine. You'll see. That is, if you don't *die* first!" Ethan made a face. "Oh fuck, sorry. Oh shit, I didn't mean to say fuck … I'm sorry, I didn't mean to … I just forget sometimes."

"It's ok."

"You wanna talk about it? I mean *the swimming hole.*"

Henry watched the state rolling over to play dead. He shook his head.

"I mean that's cool. But seriously, what made you think a church could have a ghost?"

Henry looked to the burnt field across the street. It was somehow both black and empty. The town had lost its church. More than lost. Murdered. By the pastor. Henry looked around. January, Vermont was not the kind of town you saw on TV, but it was the kind of town every American believes in and few have found. Where neighbors still stopped to talk. Where extra rockers were kept on porches in case company stopped by. Where names still went with faces. A place a man could get a free smile at the corner drug store and the mayor swapped gossip with his citizens in over a cup at The Whistling Hermit. January, Vermont was the kind of town that was fine with what it was—Church Street. Main Street, and little else. Down the street Mr. Revelli was raking leaves outside his store. Nearby, Sheriff Vault was pumping gas into his police car. Up the street the library was turning off its lights for the night. The town had been built around the church, and now carried on without it.

Henry stirred in his seat. "I'm just saying it's possible, isn't it?"

Ethan gave a suspicious look.

"I mean, theoretically." Henry bit his lips. "If people have ghosts, and live in houses, and houses can be haunted, why can't a church have a ghost?"

"Like a haunted church?"

"No. Not a ghost *in* the church, the ghost *of* a church. Have you ever thought what a ghost of a church would look like? Just picture it. An old steamer trunk of a building, where men come to deposit their worst parts. Think about it. Bad men walk in, good men walk out. Where do you think the sins go? Because they go somewhere. And I don't know where, but sins are heavy, right, will drown a man if he's not careful. Sin weighs you down, doesn't let you into Heaven, that's for certain, and where is Heaven, but way up in the sky. And how do you get to Heaven? By getting rid of all your sin, so we know sins are heavy, keep us grounded on the earth, or worse, sink you down to Hell. But a man walks into church on Sunday, his back nearly broken in two from what he did Saturday night, and walks out with a skip in his step. Where did the sin go? It had to go somewhere.

So you think about it, what is a church really? Sure you can sing there, sure they remind you about the Bible verses you've forgotten about. Sure, it's a place to talk about Jesus and make friends and take the sacrament, but what is a church *really*?"

Ethan didn't answer.

Henry kept talking.

"A church is a junkyard for sin. A repository of bad stuff. A storehouse of man's worst cravings. A dumping ground for evil thoughts. A museum of men's worst itches. A landfill for all the bad thoughts men have had chewing on toothpicks. A trunk full of broken promises. A shoe box overflowing with cat-fight marriages. A pickle jar full of abandoned children. Every travelling salesman who's gone out to make a living for his family and never came home stops by a church at some point. Every woman who's lied in bed awake thinking of her mistakes while her husband sleeps soundly next to her gets up one morning to make a deposit with Jesus. Anyone who's ended up in the bed of a stranger. Every Vietnam vet. Any boy who funneled the wrong song into his ear. Any girl who lost her virginity, any old timer salted with sin, every man who's sweat himself at night walks into those doors. And where does all that sin go?"

Ethan didn't know.

"The Pastor'd say God takes it. But takes it where?"

Ethan watched the middle leaf of autumn fall into the burnt plot. They were in an old and haunted piece of the country. Lost deep in a county, lost deep in a state, lost deep in America. A state that did everything it could to keep from being found.

"It's like melting down a car," Henry Samuel explained. "You can change the shape, mix it all together, but how do you really get rid of it? Turn it into something else, maybe. Ever think about that? God says he doesn't like sin, but he sure is ready to take it all on. Come in heavy, walk out light. That's their motto. I'll take it for free, he says, just believe in Jesus, he says. Well, what is God doing with all that sin? You ever think about *that*? You melt down a car, you reuse the metal for something else, that's what you do. So God's taking all the sin for free, well, he's doing something with it, eventually, but not yet, for my money, which means you got a church collecting sin what is really just a storehouse of raw materials. The older the church, the better, and we had one of the oldest churches in the country, old enough to collect six generations of gossip, a whole swap of headaches, a handshake over sour spit, foxhole flubs, laughter at funerals, swears at sisters, bad nights in motels, smiling over breakfast obituaries, quack doctors killing people on accident, real doctors killing people on purpose, pill makers, warmongers, wooden nickel whittlers, half-dollar henchmen, men who find something to run a carnival on, broken bones, mended hearts, lightning rod boys, storm chasing girls." Henry took a breath. "They've all dropped a dump-truck load of sin once upon a time, in that church, and where was that sin sitting? Somewhere. Maybe in the basement, maybe in the pipe organ, maybe beneath the pews, maybe out in the open aisle of the chapel for all we know, waiting for the day God decides to use it, but sitting for now, kept from hurting people by hymn singing and sermons and Bible reading and blessed walls. But what if you burnt the church down? What if you let the sin leak out into the town?"

Ethan had been wrapping and unwrapping his candy bar wrapper around his finger.

He watched another leaf fall.

Looking in at this strange burnt field across the street.

Pastor Phillip's version of a farmer's fall burn.

The boys sat on the porch of the gas station.

A man left with a pack of smokes.

A woman went inside.

The candy bar wrapper was twisted on Ethan's finger.

"This is about the swimming quarry, isn't it?"

Henry didn't respond.

"Maybe you should talk to someone ..." Ethan licked his lips. "Sometimes ... you gotta talk to someone."

"My dad started smoking again." Henry announced.

"Wait, what?"

"He smoked the whole day."

"I thought he quit."

"He started again yesterday."

Ethan blinked. "Well, I mean, they say it's the hardest thing you'll ever do, and most people have to quit like four or five times to make it stick, don't they? I think I've heard that before. I'm pretty sure I've heard that before."

"It wasn't until after the church burnt down."

"You think the church burning down had something to do with it?"

Henry nodded.

"Henry. Sometimes shit, sorry I mean *stuff*, just happens. Churches burn down, and that's a bad thing and if you take a whole town, two bad things happen at the same time, and they're not because of each other, but it just *is*. I mean, look at everything bad that happened last year, the burst pipe in Mr. Villanelle's store. Or Katherine's broken window. Then there's Rose Foquette's missing bike. What about the cow Mr. Boucher had to put down? That small fire at The Whistling Hermit? We can go back inside here and ask Mr. Fitzroy how many candy bars got stolen this year, and whaddya think he'd say? 13? Twenty? And do you think any of those happened on the same day old lady Carpenter fell and died? Probably. What else happened that day?"

"That's not what I'm saying." Henry said.

"That's what it sounds like."

"I'm saying ..." Henry knew what he was trying to say. But how to say it? How to be heard by a best friend who had just turned fourteen. He could feel the distance growing between them.

"I'm not saying bad stuff didn't happen before, I'm just saying ... what if a church burns down and something, some *things* got out. Bad things."

"Bad things? Henry, everyone makes their own sins."

Henry looked away. To the trees tapping off red leaves like tall men ashing their cigarettes over the black burial plot of the church. To the last light shafts of a southern slung sun sinking out west. To the tiny center of a miniature little town in a vacant county of a misplace-able state. Vermont didn't give a shit. Never had. The United States of blah blah blah. Vermont had stopped listening fifty years ago. Sure it picked up a word or two of the national conversation on parade. Highways? Sure. Interstates? How about one? Power lines? Ok, but no street lights.

The gas station door opened and closed.

It was still on hinges. Henry had heard Ethan talk about that big city three states over and the gas station doors that just slid like magic. No hinges. No swinging opening, swinging shut. Just a door that looked more like a window, not acting very much like a door.

Henry looked to the empty field where the church had burnt. The trees around it were black trunked. Not even a Vermont winter would scrub them clean.

Henry watched the leaves come down.

"Things are changing," he mumbled.

"Nothing ever changes here, you move away 50 years and come back, this town's still gonna be the same. It's us, we're changing Henry, it's called growing up," Ethan said.

Henry watched the leaves go. Something was different about them this year. Nature had always lit leaves on fire in very old states. Yes, the autumn leaves had always been a prayer for ordinary life, but this year ... the leaves looked like something men were pleased to call bad luck.

"They're redder this year," Henry mumbled.

"What's redder?"

"The leaves."

Ethan looked around. Noticed all the show-boating nature had been up to, but was rather unimpressed. "I guess so. They're orange up the street." Ethan pointed towards Revelli's store. "Yellow that way." Ethan pointed towards the library.

Ethan was right. They were red just across the street.

Henry Samuel stood up.

He crossed the street.

He didn't have to look, in a state sparse on traffic, a boy could hear every car coming. The blacktop river was dried up.

"Hey! Where you goin'? Henry!"

But Henry was lost in his thought. His feet did the work and when they were done, he was standing across the street in the blackened footprint of a rogue preacher's bad campfire, here thirty-four hours too late to be standing in a church, looking up at the curtain of red leaves looking very much like a drape ready to unleash a play or roadshow. Something bloody-nose-colored and velvety. Like this little corner of this tiny town in this railroaded state had a show to put on. Henry stood waiting for the curtain to part.

A single leaf fell.

Ethan was behind him now, not stepping in the black footprint of the dead church, not stepping onto the grass adjacent to the black footprint of the dead church, timid to be on the same side of the street as this match & gasoline murder scene. Not committing. One foot still in the road. Like it was his anchor to the sane world. The road. A place a boy could get run over. A saner, safer place.

"What are you looking at?"

"It's ..." Henry looked to Ethan. "You don't see it?"

"See what?"

"The leaves. They're redder here because this is where the church was."

Ethan let out a sigh.

"Don't you see?" Henry asked. "This proves it! The church was full of all the stuff that keeps men out of Heaven, and lots of it too, I mean the town was chartered in 1762, the church was built what? Twenty-five years later or something?"

"I dunno."

"They're *too* red. And why red? Well, it makes sense because Isaiah 1:18 says—*though your sins are as scarlet, they will be as white as snow; though they are red like crimson, they will be like wool.* It's moving down the street. You can tell by the colors. It's going to crawl out here until it takes over the whole town, and then, probably do nothing because maybe people would notice if it took over two towns, or three, or a whole county, or state, or country, so, no, sin's too smart. It's just going to settle for one. Just one little town in the root cellar of the country. Who would notice that?"

The day was dead.

"I'm going home," Ethan announced.

"Wait, what?"

"I'm going home," Ethan repeated.

"But I thought you were coming to my house; we always start on my street. We start with the Thibaux's and their homemade root beer, and—oh you forgot your costume? I mean, it doesn't matter, I got an extra bed sheet and we can cut—"

"I'm ... not going trick or treating this year."

"Wait, what? Are you feeling sick? I guess I can take an extra pillowcase around and—"

"No," Ethan said. "I'm going to Cindy's party."

"What?"

"Cindy Barker's house."

"Cindy? Cindy Barker?" Henry asked.

"Yeah."

"Are your parents making you?"

"No."

"Why are you going?"

Ethan scratched the back of his head. "Katherine Leblanc's gonna be there, and Fred Sindell. Bobby Thibaux, hey you should come."

"Wait, so your parents *aren't* making you go?"

"No."

"Then why are you going?"

Ethan hemmed and hawed. "It'll be fun," he said at last.

"But what about Mr. Gristle's house? We gotta see what he does this year, no way he can scare us *this* year, and what about the MacClane's? We gotta see what full sized candy bars they give out. And what about poker? With our candy tonight, and the movie, I recorded Psycho off TV last month, remember? And breakfast! What about breakfast? I've been saving a box of Frosted Flakes, and we put our Reese's Pieces in them."

Ethan didn't know what to say. He didn't understand growing up any more than the next kid. And Henry had a damn good set of ears, but he had never heard the strange breeze that comes to blow boys in different directions.

"I just thought we could do something ... different." Ethan explained. "Look, I asked Cindy, she said you could come."

"What about the candy?"

Ethan shrugged his shoulders. "There'll be candy there."

The candy wrapper Ethan had in his hand fell to the ground. Blew into the road. Wandered down the street.

"Party starts at six. I'll come by your house, we'll go together."

Across the street, in the Fitzroy's gas station, Henry saw his dad.

Smoking a cigarette.

Buying more cigarettes.

And there Henry stood, in the field where a church had been arsoned by its very own pastor just thirty-four hours ago. A field that once held a church where Henry Samuel's dad had come to repent and try to be a better dad. Across the street from this gas station where the same dad purchased lesser sins by the packful in order to thresh his lungs and distill his breath with gunpowder. And someday, his dad would come for the smokes and sit down on the porch to burn one down and look across the street and see the old growth forest through the ghost of the dead church, and without a place to store his sin, he would have to make a choice. Stay or go? Be a dad or drive off into the white-noise wilderness of America and never come home. Like a carnival with no pageant or purpose. A roadshow with no act, other than abandoning a son and wasting away a shit-rate life on odd porches across television-country to the conductor's baton of The Cattleman. Tuning himself into television static one cigarette at a time.

Suddenly, Henry Samuel didn't want to go trick or treating either.

NINETEEN

THE LITTLE TOWN OF JANUARY, Vermont sat laid out like a collection of dollhouses. A few hundred little lights the state of Vermont could blow out if it breathed too heavy. Houses shut against the cold wind. Town full of cold sunlight. Night coming out from under each tree and spreading. Getting tangled under each house. Setting up a perimeter around the corner light outside Revelli's general store. Light bulb swaying, tolling in the wind like a silent cathedral bell. Across town, men were pleased to be locking post office doors. Keys were saying goodnight to hardware and barber doors. The Cock n' Bull was opening out of duty. The after-school sun was going out. Lights were coming on, what little lights the town had in a whole state that had the power off. Dark hills. Dark bridges. Dark roads. Dark north. A whole state that used electricity suspiciously. A rough country folk wary of power lines. American's wary of being too American, hesitant of being like the other 49. Sure they spun their black spools of threaded American power through their towns, in their buildings, in their churches, but not down their roads via streetlights, as if they did not want to be connected to America through the night. By day? Sure. It could not be helped. But night was when Vermont reminded itself that it was still its own country. Only half American. It had seen too many states get drunk off the juice piped in through black chords on wooden crucifixes. Stuff spat out from factories in murder towns. It was suspicious of the stuff. Power. That's what folk called it. Power. And what did they say about power? Power corrupts. Vermont was the only state that remembered the old saying anymore. A land full of churches knows a thing or two about reverence, and Vermont still knelt before night like the pagan God it was, didn't want to risk offending it with man-made parlor tricks.

One boy stood alone in the footprint of the church.

Afraid to go home.

Tonight, no one in town noticed.

Vermont gave him the cold shoulder.

TWENTY

Meanwhile,

across town,

Angus stood in the Thibaux's front room, next to the bowl of homemade root-beer ready for trick or treaters.

The door had not been locked.

The television squawking—

"In other news the Reverend Jesse Jackson asserted the stock market's recent decline was 'the natural, logical and inevitable result of Reaganomics' and called for 'an economic Camp David.' Reverend Jackson also—"

click

Angus's hand on the television knob.

Outside hanky ghosts hung from the trees in the yard.

Two rakes lay on the ground. A pile of leaves burning in the yard.

No Bobby.

No Mr. Thibaux.

No Charlie. No Johnny.

Mrs. Thibaux's cigarette in an ash tray. Only just lit.

The house quiet. The full flame scent of leaves drifting in the house.

A thin thread rising off the cigarette.

Angus watched the cigarette come apart. Whispered to himself— *She'll come finish it ... never seen her waste one.*

...seven minutes later her cigarette went dead.

TWENTY-ONE

Far down the street, in another house, another cigarette sat wasting away.

Mr. Samuel was watching TV.

Firing shots somewhere in the tin-can kingdom in front of him. Flipping through channels looking for something specific, refusing to take the cigarette off his lips where it sat melting. Needing to be ashed. The ghost of the cigarette sat on the end, dandelion material waiting to be blown into the wind. Wished upon. Dad wasn't even smoking the idiot thing. Pushing smoke into the corners, piling it to the ceiling. Dad slung low in the chair, content to let it burn beneath his nose.

"Dad, did you eat?" Henry asked.

Click.

"Dad?"

Click

"One, three, one—"

Click

"You're not runnin'—"

Click

"Tell me Janie, tell—"

Click

"Oil has been very good—"

Henry Samuel wondered when they had gotten so many channels. Had Dad got cable?

Click

"Don't talk to—"

Click

"Leave me alone, hear?! Lea—"

Click

"Hey—"

Click

"Walter—"

Click

"Libya—"

Click

"Sh—"

Click

Click

No. Dad wasn't *watching* TV. Dad was *hunting*. Looking for something specific.

Click

Click

Click

Cable. The TV. That fuzz box was now wired to the pulse of middle America. Motor cities and murder towns. It was piping in people who lived in another land, another country, an electric country where people dragged exhaust fumes for cigarettes, where manufactorium light didn't hold off the night, but beat the shit out of it to keep it at bay. And the smells were city smells, the scent of people layered on top of each other like lasagna, the smell of burning tires, plastic sacks in the night, engines waking up, coughing, rolling over hacking their carburitic lungs free from the wreckage of last night's drive.

Click

Click

Click

The images came in sheets of rain.

Click

Lipstick smeared, one lip crushing another.

Click

Teeth chattered and fused and chattered.

Click

Everybody was laughing.

Click

The dresses swirled.

Click

The smoker's cough of a chainsaw.

Dad did not click.

Slow, lazy smoke wafted off his cigarette. He watched this chainsaw cinema. This story of gasoline-gone-wrong and butchered kids telegraphed into his living room from a place where streetlights whispered in voices understood by sewing machines, about how the city wasn't made up. Pretend or false. Rose above towns like tin-can-moons in endless rows. Where plastic sacks ran through street light like lost sheep. And pissing incandescents marked their territory. Mine. Yours. Light. Dark. Bottled daylight. Night. All cold light. City light. Cold blue-black light. Television light.

Dad did not click.

Dad did not blink.

His bent cigarette clenched in his teeth, leaking grit. America's version of incense.

The chainsaw went wild on a guy.

TWENTY-TWO

Angus walked the steps up to the Barker's porch.

The house was lit up. The T.V. talking. Jack-o'-lanterns flicking their orange smiles at him.

He knocked again.

He could only hear the canned voices, piped in from the big city.

A third knock.

Electric chatter.

The boy tried the knob. The door whined back on its hinges.

Inside he could see the full spread of the party across the table. Drinks and chips and cans and salsa and ghost and pumpkin cookies and hotdogs and hamburgers and candied apples and popcorn balls. Paper skeletons dancing in the air, witch silhouettes flying through the sky. A tub of apples, waiting for bobbers. All waiting there, alone.

"Cindy?" Angus called in.

Somewhere off in the house a light bulb tended the static scene.

"Mr. Barker ... ?"

Angus stood in the entryway, in the downpour of television.

"a summit meeting will be held next month in Washington between President Reagan and Mikhail S. Gorbachev."

He looked around the room.

The food had been set out, but not touched.

"it will include the signing of a treaty eliminating medium and shorter-range nuclear missiles."

"Mrs. Barker?!" the boy called out.

"The Gorbachev visit will be brief and will replace what the White House had hoped would be the Soviet leader's whistle-stop tour of America."

He stood in front of the squawk-box, hand on the knob.

"Israel may begin supporting Iraq in the war with Iran. A growing number of—"

The TV went dead.

Angus took his hand off the knob.

"Mrs. Barker?!"

There was only the hum of light bulbs.

The food had not been touched. Set out. Not touched. The lights on. Blazing. Chasing away Vermont after hours. Making the Barker house its own country. High noon. Angus looked out the window. The Barker's cars were still there. A smell took him to the kitchen. The oven was on. Cookies were burning. Smoking. He took them out. They were black as bedsheets. Burnt to shit. Just like the church.

"Cindy, I know you're here!" He shouted and stormed down the hall, into the bedrooms. Throwing the doors open one by one. Looking under the beds. In the closets. "Come on out!"

The television in the front room waited for him.

The boy dragged slowly back.

The box sat there cold and turned-off.

With its carved wooden legs, it looked like an animal. He felt like it was watching *him* for a change.

"Stepped out for a couple eggs," he murmured. "Went to get more pumpkins for carving." He nodded.

Angus sat down in the well-lit room.

"They'll be back soon. Becky, Fred. Bobby, Ethan. Mrs. Barker. They'll be here any minute."

He waited an hour.
He waited one more.

TWENTY-THREE

HENRY HEARD a tapping at his window.

"I changed my mind, Ethan, I don't want to go." He drew the curtain.

In the Vermont dark was not Ethan, but rather Angus Fitzroy, half lit by the light bulb spill. Henry looked at his bedroom door, it was shut, dad beyond, somewhere in the rain of television.

Henry opened the window.

"I thought you were Ethan."

"Why? He come over to lick your dick every night?"

"No, he's picking me up for Cindy's party."

"Party started two hours ago," Angus said.

"So he's late," Henry defended. "Look, you can't be here."

"You gonna help me up?"

Henry blinked. "Into my room?"

Angus shrugged, "No, into your attic. Yes, into your room."

Henry looked at his bedroom door.

"Your old man told you to stay away from me, didn't he?"

"No. I mean, kinda. Sorta. Yes. I mean, a little."

"Closet smokers don't like people who know their secret. Probably afraid I'll blab to you," Angus explained.

"You did blab to me," Henry replied.

"No." Angus climbed into the room. He smelled like cigarettes. He stood tall and took a sniff of the air; Mr. Samuel toasting his lungs in the other room. Angus knew the scent. "I didn't blab it to you. I just warned you of what you'd find when you got home. He didn't even try to hide it. Did he?"

Henry looked sheepish. "No."

Angus looked around the room, noticing the posters.

"Thundercats, huh?"

Henry was suddenly embarrassed by the posters.

"Thundercats are cool." He tried to sound convinced.

"It's a cartoon," Angus said bluntly.

"What do you got on your walls?" Henry asked.

"Metallica."

"Is that a band?"

Angus took his headphones from his neck, put them on Henry's ears. Pressed play on his Walkman.

"Ow! It's loud."

"It's supposed to be loud."

Henry squinted his eyes. Tried to listen. "Sounds like 'Nam."

"It's supposed to sound like 'Nam."

"Why would you sing about that?"

"Because there's all these ghost that didn't get funerals, because war's a quick thing, and they're pissed-off," Angus explained.

"You believe in ghosts?" Henry asked.

Angus pressed stop.

The wind blew in the window.

The curtain caught the breeze. The boys watched it play understudy to a ghost.

"Tonight's probably the most haunted night of the year," Angus said. "And Vermont's probably the most haunted state in the country."

"What makes you say that?"

"It's an old state. And old shit's always haunted. Think about the graveyards, how many dead people are in these state lines. The dead outnumber the living in Vermont. Probably seven to one."

Henry looked out the window.

Vermont was dark.

Halloween was dark.

And outside his window was dark on dark.

"You gotta go," Henry said.

"Go where?"

"I dunno, home, Cindy's party."

"No one's there."

"What do you mean no one's there?"

"They're gone."

"Maybe they moved the party?"

"All the food was there."

"Maybe they went to a corn maze."

"They left cookies in the oven."

Henry looked to the door. "You gotta go."

Angus looked to the door.

"It's your old man." Angus stared down the door, like he was in a western. "What happens to you if he finds me here?"

"I dunno."

"Whaddya mean you dunno? Don't you know your dad?"

"I used to."

Angus raised an eyebrow. "Used to?"

"*Used to.*"

Angus stared at the door. Took a step forward. Henry made a sound, but Angus lifted a hand. And then Angus was at the door, ear pressed against it, listening to the stories a house had to tell. But there were no stories in that house that night. It was the white fuzz of cities, the flashing lights of power-planted places, all kinds of alien words shipping in, stacking up in the corners of the front room. Words spoken on a made-up street in a false town, behind which was nothing and around which was nothing.

"He's watching TV?"

Henry nodded. "*Texas Chainsaw Massacre.*"

"Does he like horror movies?"

Henry shook his head. "No. They bring back memories. You know. From the war."

Angus's hand was on the knob.

"You locked it."

"I did?"

"You don't remember locking it?"

Henry shook his head.

"Do you usually lock your door?" Angus asked.

"... no."

Angus's hand clicked the lock. Turned the knob. Henry made a sound, but Angus lifted a hand. And then the door was cracked, and Angus was looking down the hall into the living room where the television spat the glow of ghosts. The dust of dad's lungs hung in the light. Dad, slunk in his chair, in his own private snowglobe that had been shook up, and now was settling, settling, settling. Dad littering his own ashes to the floor. Cremating himself from the inside out. The orange smolder of the cigarette the only strike of color in the pale blue spilling from the box.

Angus locked the door.

"Something bad's coming this way," Angus said. "Yes, bad, here it comes, feel it, way off now, but running fast ... you know that don't you? I see it. You see it. No one else sees it. But you and I do. And neither of us sees it, I mean, but we can sense it, sniff it, maybe, feel it in our thumbs, who knows, but we get it's coming. Your dad's out there watering his dreams, but you and I know something bad is coming our way, don't we? And I said coming to town, but I meant already here."

"What about your dad?" Henry asked.

"Huh?"

"You said my dad's out there watering his dreams, but what's your dad doing?"

"He's reading."

"Reading what?"

"Magazines."

"That's normal, right?" Henry asked.

Angus thought.

"No. He's reading magazines like he's at a dentist office, not reading, just thumbing, shuffling pages, stupidly passing time while he waits."

"Waits for what?"

"... whatever's coming."

Henry sat silently on his bed.

"I waited at Cindy's house," Angus said. "For two hours. It was supposed to be a party, but no one came, and you want to know what's stranger, in that whole time not a single trick-or-treater stopped by."

"Maybe they went out of town, canceled the party, forgot to tell you?"

"You listening, Henry? Cookies were burning in the oven. They had a candy bucket by the door. Food on the table. Guess what I saw on the way over here?"

"What?" Henry asked.

"Nothing. I didn't see a single kid out."

"Maybe ..."

"It's Halloween, Henry."

The wind blew outside.

"The Barker's aren't the only one's missing."

"Huh, what?"

"The Thibauxs are gone. Old lady Brogan. The Sindell's too. Fred went missing after math, so I stopped by his house after school. No one was there, Henry. Not Mr. Sindell, not Mrs. Sindell. Not Suzy. Found an iron burning the shit out of a dress shirt. And Fred's insulin was in the fridge. How far you think he'd get without that? The next meal, maybe. I pissed in their toilets. I smoked their cigarettes. They never came home."

"Maybe they went somewhere?"

"Without their cars? Lights left on? Food on the table? TV blaring to empty rooms? Electric mixers loose in the kitchen? Front doors left open? Autumn blowing in the house. Leaves burning in the yard? Cigarettes left lit waiting to burn houses down? And where's Ethan? Supposed to pick you up for the party two hours ago, right? He ever ditched you before? Not Ethan Chambers. Go call his house right now, see if anyone answers."

"I don't—"

"Do it."

Henry nodded. Opened his bedroom door. Stood in the hall, punched numbers into the phone.

ring
  ring
    ring
      ring
        ring
          ring
            ring
              ring
                ring
                  ring
                    ring
                      ring
                        ring
                          ring
                            ring
                              ring
                                ring
                                  ring
                                    ring
                                      ring
                                        ring
                                          ring
                                            Henry hung up the phone.

Returned to his room. Locked the door. Sat down quietly on his own bed.

"It's almost like someone took a pencil eraser to them." Angus said carefully.

"You mean ... killed?"

"*Murdered,*" Angus said coldly.

"What's the difference?" Henry asked.

"Killing's on accident."

The room went silent.

"You think someone's murdering people?" Henry asked.

"How else do three whole families disappear without a trace?" Angus said.

Henry glanced to his door. Behind was the front room with a TV playing Dad and a dad playing slaughterhouse porn.

"In 200 years, of all the people that shed their sins at the church, you think a murderer ain't never stopped by and dropped something off? Something that got out when Pastor Phillips burnt it down," Angus said quietly.

Henry looked off deep into his own room. "There's another way to go gone all a sudden," he said quietly.

"You mean aside from being murdered?"

Henry nodded.

"Well?" Angus asked.

"God takes you," Henry said.

"Kills you?"

"No, takes you without dying," Henry breathed. "Maybe we were wrong about the Rapture."

"We?"

"They," Henry clarified.

"Who?" Angus asked.

"Everyone."

"What's the Rapture?" Angus asked.

"Before God burns down the planet, he takes the good off it."

"Takes them where?"

"Heaven." Henry looked off into his own brain. "Maybe it doesn't happen like people thought, the whole world at once. Everyone together. Maybe Heaven can't handle the load. Maybe the Rapture comes to town. A kind of carnival rolling across the country? Hitting one town at a time. Traveling in seasons. Year by year. Family by family. A road show."

Out the window the moon was revving beneath the hills.

"Maybe God's still rolling through town?" Henry asked his bedroom.

"What happens in between?" Angus looked serious.

"In between what?"

"In between the time God takes all the good and him taking a match to the planet?"

"What do you mean?" Henry asked.

"Let's say the Rapture rolls into town, like a circus, and all the good get on board one by one, then it pulls up stakes and rattles down the road. Who's left in town Henry?"

Henry's eyes grew.

The boys looked to the bedroom door,
to the strobe-flash of chainsaw cinema beating at the foot of it.

"Oh gosh." Henry touched his lips. "In between would be the most dangerous time to be out there. With the good gone, God isn't keeping an eye on things. Isn't listening to prayers anymore. No preacher, no church, no good neighbor to steer folks straight. This town would be like a bottle rocket without a stick; who knows where it's gonna go. But it's gonna blow up."

Henry's glance wandered to the door holding back his father.

"What if he told the preacher to burn the church down?" Henry continued, "Maybe that's the sign the Rapture has come to town, a pastor burning down his own church. Churches burn down all the time and towns and people are fine, but I've never heard of *a pastor burning down their own church*, have you? What if that's the trigger? What if this is God's sign for when he's done with a town. Given up. Comes and carts the good away and leaves the rest behind. Scrap. People who didn't make the cut. Wood chips on the ground. God's a carpenter, right? So he wants to make tables and chairs. Well, he starts with a big ol' timber, cuts away all the stuff he doesn't need. What if this town is sawdust waiting to be swept away? What if he's gotten everything out of this block of wood that he needs?"

Henry blinked.

"It'd be ..." His voice got lost somewhere. "It'd be ..."

"It'd be a bad time to be in town." Angus finished Henry's sentence.

Angus looked at the door again.

The kid's bedroom door, flimsy pressed wood, hollow door, little click lock, holding back all the sights and sounds of a Halloween night horror film. Angus looked at his knuckles. "Town's gonna get drunk, Henry, and I got a feeling it's the kind where you find yourself trying to be small. Saying to yourself, not this father. Not this house. Not this night."

TWENTY-FOUR

TWO BOYS RAN from the house with a liter of dead cars in the yard on the edge of town, down Church Street, towards town, matching shadows stride for stride until both froze. Down the street was the flat shadow of the burnt church. Waiting. Pounded into the dirt by the bullfists of fire. A penny laid out on the railroad tracks. And the moon was ready behind the hills to empty itself into the town. The tall trees, like lamppost men crowded over the lot, shivering in the wind and cold, missing last night's fire that reminded them of August, last night's fire a hobo campfire for the tall trees. The ground blackened, and what grass was left in the field whispered about last night's doings, it missed the church that kept it warm.

Two boys at one end of Church Street. The burnt lot towards the other.

Two boys.

A dead church.

A street stretching out between them.

Like a western had come to Vermont. And the street was long. Smeared by moonlight. Bent crooked by the night, the gutted-pumpkin shadows of Halloween. And the wind was a revolver. A spinning chamber full of the kinds of whistles that sent men into tombstones.

"Maybe we should go home," Henry Samuel whispered.

"We are going home," Angus said.

But Henry Samuel was not sure he could trust Angus's home. A bedroom, in a building, that didn't look like home. A room above the counter where Vermonter's sheepishly paid for gasoline; some kind of cancer they could no longer escape.

The boys ran. The church carved away. The wind gonging the nothingness of the missing church. Tolling, tolling, tolling the fine, firm shape no longer there. The whole town hearing, could have heard, if only they listened, was within earshot, but was tuning their ears somewhere else, could no longer hear the wind. And none had walked to see or say goodbye. And now Henry Samuel felt a fear, brought on by the wind fiddling the space of the missing church, yes, he thought, it makes me scared, going southeast, going southwest, the wind of the country deeps, the Canadian wind from the north has come to the funeral of the church, after fanning the flames two nights ago, wants to bury it in leaves and snow, like a murderer returning to the scene of the crime to bury a body. How did he know this? He was not sure, but ... Henry was afraid of the wind.

The boys stood at the gas station door, beneath the carport.

Angus searched for his key.

Henry looked across the street. To the hole in the town, the burnt church was lost forever. In between. In a state of Limbo. Not remembering where it had been, not guessing where it would go.

Angus opened the door. They went inside. Left the wind outside, where it belonged. Outside, raw and windy. Inside, still and quiet. Dark. Henry had never been in the convenience store after hours. With the lights off. Unable to see the bright color of candy.

"This way," Angus said, and they were through the back door, up the stairs, in a space that could be confused for a house, living quarters, any regular living room, kitchen, bedrooms, bathroom, if only, if only Henry didn't already know it all rested on the shoulders of gasoline. If only Henry didn't know it was propped up by the sale of sugar, and nicotine, and spit, and cancer sold for 86 cents a gallon.

"Who's your friend?" Husked the tall voice of Mr. Fitzroy. In the deep end of a shit-lit room, under the prorated glow of a lightbulb, was an easy chair. Something big and hungry, with its back turned to the boys, leaking the voice of a late-night father.

"Henry Samuel." Angus narrowed his eyes.

"His dad know he's here?"

The boys looked at each other. "Yeah," Angus shifted. "Of course."

The boys heard a page of a magazine turn.

A cigaretted hand emerged from the mess of wood and upholstery to make a deposit in an ash tray.

"I wouldn't want anyone in town to get the idea my boy's a liar," the voice behind the chair said.

"I'd have to lie first for that to happen," Angus replied.

A plume of smoke blew out from the chair. Another magazine page fell.

"Just 'cause we don't go to church, doesn't mean we don't got morals."

"Dad, it's Halloween."

"Am I boring you, boy?"

The air of the room was stirred by another falling magazine page. Another drag of smoke.

"No sir."

"Good."

Fifteen seconds passed.

Two long drags.

One turn of a magazine page.

Angus tilted his head away from the room. The boys backed out slowly. Went to Angus's room. Shut the door.

Clicked the lock.

TWENTY-FIVE

They sat in the room. Lights off. Watching the burnt lot across the street like their own version of television. Their own magazine. Every time the wind stirred the scene, it was like the channel changing, a magazine page falling. Sometimes the boys whispering something, mostly saying nothing, just sitting, smelling cigarette smoke drifting in, hearing the hum from the fire warming Mr. Fitzroy's lungs in the next room, mostly saying nothing, just sitting on watch, looking for what could leak out of a murdered church on the deadest day of the year in the deadest state of the union, and all the while Henry wishing he had a few pieces of candy to make the night tolerable. To remind him of what Halloween had become. To keep him from thinking of Halloween before candy; an ugly holiday in an ugly month. A holiday that must be celebrated, but doesn't want to be, a day for the dead, but the mudball belongs to the living, so tucked in, out, away, thrown away, under the rug of autumn, the garbage bin of holidays thrown out in a landfill month. That's the day, the one day all the dead get. So there two boys sat. Watching. To see just what the ghost of a murdered church would look like.

An hour passed.

Maybe two ...

The boys began to get bored.

"What's your dad like?" Henry asked.

"Mean," Angus said.

"He seems nice. Always friendly, fixing things for folks around town for free. Looking after Mrs. Brogan."

"You think I get the same guy as the rest of you? All it takes is everyone in town gone to their own houses." Angus took a heavy breath. "I grew up thinking I was afraid of the dark, then I realized, I'm not afraid of the dark, I'm afraid of my dad after dark. The town gets Vern. I get Mr. Fitzroy." Something about the way Angus said it made Henry think of fists and leather belts.

Henry could see Angus's hand itch for a cigarette.

"What about your old man, kid?"

"I'm not a kid," Henry protested.

"You ever smoke a cigarette?"

"... no."

"You're still a kid."

The room was quiet. The boys watched the burnt lot out the window.

"Huh?" Angus said.

"What?"

"What about your old man?"

"What about him?" Henry replied.

"What's he like?"

"I mean, you seen him. Pretty strict. Guess that happens when you go in the army," Henry explained.

"Does he work?"

"Around the house. On his cars and stuff."

"No, like a job."

"No."

"How do you get money?" Angus asked.

"He gets disability, his injury from the war."

"Oh, right, his limp. What's wrong with his leg?"

"Dunno, he's never told me. But I think it was some kinda mistake, or you know friendly-fire or something."

"You never asked."

"I asked."

"And?"

"He ignores me. Pretends he didn't hear. He doesn't talk about things that've already happened," Henry said.

"During the war?"

"*Anything.*"

"He doesn't talk about the past?" Angus asked.

"Not really."

"What's he said about the swimming hole?"

"Nothing."

"Not one thing?"

Henry shook his head.

"He never said '*glad you're alive*' or '*stay outta the water?*'" Angus asked.

"I guess he did say, '*Don't be an idiot.*'"

"Do you remember anything?" Angus whispered, his eyes not leaving the murder scene across the street.

"About what?" Henry replied.

"Dying."

Henry was silent. Still.

Across the street the burnt lot played the most boring movie of all time.

"No one's ever asked me about it," Henry whispered.

"No one?" Angus asked, keeping watch.

Henry shook his head. "I guess everyone's afraid."

"Afraid of what?"

"Asking."

"... or maybe they're afraid of what you'll say."

Leaves ran across the burnt field like flocks of miniature black-sheep.

"I remember feeling cold," Henry whispered.
"Cold?"
Henry nodded.
"So dying is cold?" Angus asked.
"It was for me."

The street below didn't have shit to say. The lot beyond sat collecting night.

"Like winter. Here, in Vermont. It's this cold thing you survive."

Leaves across the street stirred in brown-bag papery whirls.
The boys didn't see anything out of the usual.

"Who found you?"
"Pastor Phillips."
"Wait, what?" Angus looked to Henry.
"Didn't you know?" Henry asked.
"No."
"Well, they say he did. I don't remember." Henry said.
"Now, that doesn't make sense." Angus's brow furrowed. The boy turned his gaze back to the murdered church. "You said burning down the church was like drowning the town, right?"
"Yeah."
"Why would a man of God pull your *body* out of the swimming hole and three months later try to drown your *soul*?"
Henry didn't have an answer.

The boys watched the empty lot across the street.

"Huh?" Angus pried.
"I dunno."
"Too much time in that church," Angus muttered.
"What?"

"Maybe a pastor ain't a preacher or teacher or song leader or whatever else they do in there. Maybe they're really just a warden. Like a prison. Maybe leading people through Bible verses is just part of the witches' calculus? Old kinda rites and rituals to keeps bad stuff at bay? What if his real job was to watch the sin, keep it safe, locked away, pushed back by singing Bringing In The Sheaves and reading John 3:16? What if some of it got out? Got on him? Bent his mind, made him unlock other sin, and more sin, and another, and still more sin, until he burnt down the whole goddamn church, stood in front of it frying his lungs with this biggest, sickest, most sinful cigarette any man could make?"

"What about what we were talking about at my house," Henry whispered. "God telling him to do it, 'cause The Rapture's gonna roll through town?"

"Maybe that too. Who knows?" Angus whispered. "Just trying to figure this out."

It was getting late. Henry knew his dad wouldn't notice how late he was out. No. Cable ran all night. Cigarettes burned all hours. But for some reason, he wanted to go home. Be in. Maybe it was to be tucked into a warm bed. Maybe it was the fact that without trick or treaters to push back the night the tide would come in two-fold. November was coming to drown the town. November waited all year for sweet revenge. Henry was only thirteen, but somehow he already knew he'd never be more lonesome that the walk home he had to do tonight, two hours from November.

"smoking a church ... tapping ash on the town ..." Angus was muttering. His words forming into vague liturgical patterns.

The boys hadn't seen anything but leaves play in the shadows.
Moonlight beat a dead church.

"I should probably go home ... if my dad—"
"We're doing it wrong. It's the cigarettes." Angus said.
"Huh?"
"You can't *see* sin, that's what makes it sin, right? If sin looked

like sin, no one would sin? Right?! You tell me, you're the one that goes to church."

"What?" Henry replied.

"Sin doesn't look like sin. You can't see something and *know* it's a sin. Well, I mean maybe the worst stuff, sure. Murder looks like murder, but even that, not always clear, right? I mean you think any kid that went to 'Nam was thinkin' they'd come back a murderer? ... Oh, shit, sorry Henry, I didn't mean ..."

Henry blinked away the thought. "What were you saying?"

Angus shifted. "Well, I was just trying to say sin doesn't look like sin, right? Like what about Lindsey Hale, lost her virginity, and that's a sin, right? Well you think she went out with Carl Bradford planning on it? Probably not, I mean she sang in the choir at church, right? So she's probably a good girl, or trying to be at least, so she goes out on Friday night, and says 'well there's nothing wrong with kissing, kissing ain't a sin,' and then Saturday comes around and she says 'well there's nothing wrong with kissing lips, so there's nothing wrong with kissing necks,' right? And then four months pass and she opens her eyes one night and she's naked and her virginity is gone and none of it looked like sin along the way, and maybe it doesn't even feel like sin, but somehow here she is choking to death, locked down to this millstone that only God can take, and she drags the damn thing to the church, right?"

"Uh, yeah, sure," Henry said.

"We can't see the sin escaping because *sin never looks like sin.*"

"What does it look like?"

"Fuck if I know." Angus twisted his face.

"So how do we see it?" Henry asked.

"I don't know," Angus slurred; his lungs pushing air past his tongue, saying sounds who could possibly guess what.

TWENTY-SIX

ANGUS STOOD UP. Opened one of two books he had on his shelf. Inside the book was a hole. Inside the hole were cigarettes. Next to the cigarettes were matches. A cigarette went to his lip. A match between his fingers.

"What are you doing?" Henry asked.

But Angus was looking under his bed. Fishing. Pulling out a big mason jar. His lips rolled the cigarette to the corner. Rolled it to the center. His hands struck the match on the back of his belt. He tossed the jar to Henry. "Open it," he said. And Henry did, while Angus stoked the fire attached to his face. Helping it live. Keeping it low. Not wanting his dad to know, smell, search.

He took a drag. A lungful of the only kind of pollution you can find in Vermont. Leaked it into the jar. Moved Henry's hands to cover. Trap. Make a snowglobe of the dust of his own lungs. Another drag, held in the lungs, spat in the jar. In with bedroom air, the fall burn of a boy's lungs, into the jar. Up with the cigarette, down with the cigarette. Into the lungs, into the jar. One cigarette. One mason jar. One disappearing. One filling up. A drag. A deposit. A seventh draw, followed by a pause, an eighth pull and another after that, and still another and another after that, in deadman fashion, the kind of smoking a man does when he has nothing left to lose, nothing more to gain, but saving each drag, each broken man's shudder of wasted breath, each slow and cowardly way to kill yourself.

And then the cigarette was gone.

Only stub filter.

The mason jar was full. Twisted and sealed shut. Both boys looking in this crystal ball they had made, the smoke and swirl of people's ashes on parade. The gray muddiness of people who want to commit suicide, but just don't have the guts. So *this* is what a cigarette was. Unrolled. Burnt down. Unlocked from the mad conquistador grip of the paper. That's all it was. Wasn't it? Cigarettes, just bad air mixed with smeared lungs. You could not see though it, like all crystal balls, like the future was hard to see, and yet predictable as funerals. But it was sawmill smoke, this airy-substance made from the slaughter of something. Not red, no, but murder all the same.

"So ... that's what dying looks like," Angus said, and looked to Henry for confirmation. Henry watched the stain on parade, this bottled plume of dead boy and burnt crop, something that shifted like bad dreams. Bad weather.

"I don't know," Henry said quietly.

"Whaddya mean, *'you don't know?'*"

"This is almost beautiful." Henry had never had a broken heart. Just a stopped heart. And though they're damn near close, they aren't the same thing. His hand felt his chest, knew there was this organ that pumped madly on 4,800 times an hour, had no brain, and yet was smarter still. "Dying's not something you see, really, I mean..."

"What is it?"

"Dying's something you feel."

Angus looked at this jar, once full of peaches old lady Brogan had preserved, eaten, hiding under a bed now full of the last hundred-and-eighty seconds of his life. He shook it like a snow globe. It didn't play along.

"What does dying *feel* like?"

The jar told ghost stories between them.

"Dying," Henry whispered.

"That doesn't help," Angus whispered.

"It feels ... Have you ever had a nightmare where you woke up glad it was just a dream?"

"Of course."

"You ever had the opposite?" Henry asked.

"What d'ya mean?"

"A bad part of life show up in a dream, so it feels fake as you're waking up, but then you realize, *oh god, this one's real*. Like, I have this dream I find my mom. Then I wake up and realize, I don't have a mom."

Angus nodded.

"That's what dying's like."

"So like a broken heart," Angus said, looking at the jar.

"I guess. I've never been in love."

"It's a lot like dying."

The jar played smoke-ghost cinema between them.

Angus grabbed a flashlight off his nightstand.

"It's a cop flashlight. From Detroit," he explained.

"What's it for?" Henry asked.

Angus pointed it flush into the snarl of Cattleman smoke swirling in the jar. He took the jar to the window. "Takes sin to see sin." He explained. The button rest easy in his finger. His fingers easy on the flashlight. The flashlight rest easy against the bottle, the bottle pointed at the burnt down church. The cigarette, unpacked, raw and angry in the bottle. No longer indistinguishable from the seconds sanded off the boy's life. Dancing in a pen like car-exhaust fumes, but from a human.

Angus clicked the trigger.

The light beat the shit out of the smoke. The smoke beat the shit out of the light. Tumbled together, like a 1930's catfight cartoon cloud. Came out on the other side of the jar something different.

Bruised and strengthened. Landed on the murder scene of the church with a moth-like flicker. Unsure of its landing space. Afraid. Knowing it wasn't safe. Yes, the light landed like a moth. Skittish and flighty. Ready to bolt. Afraid of the scent of the coming swat. Just like a moth. Drained and colorless. A shit-rate butterfly. Something nature'd given up on, rushed through production. The last creature God made, on the last hour, of the last day of creation, when he was tired. Didn't give a shit anymore. Had wasted his creativity on elephants and spiders. A moth.

The boy's mouths opened.

The night fluttered like a flap of bed sheets.

The camera was pointed at the screen.

This was a movie. A horror film. The flashlight, the projector. The smoke-bottle, the film.

The scene was a burnt down field,

still clutching the shape

of a church.

Like it had never burnt down.

TWENTY-SEVEN

Then it was gone.

A cockroach hit by the boom of light bulb.

"Did you see that?" Angus whispered.

"Yeah."

The boys watched the flashlight pummeling this make-shift celluloid frame. The light dirtied by the process. Flickering in and out. Getting lost through the smoke. Almost clicking like an old time movie projector. Just as yellow. Dust colored. The bottle swallowed the clear grit of batteries, and spat out coffee. Light went in white like saliva, came out snuff-colored like something meant for a spittoon.

All landing on a burnt field. A brown world.

Nothing,
at all,
was going on across the street.

"You saw that, right?" Angus said.

"Did *you* see that?" Henry replied.

"*What* did you see?" Angus asked.

"*What?* I saw the church, or like ... the ghost of the church, what did you see?"

"Yeah." Angus said seriously. "Me too."

"We both saw it?!"

Angus nodded. "We both saw it."

Another second passed.

Another second.

Another.

"Are we sure we saw it?" Angus asked.

"I'm sure, are you sure?" Henry replied.

"I'm sure, you're sure?"

Henry nodded.

"What do we do?!"

Angus clicked off the flashlight. Placed the jar on his nightstand. Sat back against the wall.

"People like you'd call the Preacher. He'd bring a Bible, and a prayer. Light a candle or something."

"Whaddya mean *'people like you?'*"

"Believers."

Henry sat in the dark. "What do people like *you* do?"

"Atheists?"

Henry nodded.

"We don't believe in this kinda shit."

Henry looked across the street, in the deep end of a little town, lost in the tornado cellar of an eighty-sixed state, misplaced in the country deeps of America. "I think it's too late for that."

TWENTY-EIGHT

"It's late." Angus whispered. "Very late in the day to start believing."

"But we both saw it," Henry said.

The boys locked eyes.

"All you Christians spend so much time believing in shit you ain't never seen. Now I've seen it, and it's hard to believe. Maybe that's God's fucked up plan? He knows once you seen it, you don't wanna believe it, but if you ain't never seen it, you'll believe it until you die?"

Henry sat silent on the bed.

He still had the question of *what do we do* swimming in his eyes.

"Why wasn't God just a scientist? Forget all this faith bullshit. Give people the facts. Knowing gravy makes you fat doesn't make it taste bad. Kinda makes it taste better. Would still be a test."

"I thought you didn't believe in God?" Henry asked.

"I don't have much of a choice, now do I?"

"Whaddya mean?"

"You can't believe in sin, and not believe in God. And we just saw a shitload of sin. Oh, I'm sure he doesn't want you to know that, but without sin there's no God. So that fucker, sitting on a star or wherever he is, just showed us his footprint, and now we can't say the Big Foot isn't real anymore. Not every atheist thinks the sky is empty. Sometimes when they say they 'don't believe in God,' it's like saying you don't believe in Reagan. Everyone knows President Reagan exists, but not everyone likes what the guy's doin'."

Angus's tongue itched his teeth.

He dumped out his backpack. School books fell. He packed up the flashlight. He packed up the jar.

"What are you doing?" Henry asked.

"Crossing the street."

"What?! You can't go over there, not after what we just saw. We need to call—"

"The preacher? Your dad lost in the cigarettes? Sheriff Vault? Who, Henry, who?"

"I don't know ..."

"My dad?"

Both boys looked to the flimsy press-wood door of Angus's bedroom. There was a hall beyond. Mr. Fitzroy in a reading room, turning back pages, one by one.

"Go on Henry. Call him," Angus said softly.

"I ..."

Angus watched Henry's mouth.

"I ..."

The boy quit trying.

"God wants you to come to him to solve all his problems because that gives him purpose," Angus said. "He wants you to drop off your sins with him because that means you need him. But what if you can solve your own problems? What if you don't have to kneel? What if there's no such thing as sin?"

"But we just saw it."

Angus looked out the window. Zipped up his bag.

"I'm going to make sure."

"Make sure of what?"

"It's sin."

"How are you going to do that?"

"Fuck if I know. But I'm guessing it has a feeling, if you get close."

Henry grabbed Angus's sleeve. "Wait, what if it's dangerous?"

"I got a feeling, Henry. If it was gonna stick to us, we'd already be acting like my dad or your dad, or hell, even Mr. Boucher."

"Mr. Boucher?"

"He came by the gas station last night to buy toothpicks."

"What's wrong with that?"

"He was chewing 'em. Like candy. Look, sit tight."

And Angus was out the window, climbing down some well-tread escape route. Something he had used before, probably to sin. And he was at the street. Crossing the street. Looking for traffic like he was a city kid, like he'd forgotten he was in Vermont where you always hear the cars coming. Across the street. Standing still, not wanting to leave the marble sidewalk. Not wanting to foot the grass. Looking at the dead thing in front of him, probably wondering how dead it really was, why it had a shape, if it had a shape, what it was made of, how much sin could breathe, sleep, rouse and wake. The jar came out, the flashlight went on. The scene was given a coat of jar-light. Two coats. Henry didn't see any more shadows of things that did not belong there. Just regular run-of-the-mill shadows. Angus stepped forward, foot after foot, like a VHS tape on play moving forward mechanically, until he was standing in the guts, the burnt and dead center of the murdered church throwing his makeshift horror film and projector on everything to see if anything would play the part of movie screen. *Here. There. Over there! Back here!* Pissing and drawing lines, looking for the footprint of God, less commonly called sin. It went on for some time, and then the light went out.

In the dark Henry lost him.

Thirty seconds passed.

Thirty more.

And thirty more.

If anyone in town had looked out over the sea of burnt churchyard dark that night, they would have seen what looked like the last firefly of the season. But no one was looking out their windows anymore, not in that town. There was only one boy who saw it, blinking in and out like a cherry light on a radio tower. Trying to pick up on invisible chatter. Tune himself into the right frequency.

Angus smoking a cigarette.

And then second, at the same time.

The last two fireflies of the season.

TWENTY-NINE

Angus had never been inside.

He didn't know he was standing in the chapel. Or where the chapel used to be.

Wedged under a weather of cold stars filtered through
Vermont's tallest.
Downstream from moonlight.
The deep, dark, wild long history of the church wanting to
swallow the boy.

The chapel. Where the choir had come to sing.
He had a cigarette in each ear.
Like Halloween had a radio broadcast he could pick up.

He stepped forward,
  adjusting himself like a metal antenna.
static
  stepped backwards.
    static
  left.

static
  right.
    static

He turned his head, like he was tuning a radio dial.

left.
static
  right.
    static
  up.
              static
  down.

he caught a signal.

  A song.

'Mama's got shoes, Mama's got clothes'
  he stepped right.

'Mama's got these and mama's got those'
  stepped right.

'But poor Papa, Poor Papa'
  stepped right.

'he's got nothin' at all'

THIRTY

Angus climbed back in the window. His two cigarette stubs coming out each ear.

"The hell were you doing?" Henry whispered.

"Henry? ... have you ever sworn before?"

"I ..." Henry touched his lips.

No. Henry Samuel had never sworn. Never had a half-dirty thought. Never cursed in his mind, or out loud or ever seen a picture of a naked woman. Never had a thimble-full of beer, never told someone he hated them. Never gone to bed without saying a prayer. Never touched his wilbur, except to pee. The only sin Henry Samuel had was smoking by association, living under the same roof as his father while he drew his own chalk outline.

Angus took the stubs out of his ears.

He smelled like cigarettes.

He dabbed Old Spice on himself.

Henry watched him silently. He did not ask. Angus did not tell.

Henry quiet on the bed.

Angus sat down. "I put them in my ears ..."

Henry nodded.

"... the cigarettes."

The wind tossed the leaves outside, spreading October leaflets and autumn propaganda.

"I heard something," Angus said.

"You *think* you heard something, or you *did?*"

"I did."

"What?"

Angus bit his tongue. "Someone singing. Some old song."

"Who?"

"I don't know."

"Are you sure it wasn't old lady Brogan, out for a—"

"Yes."

"What about Jack Foquette, playing a prank?"

"I know what I heard," Angus said. "Didn't see nothing, with the flashlight and jar, like the sin was all hiding. Didn't hear nothing until I thought, *Wait! Takes sin to see sin, must take sin to hear sin.* So I lit up two and then put them in my ears."

"What did it sound like ... the voice?"

"Sounded like an old VCR recording."

"What do you mean?"

"You know, you record something on TV, once, but watch it a lot, too much, and it starts to fuzz, and you mess with the tracking, but you can't get the lines out of the picture, and the audio starts falling apart, like it's all being lowered into a pit of television static, you know like everything born on TV has a life, and static is where it goes to die."

"It sounded static-y?"

Angus nodded. "And far away. But close. Like a VCR tape. Like something you recorded in 1983, but are watching today. But watched too much, rewound too often. Somehow you're still in 1983, watching old commercials accidentally recorded between your show, but you're not really there, the recording is wearing thin, the tape is breaking down, and every time you watch it, it gets further away."

The table lamp burned steadily in the corner.

The window hung open.

October slowly crept away. November came their way.

Henry's eyes circled hawks over the quiet, very quiet, much quiet, terribly quiet, oh so quiet room.

"What song?" Henry asked.

Angus blinked. Yes, the answer was more important than anything he'd ever heard said at a funeral. More important than any thing a teacher had said. More important than any of dad's shit-rate advice. More important than everything Cindy Barker had whispered in his ear. More important than anything Henry Samuel had ever heard passed down from pulpit to pew. More important than every State of the Union address. More important than all the things T.V. had taught him in his whole sixteen years.

'What song?'

The open window stirred his eyelashes.

Angus didn't notice.

"Yeah, ... *what* song?" He whispered to himself.

The boys met eyes.

"I don't know." Angus whispered. "Something about ... *'Poor Papa, he's got nothin' at all.'*"

Henry pondered the riddle.

"Poor Papa?"

Angus nodded.

"I've never heard it."

"Neither have I."

The table lamp burned steadily in the corner.

"How do we find it?" Henry asked.

"The record shop. Tomorrow. After school."

"You think there's a record?"

"There ain't a song ever invented that people didn't want to record. Hell," Angus snorted. "Tommy Edison invents the first sound recorder and records Mary Had A Little Lamb for Christ's sake. Someone's gotta pressed a record of this song at some point."

"Yeah." Henry said weakly. "I guess so."

"Mr. Villanelle will know." Angus said confidently.

Henry looked at the clock.

It was only one hour til November.

"Shoot. I gotta get home. Dad'll be waiting ..." Henry's voice trailed off.

The boys locked eyes.

"Yeah." Angus nodded firmly. "... your dad will be waiting." He looked outside, to the vast swarms of Halloween dark between here and home.

"I'll walk you most the way."

"Uh, yeah, sure. That's be cool. If you want."

"Yeah sure, kid."

Angus opened his bedroom door. The boys stepped into the hall. At the deep end of the next room, one lone lamp, an armchair lit, the shade tilted oddly high, spilling light that bent the room to the tune of a film noir. High contrast and crooked. The chair beneath, grainy in the grit of odd-angle lighting. The room stretched long. The corners pulled far. Depths pushed deep. All by one light bulb, wearing a hat, titled too high.

The boys heard the page of a magazine fall.

"Going out?" A voice from the chair. They could not see Mr. Fitzroy, the chair's back was towards them.

"Just walking Henry home," Angus replied.

"You wouldn't be sneaking out?"

"If we were sneaking out, we did a pretty poor job."

"You giving me lip, boy?"

Angus's eyes narrowed. "No *sir*."

"Is that a tone in your voice?"

"No."

"I thought I heard a tone. But that wouldn't be right. My boy wouldn't use a tone, with his old man, or anybody."

"No sir, I wouldn't."

Another magazine page fell.

The lamp sketched a mad world at the end of the room. All black and white. Nothing in between.

"I'm walking Henry home. So he'll be safe."

"Safe." The chair repeated the word. Like it was a stranger on his tongue. "*Safe.*" The word came again. Quiet. Lazy on his lips.

Angus waited to be dismissed. Henry waited for Angus to be dismissed. Mr. Fitzroy muttered something on low volume, something about no smoking, no drinking, no pretty women, and then his tall voice was gone. Like an unplugged TV, and the boys started down the hall when they heard a voice, almost singing, mostly muttering; *smuttering*—certainly whispering, a kind of leaky sound, sounding half-asleep, full of things easiest to lose, or just drunk on the long day.

It was Mr. Fitzroy.

"... Mama eats ham

Mama eats lamb

Mama eats bread with strawberry jam

And poor Papa,

Poor Papa,

He eats nothin' at all ..."

His voice drifted.

THIRTY-ONE

"CAN WE ... stop by Ethan's house?" Henry asked.

"I've already been there," Angus said.

"*I* haven't." Henry said.

Angus nodded. "Yeah. You're right. Best to see it yourself."

The boys walked Church Street, turned down Maple. The cold Canadian wind came out to fight. All happening alongside a match between lightweight Vermont & heavyweight Canada. All underneath the Vermont ceiling of brashful stars. The boys at this prizefight of wind. Turning up their collars, tunneling hands deeper into pockets. Their town, along with all the towns scattered across Vermont, by night a bunch of dying coals that no wind could blow to life again. And then they were there. The Chambers house rising above them. Tall as a dead tree in winter. Glowing like a carved pumpkin. The high windows flickering eyes, the low windows a toothed orange grin. Sitting there a gutted rind, like something left for the flies. Angus marched Henry up the porch.

"Go ahead. Ring the bell."

Henry took a breath. His hand hung in the air. His fingers fluttered by millimeters.

ding ..... dong .....

The sound echoing deep in the walls of this giant jack-o'-lantern.

"Again." Angus said.

ding .... dong ....

Off into the house. Littering the corners, the floors, the open space between floorboard and ceiling with tend-to-the-front-door melody.

Nothing.

"Again."
"I don't want to."
"Do it."
Henry's finger raised. Stalled. Afraid to try to summon anyone in a house that may be as empty as a carved pumpkin.
"Jesus Fuckin' Christ. *You* wanted to see it for yourself."
"I ..." Henry's finger hung in the air.
"God damnit, do it, like this!" Angus jammed his finger again and again into the bell.

dingdingdingdingdingdingdingdingdingdingdingdingdingding dingdingdingdingdingdingdingdingdingding .... dong .....

The ring finding places to die deep in the corners of the house.

Silence.

Angus tried the knob. The front door, whining back on its hinges.
"Go ahead," Angus nodded inwards.

"Ethan?" Henry called softly.

Somewhere off in the house, shadows of tree branches moved on far windowpanes.

"Mrs. Chambers . . . ?"

The boys stood in the hall by the entry door, listening to the great attic beams shift and stir in the wind.

"Mr. Chambers!" Louder.

But only mice, warmly nested, scratching works of art between the walls.

"They've gone out to a party," Henry said.

"No," Said Angus. "We know where they are."

"Where?"

"Dead. Or gone to The Rapture."

"Ethan, I know you're here!" shouted Henry suddenly, savagely, running upstairs. "Come on out you guys!"

Angus waited for him to search because Angus *had* done the search before. Twice. Once this afternoon, at the Thibaux's house. Once this evening, at the Barker's house. So now Angus stood downstairs listening, as Henry threw open closets, turned over beds, his footsteps creaking floorboards above, dust flaking off the ceiling like fleas, hangers screeching across racks, of mattresses flipped over like coins, of drawers pulled out of dressers, of the inches behind mirrors scrutinized, of shower curtains ripped, of cabinets slammed open and shut, and all the while dust drifting off the ceiling tracing the frantic path of the boy above—bedroom, bathroom, bedroom, bathroom, hall. And then Henry started breaking stuff. Something Angus had done. A kind of calculus—done in attempt to summon folks home. Angus *had* sat on the Thibaux's couch, lit up one of Mrs. Thibaux's cigarettes and waited for her to come fuming into the room. And when that didn't work, he smoked a second and didn't use an ash tray. And when that didn't work he smoked a third, and burnt holes in the couch. And when that didn't work he smoked a fourth with his pants around his ankles and his bare ass on her white leather lounge chair. And when that didn't work he'd smoked a fifth, pissing into their sink. And when that hadn't worked, he'd smoked a sixth while rifling through her panty drawer. And when that didn't work he'd smoked a seventh, sitting on her bed, with her tiny black negligee stuffed down his pants so it touched his dingdong. And when that didn't work, he'd taken a rake in the yard, and snapped it in half across his knee and gotten into the car of Mr. Thibaux and jammed the stick between the seat and the horn, so it stuck, blaring, almost breaking the frame of Vermont with noise, and he'd gone back inside, kicked his muddy feet up on Mrs. Thibaux's white lounge chair and smoked cigarette eight, and nine, ten, and eleven, twelve, thirteen, fourteen, fifteen, sixteen, and seventeen, eighteen, and nineteen. The rest of the goddamn pack.

Henry dragged slowly back downstairs.

As he reached the bottom steps, both boys smelled the wind blowing through the front door with the scent of old leaves and a burnt church.

Henry opened the door wider, and stood in the wind, as one stands in the rain.

"Do you believe it now?" Angus asked.

"I believe it," Henry said.

Henry looked back one last time at the shadows of tree branches scratching on the windows inside the front room where a best friend and he had often watched TV, played board games, Nintendo games, eaten hot cookies delivered fresh from the oven by a mother, had faux tea parties as little children, drunk hot chocolate after sledding, tasted buttered popcorn watching movies on sleep-over nights, lain under the Christmas tree looking up at the lights, blanketed in the thick evergreen scent, talking about presents, dreams and wishes. Then he stepped out and shut the door, and he and Angus ran back towards their homes, if you could call them that anymore.

THIRTY-TWO

Henry sat on his bed.

Needing to brush his teeth. Watching the slit of light beneath his door. Knowing it was spill-over from Dad's TV. He was afraid to open the door, crack the seal, let the light flood into his room. And he had to pee. Pee and brush his teeth. And the bathroom was just across the hall. *Just across the hall.* All he had to do was open the door. Cross the hall. He didn't even have to go into the living room. *Living room?* No, that wasn't right. Yes, it had always been called The Living Room, but it didn't feel right anymore. Why would you call a room where you sat down to smoke cigarettes and watch other people's lives a *living room?* Plant yourself in this chair that was more comfortable than a coffin and snort the sweet cocaine of other people living their fabricated lives piped in from big cities and bad places all while you dust yours away with cigarettes.

The Dying Room.

Henry looked at the slit of light beneath his door.
He could not tell what dad was watching, but it was something.

Something on the TV.

And he could smell cigarettes. The rotten evening gilt of cigarettes.

Henry pissed out the window.

Didn't brush his teeth.

THIRTY-THREE

3:33 a.m.

On the edge of town was a farm.

On the edge of the farm, was a barn.

The town had turned off their lights.

A single light bulb lit the wooden American castle. Yellow lines spilled into the night. Electricity leaked onto the black American soil.

A farmer stood under the bulb, casting a squat shadow.

His jaw ground.

He spat toothpick.

Wind found the cracks between the planks. The light bulb swung. His shadow shifted and stirred.

But the farmer had not moved.

He knew every centimeter of his barn, and here he stood looking at a wall of tools. Great American edge-of-the-world frontier tools.

His fingers itched.

He reached up and hefted the haft of an axe. The light bulb the sun, the blade the moon.

The gleam ran across the barn.

A mouth and chin were reflected on the axe.
The lips were whistling.

PART 2
BLACK

THIRTY-FOUR

THE NEXT DAY, Ethan Chambers was not at school.

Cindy Barker was not at school.

Fred Sindell was not at school.

Judd Barker.

Suzy Sindell.

Bobby Thibaux.

Charlie Thibaux.

Johnny Thibaux.

Jack Foquette.

Rose Foquette.

Scott Leslie.

Katherine Leblanc.

Sawyer Leblanc.

Rebecca Leblanc.

Sarah Leblanc.

Gone.

Just like that.

Henry and Angus met eyes in the hall.

They didn't talk about it.

THIRTY-FIVE

"You ever been here before?"

Henry looked at the old building. It looked like something a writer had built. Risen out of a story, a mad paragraph about a building, not built by the grit and stability of architecture but rather by the idiot will of a storyteller. A half-formed building, escaped from a part-formed paragraph, full of run on sentences, thinking in metaphors. A building built using nothing even remotely related to brick or mortar.

"Yeah, where'd you think I got my Metallica albums?"

"How many do they have?"

"Three. *Kill 'Em All. Ride the Lightning. Master of Puppets.*"

The record store stood on the loneliest corner in a lonely town that was lost in a lonely state. Vermont was a lost and found for small towns. No one ever came to claim them. So here they sat, in this bin called a state, all these lost and forgotten towns, too small to claim, two hundred and forty three, lost together. The building slouched, as if it knew it was a little lost screw in a misplaced town collecting dust in a lost and found.

It was 4 p.m. and already starting to dark.

"Come on," Angus opened the door.

Inside was part starlight, part dying carnival glow. The stomach of some monster that ate whatever it could find. And the boys alone in its territory. Angus shuffled the trash, stirred through the mess. Looking for something about '*Poor Papa,*' here in this building that *said* it sold records, but felt like a business of shadows.

"How do we find it?" Henry asked.

"Dunno. Just keep looking."

"There's like a million records in here."

"There ain't a million."

"There's a lot."

Henry thumbed a few albums. "Who are The Beatles?"

"You never heard of The Beatles?"

"No ..." Henry said sheepishly.

Angus waved a hand like he was pushing away the conversation. "They suck anyways."

The boys sifted. Fingers crawling through records. Somehow Henry knew he was passing through the soundtrack of America, and he felt left out. He didn't know the songs. The boys drifted to different parts of the store. Thumbing back records one by one, watching America grow out its hair, become strung out, apologize, relapse. Sometimes it overdosed, and went away. Died alone and forgotten. Had poorly attended funerals. Henry wandered back over to Angus. He was lost somewhere deep in an album. Henry saw the ladies. A sea of flesh. Naked. Twelve? Twenty? He'd never seen so much. He'd never needed so little. Just this image and he would be happy. Just this album and nothing more.

"Electric Ladyland," Angus whispered. "Jimi Hendrix."

"Is it good? I mean, the music?" Henry asked.

"Who cares?"

The boys looked.

"We shouldn't be looking at this." Henry whispered.

"Why not?"

"It's a sin."

"I thought sin was supposed to feel bad?"

"It is," Henry said.

"This doesn't."

"Sometimes it feels bad after," Henry pointed out.

"Is that 'cause it actually feels bad, or 'cause someone told you to feel bad?"

The boys took it all in.

Henry tried to close the album.

"Don't!" Angus scolded.

"*Don't?* Listen to yourself." Henry said.

Angus blinked.

"I don't like the way you were looking at it," Henry said. He closed the album. Buried it in vinyl.

"God, Henry, there's nothing wrong with naked bodies, God made us naked."

"I'm not so sure."

The record store was silent. Oddly silent for a store that brokered in sound, music, noise.

"You had a look in your eyes," Henry said. "A sound in your throat."

"A sound like what?" Angus asked.

"An answering machine. No one is home, but here's my pre-recorded voice. I've seen that look before, recently, when my dad watches TV. I've heard that checked-out-of-your-throat voice too. With your dad. Last night. Thumbing through magazines."

Angus blinked.

"What are we doing here?"

"*Poor Papa,*" Henry answered.

"Right. Where's Mr. Villanelle? We should ask him." Angus peered off into the record store deeps. "Maybe in back." And deeper they went. Deeper and deeper and deeper still. Wishing they had flashlights, matchlight, starlight, moonlight, sunlight, remembering where they were. Vermont. Indoors. Arithmetic that always equaled darkness.

They heard humming.

Some kind of old time tune.

They followed the sound. Deeper went the store. Clearer came the humming. Foot over foot. Swimming their skin in pools of record store darkness. No longer able to see anything, but following the light leaking from the back room. Following a voice ticking with the mechanical lurch of a music box.

The humming stopped.

The boys stood inches to the back room, eyes washed with 40w spillage. Angus moved to look in. A shape stormed the doorway.

The boys jumped.

"Jesus! Mr. Villanelle?"

"What are you doing here?" Voice like heavy rain on a window. Form blocked the shadeless lamp. Like a shadow puppet standing in the doorway. Black as socks. No man. Only shadow.

"Here? Records." Angus squinted his eyes. "Looking for a record."

"I don't have any records."

The boys looked behind them, at the private pews servicing a million different artists and their electric mementos.

"What are all these?" Angus pointed.

"Not for sale. Store's closed." Words swept past the boys like rain-gutter water.

"Not for sale? Since when?" Angus eyed the shape.

"Since, since, since!"

The boys looked at each other. Felt the clouds opening up.

The shape did not say.

"Ok. I guess we'll go?" Angus muttered.

"Get. Go. Gone."

The shape turned. Taken by the corner. Left the boys wet. Soggy. Cold. Chilled by some Atlantic bomb. Angus took a step back. Another. Kept eyes on the door, the lamp, the bulb pounding the shit out of the dark, trying to look *around* the corner of the back office, not knowing what he would see, wishing his eyes could do the circus act, but really looking at nothing; a blank wall, a lamp without a shade, a piss-poor understudy of a bulb.

"Let's go," Henry whispered.

Angus waved his hand, took another step back. A second. Kept his eyes on this still life. A meaningless door, a pictureless wall, a lamp without a shade, a bulb without a spirit.

"Come on!" Henry hissed.

Angus waved his hand again. Never took his eyes off the scene. This post-modernist still life waiting to be painted, photographed, written about, redeemed.

But nothing happened.

Angus finally turned.

At his back came a small tide of sound. Old timey. Some ancient crooner long dead, speaking from the grave. Resurrected by machinery and Edison instead of Jesus.

"... Now, Christmas come
And Mama gets
The most expensive frocks
Papa gets a necktie
And a pair of ten-cent socks
Everyone cheers
When Mama appears
And she's got diamonds
Stuck in her ears
But poor Papa
Poor Papa, he's got nothin' at all."

THIRTY-SIX

OUTSIDE, around the corner, between a couple of buildings, the boys tried to catch their breath. They'd run like hell. And one was a smoker anyways. Or had been, for the better part of a year, which was enough to singe a boy's lungs.

Vermont was quiet.

Usually is, but always at the start of winter. Like it knows what's coming.

The boys trembled outside, in the 4:30 p.m. dark, between the buildings, while out there in the trees, lay a typical Vermont silence. The sound made after grandma's last breath. Out there was Vermont, the largest manufacturer of silence in the country. Madly carrying on production.

The wind came in from the north.

It smelled of Canadian winters.

"There *is* a record," Angus said.

"He's got it," Henry added.

"But why? You got a guy who suddenly is hungry for all his own stock of records, and he listens to the one record nobody would ever come asking for. A record he himself probably forgot he had. Something he had to dust off before playing. Sounds like something that should a been on cylinders. A song sung by a guy nobody would remember if it weren't for Tommy Edison. He could listen to any record in that store, and *that's* the one he chooses?"

Henry didn't have an answer.

Out on the highways the very last memory of the drifter sun was hitchhiking away.

"We gotta get that record," Angus said.

"Wait, what?!"

"Sneak in there, after he closes."

"You mean *break* in?"

"It's not breaking in if you don't actually break anything."

"I think it still is."

"Whatever. Look, you saying we don't need to get that record? Listen to it? Write down the lyrics?"

"No," Henry replied quietly.

"I mean, God, that's the same song from the church yard."

"Maybe Mr. Villanelle was out for a—"

"He wasn't."

"Maybe Mr. Villanelle has been humming that tune for two weeks around town, getting it stuck in people's—"

"You know that's not true." Angus said.

"But it *could* be true."

Angus took a drag of Vermont. "We both know what is true. You can feel it in the part of your heart that remembers being dead, and I can feel it in my bones. That record was pressed in the 20's or something and forgotten about by the 30's and passed on from collector to collector ever since only on account of being old, and how long has it sat in this building with that man? Probably since 1963, the day Kennedy got his brains blown out all over the country, I bet. The darkest day in history, because Kennedy dying meant every American boy was gonna die in jungles impaled by bullets and punji sticks. But the point is *we know what's true*, don't we Henry. We know that record sat in the back of that store collecting dust for the better part of twenty-five years without a listen, without a thumbprint without a single eyelash falling upon it until the night Preacher Phillips burnt down the church."

"Pastor," Henry corrected.

Angus ignored him. "And while the church was crackling like a boy scout campfire, while Preacher Phillips was dragging all the fumes of a burnt religion like a giant cigarette, somewhere, on the other end of town, walking distance from the church, Mr. Villanelle sat up in bed, thinking he needed a drink of water, and got up, and wandered to the sink, only to realize he was mistaken, and shook his head, like he couldn't believe he had been so silly, maybe laughed at himself, and without thinking wandered downstairs into the record store, and found himself at the very back, looking at a box of records even he'd forgotten he had, thumbing through, looking for something specific he didn't even know was there, finding *that* record, going to the back room, turning on the player, and alone, spent the rest of the night listening to one goddamn song repeating over, and over, and over, and over and over and over, and over ...

... listening to it, ever since."

A gust blew from the north.

It was November 1st, and the wind knew it.

"Henry?"

Henry looked at the wind.

He couldn't see it.

"It's a lonely wind," Henry whispered. And he was lost in Vermont. Vermont's a strange land. All the forests and bridges and lonely stretches of unlit highways and here and there a plaything town, built around a dollhouse church with a few lights burning you could put out if you breathe too heavy. The towns, by night, a bunch of dying coals that no wind can blow to life again. A small state; a big country—that's Vermont. Something you could get lost in. Maybe ... the boys already had?

"Henry?"

Henry snapped awake. "Huh?"

"What the hell are you talking about?"

Henry squinted his eyes.

He couldn't see the wind. But somehow he knew it was from the North. He realized he'd always thought of the wind as a singular thing. Each blow and breeze a new shot fired from an old gun. A different bullet. But that wasn't how the wind was at all, was it? No. The wind wasn't something new every day, every season, the wind was something old. Something that had been here before. Knew the town by name. Maybe, had a name of its own. Henry shivered. Somehow, he knew the wind that was ruffling his clothes *right now* had been here before, to this town, just two nights ago. It was the smell of burnt maple leaves, autumn incense, ash-pile prayers. It was the same wind that had blown the church into a boy scout's campfire. A kind of accomplice to murder. Returning to the scene of the crime.

"You smell that?" Henry sniffed North.

"Smell what?" Angus asked.

"Sniff."

Angus snorted raw November. Narrowed his eyes. "Smells burnt."

THIRTY-SEVEN

Across town the bell on the gas station door rang.

Mr. Fitzroy did not look up.

On the counter, a magazine page turned.

Mr. Samuel walked to the counter, pointed at the cigarettes.

The two men's eyes did not meet.

The magazine page turned.

A pair of lips, burnt with nicotine, licked themselves.

One blind hand reached up for a pack of Cattleman Rough Cuts, came down with a carton.

A fistful of dollars was left on the counter.

The bell on the door rang.

THIRTY-EIGHT

The boys sat between a couple buildings off Main street, around the corner from Villanelle's record store.

"We need to get that record," Angus said.

"Why?" Henry asked.

"Do I need to explain why?"

"Maybe," Henry said.

"Because the whole goddamn town is tapping their toes to the tune of a dead, forgotten crooner. Everyone's become someone you wouldn't want to meet whistling in the woods, a gross chorus that's all fucked up, because they're all humming the same tune at the same time, but all alone in their own corners of themselves, that's why. I heard that tune in the burnt lot of the church. Because Mr. Villanelle was listening to the same goddamn record in the backroom of his record store. Because now that I've heard that song I'm remembering what drifted out of my dad's mouth last night, on accident. It was part of the lyrics, Henry! Don't you remember? Halloween night, my dad thumbing through magazines, mumbling something about Mama eating lamb and ham and strawberry jam and Papa not eating nothing? Don't you remember the way he said it? It was almost musical. The way people who know they got a" shitty voice sing the hymns, mostly talking, almost singing, not brave enough to belt it out, testing the waters of song, but only really talking, so no one can accuse them of singing badly, because they weren't actually singing. Just talking. And nobody can make fun of someone for *talking* in church. God, that's what it's for. *Talking is how you unload your sins.* So the church can't shame that, because they need to collect sins. Stockpile them for The Rapture, for some reason." Angus blew hot boy-air into the wind coming down from Canada. "God, fuck Canada," he said.

"What?" Henry asked.

"Just ... they should keep their cold to themselves. Across their border."

"What's that have to do with anything?"

Angus shrugged. "I need a cigarette."

"*Need?*"

The boys met eyes.

"Why not *want?*" Henry asked.

Their conversation suddenly was out of gas. The entire machine, imbalanced. Dead.

Lying between them.

"The record," Henry said.

"The record," Angus replied.

The boys nodded at each other.

"We need to get it," Angus said to himself, and the wind, and Henry. "The whole town is mumbling it together, alone in their own houses, and we need to figure out what they are singing about."

"You mean, listen to the lyrics?" Henry asked.

"I mean, write 'em fuckin' down."

"Then what?" Henry asked.

Angus pulled a cigarette from his pocket. Planted it on his lips. Didn't look for a match. Didn't pat down his coat, or fish his pockets.

"See what they say."

THIRTY-EIGHT
THE SIGNAL

HENRY STOOD on his own porch. The house with the liter of dead cars in the yard.

He smelled smoke.

Smoke and his dad.

He opened the door.

The house was dark. Light spilled from the TV. Dad's face was in shadow, his body in static. Fuzz filled the screen, angry insects, buzzing and screaming like bees. The sound droned on. There was no honey.

The blinking red light of a radio tower showed up in the room. On dad's lips.

On.

Off.

Blinking in.

Blinking out.

Red. Dark. Red.

Going away, coming back. Dad's face. Moldy light.

Red. Dark.

The cigarette planted on his lips like a dead flower. Ashing itself on occasion; when gravity said so. Watching TV static. The remote clutched in a mad conquistador grip.

In came the smoke.

Out went the smoke.

Red. Off.

Red. Off.

Dad wasn't using the ash tray. It was like he was cremating himself from the inside out. Inside parts of dad, burnt and hanging in the room. The ash down his flannel shirt part of the poetry.

Blinking in.

Blinking out.

Red.

Dark.

Red.

Going away, coming back.

The TV was full of electric snow. There was no signal.

THIRTY-NINE

ABOVE THE GAS STATION. In the hallway of the faux house propped up by gasoline.

Angus Fitzroy stood in the doorway to dad's reading room.

Another magazine page fell.

And another.

And another.

"Dad?" he called out softly.

Another magazine page fell.

And another.

And another.

"Dad. Did you eat dinner?"

The kitchen was cold. A layer of dust two days old.

"No dinner ..." Mr. Fitzroy's voice grinded.

"No dinner? But Dad—"

Mr. Fitzroy's tall hand stopped turning pages. Started cracking knuckles.

Angus was gone before the third crack.

FORTY

L ONG AFTER MIDNIGHT.

The deep end of Main Street. The edge of town. The road lonely and silent.

Boucher's dairy farm off the road.

Barn glowing under the thin muscle of one 40w.

Canned light swaying. Light pushed through planks like Play-Doh. Wind howling at the knot holes. Swinging bulb crowding shadows into the corners, letting them come out to play. Back and forth.

Half between farm and forest, just out of reach of the high swing of the bulb, stood a farmer.

His breath a fist of smoke from the cold.

Tucked under his John Deere hat.

Hands fastened along the throat and shoulder of his axe.

The taste of splinters on his lips.

The mark of toothpicks.

Reading the Vermont forest. Each tree a word in a book. Trying to swallow a story.

Jaw rigid as a horseshoe.

FORTY-ONE

Christopher Burmaster was not at school.

Annette Burmaster was not at school.

Jenny Holdridge.

Jane Franklin.

Meg Martain.

Jared Martain.

Jillian Martain.

John Farr was not at school.

Anthony DeWitt.

John DeWitt.

Matt DeWitt.

None of the Brooks boys.

Not a single Chevalier girl.

School couldn't save them. Because school had never saved any kid. It took a lot of credit, sure. But kids were saved or lost on their own terms. Sitting in a desk never cured any kid. Stuffing in math never fixed one. It was a lie everyone in the country believed. Even Vermonters. Henry believe in school like Catholics believed in St. Michael. The world was built of ones and twos, and if he looked at it hard enough he could get the answer. But the world wasn't a math problem. It was just a story. Something we started telling ourselves a long time ago beneath the stars, continued to tell ourselves by our electric campfires. There was no math to it. Science, just a plot device, this weak little can-trip that'd tell a boy *how* grandma died, but never *why* grandma had to die. Kill or cure. That was the motto of the American school system. A boy like Henry could be cured. A boy like Angus would have to be put down. A horse with a broken leg, that boy.

Henry worked extra math problems that day.

Angus, less than usual.

And Ms. Hewett couldn't meet the needs of either boy anymore. Sat in the corner, by the windows, with a magnifying glass and a book, pretending she was reading, burning away the literary world, one word at a time.

FORTY-TWO

T HE SCHOOL BELL rang and no one yelled. It was like library hour, and Henry and Angus found themselves walking away as fast as possible, now crossing town with nothing to say. They had every single combination of words in the English language running drills in their heads. Every single thought performing some duck-and-cover strategy. *What if? Then what? But if they? Could they? And what about? And night is coming. And winter.* But most of all—*what if good, what if bad, what if, what if, what if?*

They were asking the kinds of questions no boy should ever be asking.

Sometimes you're just born in the wrong place, at the wrong time, and someone responsible for leading your church, burns it the fuck down.

"How are we ..." Henry's voice trailed off.

"I don't ..." Angus's voice went to find it.

Both voices got lost. Never came home.

They walked the town.

Going where they knew they needed to go to try to get some kind of mathematical answers that didn't exist. The record had words, and words made sense, so if they could listen to the words, then the town would make sense again. Neither thought it out loud. But their bones wanted it to be true so bad they were quivering like tuning forks.

Pastor Phillips had said something like that once. Some sermon, on some forgotten Sunday—Henry had sat reverently in the pew. Angus had stirred across the street—*'We're all going where we have always known we must go. To get some kind of answer we have always known we must have. God's words are nuts and bolts. With them he will build sense into the world.'*

"It's nine more families," Henry said. "That's in addition to the five from yesterday, or was it the day before that?"

Angus kept walking.

"Aren't you gonna say something?" Henry said.

"What do you want me to say, Henry?"

"Anything!"

"I don't know Henry ... I don't fucking know. God's plucking them like flowers, or someone in town is hacking them to pieces. That's what we decided right?"

Henry walked quietly.

The ghost town passed by.

No cars.

No people.

"The thing is, Henry, it doesn't really matter."

"How can you say that, of course it matters!"

"Yeah it matters, I meant it doesn't make no difference. If someone's out there with a murder bug in their ear, the town's gonna get smaller and smaller until ..." Angus paused. "If God's bottling good folk one by one for his big bug collection in the sky, town's gonna get worse and worse until

...

either way,

Henry, in the end, something bad is coming for you and me."

"We gotta go to the police!"

"Sheriff Vault? How do you know he ain't the one making folk disappear?"

"He's a cop!"

"You said it yourself, The Rapture comes to town and takes the good. So, more and more, who's left? The bad, and the ugly."

"But ..." Henry's voice fell down his throat.

"Get rid of the good and suddenly this town starts to make sense," Angus said. "Everyone's here for a reason. So what was it? What's Sheriff Vault's reason? Maybe he went out on the highway and pulled over young girls, slapped them with big tickets, but gave 'em a chance to work something out, no money required. Maybe he shot someone dead who already had their hands up. Maybe putting on a gun every morning like a piece of jewelry is enough? It's a tool built to kill after all. Maybe you wear that badge long enough and it rots you from the outside. Maybe he and Ms. Hewett ... we'll never know. They'll never tell. We could guess, and probably guess wrong, on ten dozen things. But if you're right about The Rapture, and he's still here ... he deserves to be."

The boys were outside the record shop.

It looked closed.

The sign said so.

But the boys knew what was going on in there—in the back was a room. In the room was a lamp without a shade. Under the glow of an unfiltered bulb was a man. On the man was a pair of lips. On the lips was a tune. Synchronized with the tune was a record. On the record was one song playing over, and over, and over, and over, and over, and over, and over ...

"What do we do?" Henry whispered.

Angus narrowed his gunslinger eyes. "We get the record."

"But how? You know he's in there listening to it over and over and over."

"We take it."

"But he's bigger than us, and stronger!"

"We distract him," Angus said.

"But that's the problem," Henry replied.

"He's distracted?"

Henry nodded.

Angus nodded with him.

"We can't get it," Henry said. "The store's closed, the door is locked and in there is a man falling into a pit of something we don't understand. Shuffling his life into the breeze cast off a spinning record. Wasting away listening to something not bad, or good, but just *there*. Building a life around it. How much you wanna bet he skipped dinner last night. Fell asleep in the chair. Woke up and cursed at himself for being so stupid and went upstairs and got in bed only to lie awake listening to the rattling yarn of the country turning towards a cold winter. Catching himself humming the tune. Cursing at himself. Blinking and finding himself back in that back room, with a window so small he could barely tell if it's day or night anymore, and who cares? Day and night don't mean anything anymore. Stupid little poems, written by kindergarteners. So what do we do? The record store closed, lights off, a whole town herded off. Even if the door wasn't locked, we couldn't get the record away from him, or him away from the record, I don't even know which it is anymore."

Angus planted a cigarette on his lips.

"What the heck are you doing?" Henry exclaimed.

"They help me think," Angus defended.

Henry looked to the cigarette.

"Why are you looking at me like that?" Angus asked, cigarette slurring his words, match in hand, waiting to be struck.

"Like what?"

"Like *that*," Angus said.

"I don't know what you're talking about."

"You're looking at me the same way you were looking at Mr. Villanelle yesterday. The same way you looked at the chair that had swallowed my dad. Probably the same way you look at your own old man every night you go home and he's thirty-two channels and forty-eight cigarettes deeper in ... whatever this is."

"It's just ... why do you gotta smoke?" Henry asked.

"I told you, smoking is who I am. What I'm meant to be. You got a name like Henry, that means teachers like you. You listen in school, get good grades, will grow up and fit in. Be a lawyer, or a doctor or even a goddamn preacher, hell if I know, but I know it will be something legitimate. But I was never gonna be there. You know what my destiny is in life. Lay tile in someone's bathroom. Cobble together tips from waiting on people. Lord over a tiny little empire of candy bars and gasoline with cigarette pitstop out back once an hour. Seventeen bucks on pump two, you got it. A pack of Cattleman Rough Cuts, that'll be 94 cents. You know how my story ends Henry Samuel? I end up impregnating some girl I don't actually care about, and we have a miserable life together and pop out four more fucking kids who will grow up thinking love is chewing your spouse up one side and down the other. We'll get fat and ugly and the only peace I'll have is when I smoke because the goddamn kids will know their mother said to not to be around me when I smoke." Angus stuck the match hard. Sucked cigarette heavily. Blew smoke bitterly.

Vermont took the smoke easily.

"Why don't you just change your name?" Henry said quietly.

"What?"

"Why don't you just change your name?"

"You need a lawyer or something to do that."

"Says who?"

"The State of Vermont. The United States of America."

"Screw them."

"What did you just say?"

"I said screw them."

"Did Henry Samuel just use the word *screw*?"

"You bet I did, just pick a new name. Something you can grow into. Something you like. Something that lets you become a doctor or a banker or a writer or even mayor of the town, or heck, President of the United States. Just pick something new and tell everyone I want to be called so-and-so now. And stop responding to Angus. Someone says Angus, you don't respond until they remember that now you're Michael or Thomas, or Walter. Walter is a fine name. The name of a singer. Something on stage, in New York. Walter

Fitzroy, that's a name that could take you places. Away from here. That's a name that would look good in lights."

Angus shook his head. Tapped his cigarette. Dragged.

"Why not?" Henry asked.

"My name's Angus."

"Says who, your mom and dad?"

"Vern. The whole goddamn town. The state outside that. The country outside that."

"Sixteen years ago? Times have changed. Maybe your parents made a mistake. Maybe you were supposed to be a Christopher? Parents make mistakes."

Smoke.

"I'm an Angus, through and through."

"But you don't have to be," Henry said softly.

Angus shook his head.

Burnt spice went in his lungs.

Mortuary dust came out his mouth.

"I don't know what name I'd pick."

FORTY-THREE

AND HENRY DIDN'T REPLY to that. No. Henry knew he'd said too much. Too, too much. And part of him wanted to take it back. All the talk about names. Because although he wouldn't be a parent for another twenty years give or take, although he wouldn't bear the full burden of naming a chunk of clay he'd help bring into existence, he understood something about parenting in his teeth and toes. Something about loosening the reins, letting humans figure out their own answers, the defeatist notion of ever trying to convince anyone of anything, the corrupt morality of it, the absurd practice, the raw stupidity and waste of voice. Most parents bark at their kids, constantly crying wolf, but, even at thirteen, Henry Samuel's bones understood it was best to teach a kid what a wolf was. Let the child warn itself. Someday, Henry Samuel would make a fine parent. Not a perfect parent. A parent who made a lot of the kind of mistakes that come from trying, and caring too much, which all things considered may be the best kind of mistakes to make.

Angus finished his cigarette.

He dropped the stub and ground it into the state.

Vermont took it and didn't complain.

"Ok, we come back tomorrow, when it's open," Henry said, "and

I knock something over, you know, on purpose, and the ruckus should bring Mr. Villanelle out of the back room, and then you sneak in the back and lift the record, right? I mean borrow. We'll bring it back."

Angus shook his head.

"Ok, so we go to the back, and find the power breaker, right? And we shut it off, Baxter Boyd told me about that. Then when Mr. Villanelle comes outside to turn it back on, we go inside and get the record."

Angus shook his head.

"I don't know?" Henry huffed. "You got a better plan?"

"Yeah. I do."

"Your cigarette tell you it?" Henry said.

"They can tell you a thing or two. If you listen. Most people smoke to shut up the world, not to tune into it."

"Still killing you."

"Living is killing you," Angus pointed out.

"Not as fast."

"Strange thing for a boy like you to say."

"What do you mean?" Henry asked.

"How many boys you think went down to that swimming hole for a summer swim and never came home? Thirty? Forty? Counting Indians, God knows? Being alive is like being a match, any breeze too rough and you're gone, you burn too long, you're out. But cigarettes ... you ever try to blow one of those things out? Good luck. It burns away as fast as you're ready. Suck it down quick, suck it down slow, just let it smoke itself. Someone will wake up with cancer tomorrow. For no good reason. But if you smoke all your life, and end up with cancer, at least you earned it."

Henry didn't want to talk about dying.

He'd been there and hadn't liked it.

"I bet you're the only one," Angus said.

"The only one what?"

"To drown and come back. Thirty, forty kids that swimming hole ate alive, and you're the only one that got away."

"But I didn't, according to you. I'm dead anyways. Might as well start smoking."

"Smoking? You? Nah. It doesn't suit you, kid." Angus narrowed his eyes. "But something about you is different. Yeah. Something about you didn't come back, and I'm not talking about the pinky toe of your spirit."

"I don't know what you're talking about." Henry looked around the town. There wasn't much to see.

"I've been trying to put my finger on it ever since that day last summer. I knew you'd come back different. Not in a horror-movie kinda way. Not in a high-strung evangelist kinda way. Nah ... something more subtle. Something you can't see, but something that let you see the missing church when no one else could."

"I don't know what you're talking about."

"Not yet."

"Sounds like you know, so you tell me."

"I don't got an answer yet. Maybe I haven't smoked enough cigarettes. That's how great minds think."

"Says who?"

"Sherlock Holmes."

"Doesn't seem like something you would read," Henry pointed out.

"That's because most people assume I can't."

"Read?"

Angus nodded.

"Didn't he smoke a pipe?" Henry asked.

"It's all tobacco."

Vermont sifted around them. On the edge of town they stood on the side of a road that both lead to nowhere, and everywhere. They looked to the squatty two-story building across the street looming above them. Now that the church was gone, it stood a little taller. The way the bricks sagged slightly in the center, almost looked like a smile.

"We need that record," Henry whispered.

"We don't need the record," Angus replied. "Just the words."

FORTY-FOUR

IT LOOKED like school behind Mr. Villanelle's record store. A couple boys sat on a gritty strip of concrete pencil and paper out looking like some valedictorians sitting in their desks first day of school, starved by the summer drought, paper ready, pencils in hand, just waiting, itching for the teacher's mouth to open and pour out a thousand old and useful things.

The boys listened.

They heard music. The brick blocked it. The window mumbled song. It was all stirred together. Some kind of jumbled mess. Angus cocked an ear. Stood up. Raised it toward the window just above his head.

"I can't hear it," Henry whispered.

"*Shhhh.*"

There was a tune in there. There was a man in there. One was playing off a record. One was coming out a throat. Both were dancing together. Maybe Angus could have followed the tune if only he'd known it. Maybe Henry could have picked up the words if only he'd heard them before. The boys tilted ears. Looked at paper. Commanded pencils to go, but they stood still. Their pencils would not tell lies. They did some scribbling, kickstarts at words, but nothing came out. Only the word *'Papa.'* Only because they already knew it was there in the room.

"Fuck!" Angus hissed. He fished his pockets for a pack of smokes.

"What are you doing?"

"Thinking."

"You mean smoking?"

"Thinking."

Henry looked to the window above. "He'll smell."

"Through a shut window?"

"Maybe."

Angus looked to the window above. Beyond, there was a raw record going on. But the window beat the shit out of it by the time it got to the other side. "I don't think he can smell much of anything anymore."

Angus sliced a match. Took a few breaths. The wind tossed the last pieces of daylight around. Angus breathed in. Breathed out. Left behind a vanishing trail of exhaust. Curled his lips around the cigarette. Let it go. Up with the cigarette. Down with the cigarette. Blew smoke down the alley.

He ashed.

Stood up.

"I'll be back," he announced.

"Where are you going?"

But Angus was gone. Around the corner. Out of sight. Leaving Henry sitting alone, behind an old brick building that served as house and record store to a man named after a type of poem. The record store. The only outlet to the mad world beyond the borders of Vermont save for the TV. Something, somehow more pure, because electric roadshows pumped in from big cities through tiny little wires didn't have a scent, smell, or musk. Hadn't really touched anything on their way to Vermont. But records had been somewhere else. Maybe lots of places else. And landed here. Each one, its own ghost story—about an owner who didn't survive the record.

Angus came back, smoking a different cigarette. With a baseball. Brand new. Ripping it out of the box. Never been used before.

"Baseball? You wanna play a game at a—"

Angus wound up.

C-R-A-S-H-!

A thousand light-speed spiders spun their webs over the glass, and then there was only the sound of the ocean. The slush and surf of falling glass. Spilling out the frame, dripping down the brick. Settling on the street.

The record stopped.

A shadow moved in the room. The boys could only see shape, the day was gone, electricity boxed away in a switch somewhere on Mr. Villanelle's wall. It was dark. The room. The figure. "The Hell's wrong with you kids?" His voice came like heavy rain. Rain meant to beat the shit out of the planet.

Angus's cigarette hung, smoldering, off his lip.

"Oh, geez, sorry, Mr. Villanelle. Gosh, we're awful sorry, we'll pay for it. Honest. I got sixteen dollars saved up at home. Really."

Henry stood still between them.

One loose paper blew down the alley. Vermont's version of high noon and tumbleweeds.

November flowed past them, winter in its teeth.

Angus's lips rolled his cigarette to the far side.

His fingers itched.

"Can't go breaking another man's property." Came the storm. The boys stood in the rain. It did not put out Angus's cigarette. It did not drench them, but it did chill them. It made them long for summer, when Vermont was leaning *into* the sun, made them long for fireplaces, chopped-wood, matches, campfires, electric blankets, hot chocolate, tea, warm cookies, wool socks, ovens, hot showers, chicken noodle soup. There was a storm in Mr. Villanelle's voice, broken, chaotic, angry, unblamable, and it made the boys cold. Winter was coming down from Canada, winter, this thing you survive in Vermont, but it was already here in Mr. Villanelle's voice, and it made the boys long for anything and everything warm, hot or cozy, or even lukewarm. But standing outside, in Vermont, in November, they didn't have any of those things. Angus dragged his cigarette. It burnt his lungs. It was the only warmth he had.

The clouds opened up,

a drizzle fell on the boys,

weak and passing, "*Smoking causes lung cancer.*"

The shape slurred, turned.

Left.

Swallowed by the room.

Leaving the boys alone.

Cold.

Angus passed the cigarette.

Henry took it. Did not smoke. Did not put it on his lips. Just held in between his fingers like his own private campfire to keep him warm.

The record turned back on.

The boys heard Mr. Villanelle muttering.

Vinyl words came clearly out the window.

Angus grabbed his pencil.

———

no teeth at all.

Angus finished writing the last words. Somewhere close Mr. Villanelle picked up the needle. Set it down. The old time piano scratched into existence again. The crooner began to sing. '*Now, don't get married, don't get married, said my friend Nick Brown.*' Some kind of ghost, risen from the grave by the necromancy of Edison. They'd listened to it three times. Twice to get the lyrics. Once to check the lyrics. Three times. And how many times had Mr. Villanelle listened? God knows, thought Henry. But God didn't know. God was too busy picking up stakes. Packing up The Rapture to roll down the road.

no teeth at all.

Angus closed his notebook. Looked at Henry. The boy was still holding the cigarette, or what was left of it, only the filter, and a pile of ash waiting to be tapped. It'd felt warm in his hands, and now it was gone. He moved his hands, ash wasted away snowing the skin of his hand. Henry dropped the filter like a spider. And Angus was about to say *let's go read these, someplace safe*—by which he meant his room, but *safe* suddenly seemed a strange word to sling.

Somehow didn't fit the town anymore.

Like old clothes.

"Let's go," he whispered. A fragment of his original sentence. Line-edited to shit.

"Where?" Henry Samuel whispered.

And Angus almost needed a cigarette to come up with an answer. Probably would have fired one up to kickstart his brain, but something else came their way.

T-H-U-N-K

T-H-U-N-K

T-H-U-N-K

A sound out the alley.
Angus stood.
Made his way down the alley.

T-H-U-N-K

T-H-U-N-K

T-H-U-N-K

Henry watched him go. Walk to the beat of something bad.
It was the sound of a tree being hacked.

Slow.

Steady.

Axe whistling through November woods. Wood being slaughtered is an awfully normal sound. Metronomic. Angus came to the end of the alley. Peered around the buildings. But Henry already knew what was out that direction. The last place in town. Boucher's farm.

"It's Mr. Boucher." Angus tossed the words carefully back down the alley.

"Stocking up on firewood, right?" Henry replied.

Angus turned back to watch.

"That's normal, this time of year," Henry said. "He always does that."

Angus didn't answer.

"Right?" Henry said.

No answer.

"Right?!"

"I don't think so," Angus whispered.

"Why not?"

"He's not chopping up the trees. He's just chopping them down."

T-H-U-N-K

T-H-U-N-K

T-H-U-N-K

C-R-A-S-H

Another tree came down.

Mr. Boucher started on a new tree.

T-H-U-N-K

T-H-U-N-K

T-H-U-N-K

Angus could still hear the ghost song spilling from Mr. Villanelle's broken window behind ... *But poor Papa, poor Papa, he's got nothin' at all ...*

It was quiet.

There was no way the dollhouse figure of Mr. Boucher, a hundred yards off, could hear the record.

Yet, Mr. Boucher hacked in tune.

On the beat.

Like he was humming along.

FORTY-FIVE

ACROSS TOWN A MAN sat low in the light-spill of television static.

A radio tower blinking on his lips.

In.

Out.

The room was pregnant with smoke. Cartons in the corner. Empty packs scattered like landmines across the living room.

On.

Off.

The red light.

On.

Off.

A pair of hands clutched the armrests.

The electric gust from the box stormed on.

FORTY-SIX

"I DIDN'T EVEN HAVE to pay for the baseball," Angus announced strangely.

"What?"

The boys were walking down the street. Feeling more and more they were on a stage. The buildings, just props. The town, something made up.

"I hollered at the backroom. I heard someone tuning the radio, but no one came to the counter. The baseball. I didn't even pay for it."

"Wait, what do you mean?"

"Mr. Revelli. He wouldn't come to the counter. I called out like six times. I heard him moving around in the back room, lights off, fiddling with a radio, trying to tune into..."

Angus stopped walking.

"Well?"

"It was weird," Angus said, looking somewhere. Nowhere. Trying to recreate the scene in his mind. "You know how you tune into a station? Like you get static and then you start picking up the station, and you move the dial into the signal until the static is gone?"

"Yeah."

"I think Mr. Revelli was doing the opposite."

"What's the opposite?"

"Tuning into the static."

The wind stirred a plastic sack, it ran the empty street. Sounded like radio static. It ran away.

The boys were alone on the street.

Main Street.

There were no lights on anywhere. They knew there were people in the buildings, at least some of them, but they were no longer leaving lightbulb footprints.

Henry looked around the town. Suddenly he felt something in his stomach.

"Angus."

"Yeah."

"I'm homesick."

And Angus knew what he meant. Knew the feeling. Had felt the same way before. For a person.

His mother.

"Yeah," Angus nodded. "I get that."

The boys got quiet.

The wind got loud. Funny how that happens.

Wind going here. Wind going there. Passing by. Not wanting to stay. Not wanting to get stuck in Vermont for the winter. Running like Hell from the north. Away from Canada. Headed south.

"You got a mom?" Angus asked.

"Everyone's got a mom."

"Not everyone. What's the deal with her?" Angus scratched the edge of his lips.

"Whaddya mean what's the deal?" Henry replied.

"Where is she?"

"I dunno."

"How do you not know?"

"I dunno," Henry explained. "My dad never said anything about her. I asked, he pretends he doesn't hear me. I found a picture. He keeps it in his dresser drawer, under a little plate thing where he keeps his watches."

"And?"

"They looked happy. I think she was pregnant with me."

Vermont was library-quiet for the boys.

"What about your mom?" Henry asked.

"What about her?"

"Where is she?"

"She's dead." Angus said plainly.

"Oh. ... how'd she die?"

"Giving birth."

"So your dad named you ... alone?"

Angus shrugged. "Probably. I guess so. I don't think they had names picked out if that's what you're asking."

"Maybe that's why," Henry said.

"Why what?"

"Why your name ..."

"Sucks?"

"No." Henry spoke quickly. "It's doesn't suck ... it's just ... *stuck.*"

"Stuck?"

"Yeah. You were named by one parent. Planning a funeral. No wonder."

"No wonder what?"

"You got a name with a lot of hurt."

"*A lot of hurt,*" Angus repeated.

"I mean having a kid is supposed to be the happiest day of your life, especially for dads and sons, and they say when you meet the kid sometimes the name just pops into your head. And imagine your dad watching the birth, and the monitor starts beeping and the nurses look scared, and the doctor starts to sweat, and your mom passes out and your dad asks 'what the hell is going on?' and someone says 'get him out of here,' and he's pushed out, to the lonely halls of a hospital. Long after midnight, empty and dim, and no sound but nurses clucking at some station down the hall. And he waits for one hour? Two hours? Three? And it's three, now, Christ, 3 a.m.! And finally someone comes out, and all his life he's been waiting for the moment where a doctor would tell him 'congratulations, you're a father,' and the doctor doesn't say 'you're a father.' The doctor leads with the bad news. Your wife ... didn't make it. And you, *you* Angus, are the good news. But the bad news came first, right? And what do you do when someone beats the crap out of you like that? A one-two punch like that—your wife is dead, and you're a dad. And your kid needs you. And he needs a name. And what's the name of your mortuary, and we'll send your wife's body there. And your boy needs a name. What will you call him? Mr. Fitzroy? Sir? Sir? Sir?"

Angus sat down on the side of the street.

He looked the state sidewise.

"Fuck my name," he mumbled.

Henry sat down beside him.

He put an arm around. The boy shifted it off. Sat alone.

He could almost hear Angus shuffling the trash, stirring the mess of memories.

"You think he thought I did it?" Angus asked.

"Did what?"

"Killed her?"

"Oh Angus, I don't—"

"Why are we the only two in town that can see this shit? I'll give you two answers. You've been dead. I killed my mom. You know what a life is like starting out on the left foot of murder? Knowing you're already guilty of the worst crime we got?"

"Angus ... I just ... don't think like that. Dyin's just ..." Henry lost his words.

"... part of living," Angus finished the sentence.

Angus planted a cigarette on his lips. He fired up a match. He dusted a few seconds off his life. Looked at the idiot thing between his fingers. Burnt a hole in his jeans. Put the cigarette on his lips.

Dragged. Sanded away part of himself, an odd thirty seconds from a bad day. *A lot of hurt*. He muttered.

"So that's my name, huh?" He blew smoke. "The first thing my dad said after they told him his wife was dead."

He dragged on the Cattleman.

It said something.

But not at a frequency a boy could hear.

FORTY-SEVEN

A FIGURE in a dress stood in the school library, a cold cigarette on her lips.

Doors locked.

Lights off.

Night out.

Cold. Raw Vermont. On the other side of the windows.

A hand sparked a plastic *Bic* lighter.

Felt *now-here now-gone* warmth.

Sparked the lighter.

Warmth.

Cold.

Sparked the lighter, held down the fuel line.

Flame whispered in the library.

The hand toasted to perfection.

The book spines flickering in the night—

200 - Religion

400 - Language

900 - History & Geography

800 - Literature

The lighter went to a pair of lips.

A cigarette waited there.

A hand pulled a book off the shelf in a cloud of smoke.

Tore a page out.

Jack-o'-lantern glow filled the library.

The cigarette demolished each word, one by one, like a pencil eraser. With the words bulldozed, the page collapsed. The cigarette dead between her lips.

Night swept in.

Cold.

The figure reached for more words.

A hand sparked the lighter.

FORTY-EIGHT

Henry looked up.

They were across the street from the pastor's house. It sat lean in the season. Collecting shadows. Reclining in darkness. Ready for the Vermont winter, the low daylight, the cold, the cold, the cold. There would be no fire inside this house this winter. No more lights turning on.

"Whatd'ya think will happen to it?" Angus wondered aloud.

"I dunno," Henry replied. "I mean, I guess it depends how long he gets. If you don't pay your house payment I think the bank sells it off."

"How long does that take?"

"I don't know. Maybe a year?"

"He could be back in a year," Angus said through his cigarette.

"How long do you get for arson? Is that what you'd call it?" Henry asked.

"Guess it depends if the judge is Christian."

"You think that makes a difference?"

Angus shrugged. "Maybe. An atheist would say you burnt down your own building, maybe a community building. A believer'd say you burnt down a house of God."

The house sat quiet. Full of stories and secrets.

"I bet it knows." Angus tapped his cigarette.

"The house? Knows what?"

"Why he did it."

The boys looked to the house. It took their gaze and didn't blink.

"We need to find someplace safe to read over these lyrics," Angus said.

Safe, Henry Samuel thought. *Safe.* The word felt so far away.

Safe.

Dead and gone. Never having been there. Angus was homesick for his mother. Always had been. Always would be.

Neither boy had gotten the first dose of safety life was supposed to give you.

Had Henry Samuel even had the security of breast milk?

He could not say.

Dad would not tell.

Safe.

Mothers are director-writer-producers of little films played on tiny sets of bones. What they say goes. What they don't falls by the wayside. And some kids get a family film, something that colors the world free from harm. They walk out into the world understanding it's there to meet their needs, something they can trust. But Henry and Angus got something slid to ruin. Unplanned horror films. Neither boy had ever felt safe before, so how could they now?

Safe.

"But ... where?" Henry Samuel asked aloud.

"I don't know," Angus replied. He racked his brain. Where? Where? Where?

He fished for a new cigarette.

"Wait," Henry said softly.

The cigarette hung on a pair of lips.

"Maybe ... try it this time, without smoking."

Angus looked to the cigarette. It was easy to mistake it for safety, because it was certain. And safety and certainty seem like the same thing, but they aren't the same thing. Smoking cigarettes is certain you will die. But it doesn't make them safe.

Angus dragged his unlit cigarette. Tasted raw, dried, un-immolate tobacco.

It didn't taste the same.

"We need to find someplace to read over these lyrics," Angus said.

Henry noticed it was the same sentence as before, line-edited for two boys who'd never had mothers.

FORTY-NINE

The door whined back on its hinges. A dark and deserted house expanding. The door had not been locked. Like the pastor had expected to come home. Dinner was left out, not put away, like he understood the errand would be small. To the gas station for a quart of milk, batteries for the smoke detector, and burn down the town church, it should only take ten minutes.

"Not his house," Henry replied.

"Why not?"

"I dunno. Just ... haven't."

"I thought it would look more ... churchy," Angus said looking around.

"Yeah ..." Henry said. "Me too."

"He doesn't even have a cross. Or a picture of Jesus or a psalm cross-stitched and hung on the wall."

The smoke detector chirped. The boys looked up at it.

"Needs a new battery," Angus said.

"You mean like this," Henry pointed. On the kitchen table, next to dinner barely started, sat a white plastic sack holding a brand new nine-volt battery.

"Yeah ..." Angus's eyes narrowed. "Like *that.*"

The boys stared.

"Looks like one of your sacks. From the gas station."

Angus nodded. "It is." His eyes narrowed even more. "So lemme get this straight, the pastor sits down to mac 'n cheese, green beans, mashed potatoes and a glass of milk, has two bites, hears the smoke detector beep about being low on battery, stands up, goes and buys a battery from my dad, because the thought of burning up asleep in his own bedroom is too awful to tolerate for even ten minutes, can't even wait until he finishes his dinner, *but* doesn't even install the battery? Doesn't even get it out of the plastic sack, out of the packaging, doesn't even slide a chair over here against the wall to reach the smoke detector, but instead sets it on the table and goes back to the gas station for three canisters of gas to burn down his own fucking church and stand in front of the inferno like a goddamn campfire, huffing in all the smoke like a top-shelf cigarette, roasting marshmallows on a stick for all we know?"

Angus looked around.

Somewhere off in the house, shadows of tree branches moved on far windowpanes.

"It's strange."

The boys stood in the dining room listening to the attic beams shiver. Now and then hearing a tree limb scratch the house in the wind.

"Don't you think that's strange?"

The smoke detector chirped.

Angus thrust a hand into the plastic sack, ripped the nine-volt out of the packaging, threw a chair against the wall, stepped up, clawed the cover off, pulled out the geriatric battery and plugged in the new one. He stopped before he put the cover back on. Looking at the fool plastic thing, turning his gaze to the mesh of colorful wires in the exposed smoke detector. He threw the cover on the table. Sat down in the chair. The smoke detector no longer talked about dying.

"I guess it doesn't matter ..." he said, "you know, if the smoke detector's got a new battery or not."

"Yeah," Henry Samuel said. "I guess not."

Outside Vermont hummed a tuneless tune. Wind passed through town like migratory birds headed south.

"Maybe we should look at those lyrics," Angus said.

Henry nodded.

Angus flipped a light switch.

"Wait! Someone will see!"

"Who?"

Henry thought.

"I guess you're right."

Angus got out his notebook. Pushed the pastor's last meal to the far side of the table. The boys crowded over the words.

"Now, don't get married, don't get married," said my friend Nick
Brown
If you take a wife, you're out of luck for life
He had all his little sons and daughters by his side
Like happy hooligans, sixteen kids, they all lined up and cried

Mama's got shoes, Mama's got clothes
Mama's got these and Mama's got those
But poor Papa, poor Papa, he's got nothin' at all

Mama goes here, mama goes there
Mama goes out to every affair
But poor Papa, poor Papa, he waits out in the hall

Now, Christmas come and Mama gets
The most expensive frocks
Papa gets a necktie
And a pair of ten-cent socks

Everyone cheers when Mama appears
And she's got diamonds stuck in her ears

But poor Papa, poor Papa, he's got nothin' at all

And Mama eats ham, Mama eats lamb
Mama eats bread with strawberry jam
And poor Papa, poor Papa, he eats nothin' at all

Mama says, "Oh!" Mama says, "Ah!"
Mama says, "Boo!" And mama says, "Bah!"
But poor Papa, poor Papa, he says nothing at all

Papa bought a limousine
And the most expensive kind
Now he wears a chauffeur's suit, heh-heh
And Mama rides behind

Mama's got silk, satin beneath
She's got gold in all of her teeth
But poor Papa, poor Papa, he's got no teeth at all

The boys looked at each other.

"What do you think it means?" Henry asked.

Angus reached for a cigarette. He caught Henry's gaze.

"Sherlock Holmes smoked to clear his mind," Angus explained.

"In the pastor's house?"

"He burnt down your church. I think I can smoke a cigarette in his house."

The cigarette went off. Leaking smoke into the dining room.

Angus tapped his chin.

Dragged.

"*Poor Papa.* That's it. The tune of the town," Angus said.

"What do you mean?" Henry asked.

"Look at this guy, he doesn't get shit. He's left behind. He gets married and *BAM!* Suddenly, he's not getting anything, and she's getting everything. That's what's going on, in this town, look, my dad, your dad, Mr. Villanelle and Mr. Boucher and Mr. Revelli, what's going on? They got hitched, that's what. Married to something that's bleeding them dry. Something that got out when the church went down. Something that only cares about itself." Angus tap ash off his cigarette over the pastor's last meal in lieu of an ashtray. *"'Don't get married. Don't get married. You take a wife, you're out of luck for life.'* Mr. Villanelle knows it, or some part of him. He's trying to say it the only way he knows how. He's screaming inside. But he doesn't got a voice no more, so he has to speak the only way he knows how. And a record store owner's got a brain full of lyrics. He's telling us, he's telling himself, he's telling the town how it's gonna go."

Henry Samuel nodded.

Angus smoldered on his cigarette.

His eyes looked over the lyrics again.

He took a long draw of his cigarette.

"And it gets worse the longer you're married."

"What?"

"Look." Angus pointed to the words. His finger moved down the page. "First you give up your shoes, you give up your clothes, Mama goes out and you stays home. Sound familiar? When's the last time your dad left the house?"

"Um . . ."

"Not since the church burnt down," Angus answered.

Henry didn't blink.

"Mama gets the best clothes, you get a pair of ten-cent socks. Your dad changed his clothes in the last few days?"

Henry Samuel shook his head.

"And *here,*" Angus jabbed his finger on the page. "This is where we are. *Mama eats ham, Mama eats lamb. Mama eats bread with strawberry jam. And poor Papa, poor Papa, he eats nothin' at all.*" Angus's cigarette sifted smoke. He took a long draw.

"My dad didn't eat last night. Or the night before."

Henry nodded, like he'd know it all along.

Angus took another drag.

The cigarette burned up his breath and threw it away.

"These last three verses tell us how it's gonna go." Angus said into his cigarette. "'*Oh!*' and '*Ah!*' that's where we are right now, the way my dad looks at magazines, the way Mr. Revelli's tuning into static, Mr. Boucher chopping down trees."

"The way my dad's watching TV static."

"Right," Angus nodded. "Something exciting about it right now, that ain't the right word, but whatever. Thing is . . . it's going to '*Boo!*' and '*Bah!*'"

"What do you mean?"

"It's gonna go bad. It's gonna go scary."

The pastor's clock ticked on the wall.

tick

tick

tick

Angus tapped the word *chauffeur*. "Whatever got outta that church is gonna start puttin' people *to work*."

"What kind of work?"

tick

tick

tick

The clock ticked its own measure song. And suddenly Angus thought of the rhythm of Mr. Boucher's afternoon axe. Chopping down the forest in perfect timing.

"I don't think we want to find out. But we know how this ends. For my dad. For your dad."

Henry read the last line again.

But poor Papa, poor Papa, he's got no teeth at all.

FIFTY

He hadn't struck a match in two days.

There was no need.

He'd been chaining the cigarettes. Using one to light another. Dragging himself through this killing chemistry of broken men.

The television played electricity's idea of a snowstorm.

It was loud.

Noise and light owned the room,

a blistering dispatch from a paranoid world.

Noise.

Light.

Two bit parts compared to the cigarette.

FIFTY-ONE

"How long has it been?" Henry asked.

And for some reason, Henry didn't have to say *since the church burnt down.*

"Three days. No, two? Maybe two?" Angus thought. "Three. I think three."

"It feels like a long time."

Angus nodded.

"Yeah," he said. "Feels like the week got burnt and melted too."

Henry nodded.

They listened to the empty house waiting patiently for the preacher to come home. It would be a wait. Dust would have to settle. Maybe he never would come back. Maybe he never would get back inside. Maybe the bank would take it and sell it off and by the time he got out he'd have to watch from across the street on the marble sidewalk? But of course, none of that would ever happen.

"You're right. I haven't seen my dad eat," Henry said.

"Nothing?"

"Cigarettes."

"Those don't count. You don't chew 'em."

"But I haven't been home, maybe he ate while I was out?" Henry said.

"Have you seen any dishes in the sink?" Angus asked.

"Wait, he buys cigarettes." Henry said.

"So?"

"Maybe he's eating stuff from your gas station? Candy bars, hot dogs, stuff like that. Could you check?"

"How?"

"Don't you have some kinda inventory system?" Henry asked.

"No. We just order stuff when we run low."

"Oh."

He shifted in his seat. Suddenly uncomfortable being in the pastor's house.

"Could you ... ask your dad?" Henry asked.

"Ask *my* dad?" Angus repeated.

"Yeah, ask your dad if my dad's bought any food."

Just out the window the streets knew things by night. Kept secrets.

And Angus Fitzroy didn't know how to say *I'm afraid of my dad...*

...more than usual.

FIFTY-TWO

Somewhere, on the edge of town, a man stood looking over the fresh corpses of a litany of trees. He could almost hear their last breaths.

How many had he killed?

Seven. Eight. Nine.

His eyes floated.

Ten. Eleven. Twelve.

Twelve. He said it out loud.

He looked to forest. His hand clutched axe. The moonlight came down like a projector. The blade played the part of movie screen. Smoke came out of the man's mouth. There was no cigarette. Just November. The season was smoking him.

The vague shape of a bundled man surveyed the forest.

How many were left?

One hundred and twenty. Twenty-one. Twenty-two.

His eyes stirred.

One hundred and twenty-three. Twenty-four. He lost count.

... a million ... He said it out loud.

A hand let go of the axe. It fell to the dirt. The moon spilled aimlessly, a projector turned on its side. The horror film slopped all over the farm.

The man walked to the barn.

The light bulb spilled.

A shape surveyed the museum of tools.

A million, said a voice. *A million. A million. A million.*

FIFTY-THREE

HENRY CAME in the front door for the first time in a couple days. He'd been using his window. Hiding in his room. Not brushing his teeth. Pissing outside. Eating lunch at school. Using their restrooms to shit. His home had shrunk. He only had his room. A bed, a dresser, a window, a door that might as well have been a wall.

The front door whined back. The front room sketching out in charcoal. Blue light spilled like oceans.

Henry took a step inside.

The kitchen was cold. There were no dinner scents.

A white tide coming in from the TV.

Rolling over, and over, and over the room. Churning the room in surf. Angry, pissed-off, moon-stretched waves. Dad sat in his arm chair. Fingers clutched to the armrest like he was on a ride. A cigarette clenched between his teeth.

Dad did not move.

Did not blink.

Did not even drag his cigarette. It just smoked itself, like a piece of incense.

Dad was caught out in the storm.

Henry approached. His father didn't notice.

"Dad?" Henry said.

No answer.

"Dad?" Henry said louder.

No response.

"Dad?!"

Not even the cigarette answered.

The TV splashed and surfed. It had drowned many men. Why not one more?

Henry picked up the remote. Shut it off.

"The Hell's wrong with you?!"

Dad snatched the remote. Turned back on the static.

"Dad?"

No answer.

"Dad?"

No response.

"Have you had anything to eat?" Henry yelled above the crash.

The cigarette did not catch wind of Dad's breath. Sat, smoldering low on his lip.

"Dad?!" Henry yelled. "You have anything to eat?!"

Dad said nothing.

Henry watched Dad watch television static. The waves came in, came in, came in. Dad's diet was this now. He'd been drinking ocean water. Salt water. Kidneys can only make piss that is less salty that ocean water Henry had read once, somewhere, he couldn't remember. To get rid of all the extras salt taken in by drinking sea water, you have to piss more water than you drink. That extra water comes from your body. Eventually, you die of dehydration.

"Dad, you gotta eat," Henry said.

Another wave came in. Dad took it.

"Dad?"

No answer.

"Dad?!"

No response.

Henry unplugged the television. The ocean drained.

Dad grabbed Henry's arm. Stoked his cigarette.

"Don't you *ever* turn off the TV when I'm watching something, you hear?!"

He jammed the cigarette into Henry's arm.

Flesh burnt, cigarette squealed.

Henry cried out. Felt himself cry. Dad threw Henry's arm away, puffed his cigarette back to life.

"Plug that back in," Dad pointed, the cigarette humming power between his teeth.

And Henry did.

FIFTY-FOUR

Angus Fitzroy tapped the last thirty seconds of his life off the end of his cigarette.

Flinting his eyes over the loss,

himself, scattered to the wind.

The gas station rose before him. A squatty two story building by day. Tall and lean and lank by night. Or at least, this night. Because the church wasn't across the street anymore. The gas station had grown. It was only 1987, so Angus wouldn't know for another fourteen years, but there was a single day coming when all the buildings in New York grew a little bit taller.

His little town in Vermont learnt the lesson fourteen years early.

They boy's smoke ran away into the hills. The wind took it there.

Angus opened the door.

The bell rang.

The lights were off. The door had not been locked.

Closed, but not *closed*.

He looked over the candy bars, the hot dogs, the popcorn machine.

Cold and unattended.

He stood in the dark, missing warm lights, safe streets, good town, home cooked meals.

There were no smells of food.

He stood missing fine October air, Sunday night town, warm church, lit like a lantern across the street. Yes. Even the church.

No smells. Not even from the kitchen.

The boy went upstairs. He could see the bent shaft of light coming out of his father's reading room. One bulb sitting high and wild. Spitting noon. Wearing a lampshade fedora. Tilted low. It made the room noir. Long, like a trench coat. Crooked, like a city.

A magazine page fell.

"Dad?" Angus called out to the back of the arm chair.

The bulb hummed.

A magazine page fell.

"Dad?"

No answer.

"Did Mr. Samuel come buy anything to eat? Hot dogs, candy bars?"

A magazine page fell.

"... popcorn?"

"Dad? ... did *you* eat?"

Angus stepped into the room. It was like stepping into a mountain. Steep angles. Unknowable geometry. Because of one bulb and one lampshade slanted in the deep end of the room.

Mr. Fitzroy's tall voice stirred the mess of his own throat.

Voice-box static trying to find a station—

"... *Come to Cattle Country* ..."

The signal was lost.

Angus took another step forward.

And another.

He peered past the high-back of the chair.

Dad was on a two-page spread of Cattle Country. His voice fuzzed. Came into tune—

"*... Follow the flavor ...*"

Something disturbed the signal.

Angus couldn't take his eye off the pastoral vista sitting in Dad's lap.

"Dad? Dad, are you still there?"

FIFTY-FIVE

Inside Revelli's General Store on the corner of Church and Main a radio buzzed. A man's hand tuned a dial.

Voices popped and sizzled in the static.

Waves came in.

Waves went out.

The antenna picked up the surf of the invisible ocean.

...

...

...came back...

...can't...

a sad, lost whistle tried to find its way

a pissed off storm

fuzz

...johnny...

...have a story...

Twelve voices stirred together. Different tones, genders, enthusiasm, vocabularies.

The hand switched the receiver to AM.
AM.
Less stations.
More static.

...Palestinian...
...cleaning woman...
...
...
...what ...
Mr. Pop ...
me ...
...
...
...
...

The voices got lost.
The radio whistled to itself.
It brewed a storm.

Static.

Snow white *static.*

The hand left the tuner.

waves came in
waves came in
waves came in

FIFTY-SIX

ANGUS WAS in his room alone. Door shut. Locked, he wasn't sure why, but ... Dad.

He looked out his window.

There used to be a church there.

A bell in the sky.

A home for birds.

No. They'd flown south for the winter. Before or because of the fire? He couldn't say.

They were just gone ...

like the church.

The town had always just assumed the church would be there. Because it had been. So that meant it would be. The church was how the town remembered who it was. And without it ... ? Angus only saw nothing. A line of trees and beyond that another line of trees, and beyond that more trees and a road somewhere that went some where, so they said.

They were lost.

Sure, Angus knew where he was, could name the town, point it out on a map, but they were lost. Hadn't gotten lost by wandering off. They'd gotten lost by staying put. The whole town had. Naming a town didn't find it. Laying roads didn't make it. Stringing power didn't keep it.

Angus looked over the tree line. He might as well have seen the whole damn state. It was all the same.

Nothing.

Nothing, Vermont.

Out his window he could see the far country, the country deeps, the dark country, the straggling territory off in night country, out country, the backside of nowhere, autumn country, bedtime country, out in the sticks, the shut-off night, the shut-in night, shut up, the good way gone country, far flung, the lights-off country, the long after midnight land.

They were lost. He and Henry.

There were no adults to save them.

FIFTY-SEVEN

T HE S O N G of gasoline shut down.

A shape stood in the slaughter of trees.

The forest trembled. Or was it the wind?

Red flannel. Blue overalls. Brown boots. Machine.

The fallen trees surrounding the man were reminiscent of pews. Some kind of hellish and disorganized church service.

The man a type of pastor.

The chainsaw ticked and cooled. It was hungry. Needed more gasoline.

The lightbulb clicked on. The barn flooded with city-farmed daylight. The barn couldn't hold it all. It leaked through the cracks. Shot out of the roof. Pushed back the night. Argued with the stars.

Inside a man underneath a John Deere hat fed his machine. Like a mother bottling a baby. He patted the machine to calm it. Soothe it. It had so much work left. He hummed a song. Some tune never intended to be a lullaby. The machine had enough to drink.

The man stood, chainsaw in hand, gaze lost at the end of the light bulb's reach.

He saw a cardboard box.

And then he was standing over it.

Holding it in his free hand. It would need eye holes.

He whistled while he worked.

Chainsaw waiting, like a shut-down carousel.

FIFTY-EIGHT

HENRY HEARD a knock at his window.

He got out of bed.

It was Angus.

"The hell were you?" Angus asked as Henry raised the window.

"Huh?"

"School started an hour ago."

Henry panicked in his eyes. Looked at his clock.

"Don't bother." Angus crawled through. "No one is there."

"What do you mean *no one is there?*"

"I was the only one who showed up," Angus said.

Henry stopped getting dressed. "*You* were the only one who showed up?"

"It's not funny."

"I wasn't trying to be funny."

Henry looked off towards school. There was a bedroom wall in his way.

"No teacher, no janitor..." Angus paused. "No other kids."

Henry blinked. "No other kids?"

Angus shook his head.

"Where are they?"

"... I don't know."

"The school's locked up tight?" Henry asked.

"Like it was Sunday."

"Is it Sunday?"

"No. I checked the calendar."

"What about the teachers?"

"Told you. Not there."

"Mr. Van Grohl?"

"No. Henry. Nobody means nobody."

Henry sat down on the bed. He stared blankly at the wall. *"The Rapture."* He whispered, "That means everyone but the bad ..." He looked at Angus. But Angus was looking at Henry's arm. "What's that?"

Henry hid it.

"It's nothing."

"Henry."

"What?"

"The hell is on your arm?"

"Nothing, I just ..." Henry had never lied before. He didn't know how.

His eyes darted to the door. Angus saw.

"He did it. Didn't he?"

There was water in Henry's eyes. He nodded.

A cigarette twirled into existence between Angus's fingers left. A lighter sparked in his right. "I have half a mind to fire this up and snuff it on his neck."

"Don't," Henry protested weakly.

"I'm not gonna."

Angus planted his cigarette on his lips, dry-fired it with his lungs.

"He ever done that before?"

"What?"

Angus pointed to Henry's arm.

Henry shook his head.

"Why did he do it?"

"... because I unplugged the TV."

Angus nodded, like he'd known it all along.

Pointed his chin towards the door, "He's watching TV?"

The electric-storm scratched on the other side of the door.

"Kinda."

"Whaddya mean *kinda?*"

"Just static."

"Strange. I think my dad only reads the ads. The static of magazines. And Mr. Revelli only listens to the space between radio stations, and Mr. Villanelle is only repeating one scratchy song from 1920-whatever, which is basically half static and Mr. Boucher is ..."

Suddenly Angus recalled a far off noise, last night, filling his dreams with gasoline static.

"What?" Henry asked.

"... oh, no, no, no, no, no," someone murmured.

Henry Samuel touched Angus's arm. Angus stopped saying, "Oh, no, no, no."

Suddenly, the small storm scratching against the door stopped.

The boys looked to the silence, lurking, on the other side of the door.

Looked to each other.

Looked to the door.

It said nothing. It meant nothing. Had nothing to say. The door had damned back the storm of static, but was no longer needed. Stood there, strange and awkward, unsure of itself. Gangly. Ungainly. All thumbs. Two left feet.

Then, the storm came back.

Pawed at the door.

And next it did something neither boy expected.

"It's like he's ... turning it down," Henry whispered.

"No ..." Angus stood. Eyed the door. His fingers fluttered in millimeters, like it was gunslinging noon. He tilted his head, but the answer was there, sifting away into the day.

"Not down. No ... the TV's moving *away.*"

Angus moved for the door. Henry raised his fingers to stop him, fingers, not his whole hand, or arm, just his fingers, blindly, stupidly, secretly. Angus did not see them, not that it would have stopped him.

The boy unlocked the door. Twisted the knob.

The door hinges whimpered.

The tar pit of living room fell open at his feet. Mr. Samuel had blocked out the windows with something. But one crack of light spoiled the near-perfect dark. One sliver running high through the house like a slit in a film noir dress. The front door, left open slightly, spilling a crack of golden daylight, running through the house like the yolk of a broken egg. Mr. Samuel was not there. Mr. Samuel's TV was not there. Only cigarette smoke was left behind; an old broadcast of Mr. Samuel's lungs hanging in the room. Angus crossed the idiot-wilderness of dark. Pulled the cracked door open. Took the daylight in the face. Mr. Samuel was gone. He'd taken the TV with him. But he would be easy to find.

All they had to do was follow the extension cord.

"Where did he go?" Henry asked.

"I don't know," Angus said.

Henry sat on his bed. From his bedroom door he could see the orange snake of an extension cord running away into Vermont. Vermont did not like it there.

"Do we follow it?" Henry asked.

"I don't know," Angus said.

Henry looked around the room. He missed so many things about being a boy.

"I don't think we have a choice, do we?"

Angus looked around the same room, like he missed never having had the chance to be a boy.

"Sometimes you don't."

FIFTY-NINE

The bell rang.

A storm came in the door.

Static and storm.

Manmade.

Piped in from a big city.

A shape stood in the doorway, drenched in static.

Leaking all over the mat.

On the second floor, almost exactly above the first man, a shape stood in what was once a reading room. It's likely he heard the storm, he was conditioned to respond to the bell, like Pavlov's dog.

But he did not move.

Did not stir.

He was looking at another ad—*Come to Cattle Country.*

He ripped it from the magazine.

Taped it to the wall.

It was not the first. It would not be the last.

A pile of magazines fluttered at his feet.

He shut the window.

He picked up another magazine. Thumbed through it. Skipped

the articles. Found the ads—*Follow the flavor.* The room filled with the sound of a page being torn out.

Below, a man carrying an electric storm in a box, leashed to an outlet within walking distance, stood in front of the counter. The downpour tucked under his arm. His eyes scanned the back-shelving. *Parliament. Camel. Pall Mall. Lariat. American Spirit. Newport. Lucky Strike. Old Gold. Prairie Creek.*

His eyes darted.

Cattleman.

Come to Cattle Country. Follow the flavor.

A hand cracked a carton, it worked by itself, the other hand would not set down the television. The storm raged on. A cigarette was worked free. A lighter was sparked. A pair of lips made a draft. A pair of lungs took the wind.

Cattle Country music played;

a tune of tar and fire and bodily arson.

The song of a cigarette being smoked.

But neither man could hear. It was drown out by the storm.

Four cartons were stacked under arm.

The bell rang.

SIXTY

T HE BOYS FOLLOWED the extension chord.

Like a *Wizard of Oz / Nightmare on Elm Street* mash-up. Follow the yellow brick road. Follow the orange extension chord.

"Wait," Henry stopped.

"What?" Angus said.

"Maybe we should go back?"

"Go back? Why?"

"You know, unplug it from the wall." Henry felt his arm.

Angus looked at the cord. They were somewhere in the middle. One extension cord plugged into another. He looked back. It was all orange snake. He looked forward. It was all tangerine serpent.

"Just unplug it right here," Angus nodded towards the ground.

The boys stared at the end of one extension chord, the beginning of another. Knew there was power running through it. Gross, raw, Edisonian power.

The wind blew. Clothes ruffled.

"I dunno ..." Henry mumbled. "You know what happened last time I did that."

Both the boys looked to Henry's arm. It was covered in coat and sleeve. They looked anyways.

"What do we do, Angus? We can't let him starve to death," Henry said.

"Maybe he went to get food."

"Yeah," Henry nodded. "Maybe he went to get food."

The boys knew it wasn't true. They just needed it to be.

"Do it for me," Henry asked.

Angus stared at the bond. One snake eating another. "I ..." his voice cracked. "... I feel like you need to do it. It's your dad."

"What about your dad?" Henry pointed off in the direction of the gas station.

"What about him?"

"You going to take his magazines?"

Angus paused. He touched the chord with his foot, as if he was trying to feel the flow of power.

"Then what?" Angus said.

"Huh?" Henry replied.

"So I unplug it. You take my dad's magazines. Then what?"

"What do you mean?"

"We unplug this and hide, your dad comes back here, plugs it back in. We wait here, he burns us with cigarettes."

"Then we cut it," Henry made a fist.

"We'll get shocked."

"Unplug it. Cut the dead line. So he can't plug it back in. Maybe we find a way to cut the line on the goddamn TV itself!"

"Henry?!"

"What?"

"Have you ever taken God's name in vain?"

Henry touched his lips.

The orange trail sat below them. Going back where they could not see. Going forward where they had not been. It did not belong in Vermont. Vermont hated it being there and couldn't do shit about it.

"Henry, you unplug the TV, and he burns you with a cigarette. What do you think happens if you cut the line?"

"What do you mean?" Henry said.

"You cut power temporarily, he hurts you temporarily. You cut power permanently ..."

Angus did not finish his sentence.

Vermont took it away.

"What do we do?" Henry stirred in his shoes.

"I don't know. For the first time in my life I feel like praying." Angus looked east. The direction of the burnt-to-shit church. "But even if God's real, I think our phone line's out."

A shape appeared off in Vermont.

Down the line.

Limping.

Stout.

A scream carried under arm. Scratching the day.

Coming their way.

"It's your dad!" Angus said.

"Hide!"

The storm neared. Snow fell in static sheets.

The boys cowered behind a building, but out in the storm.

Angus turned to look. Two black boxes, one under each arm. Beneath left was a box plugged into the wings of flies. Below right was a hole into the universe. A pit of nothing without power.

The spark-throwing tumult passed. Mr. Samuel and his pet storm. A black chord trailed behind like a dog's tail. Angus stepped out from the building. Stood in plain view. Watched the storm go.

Asked a question to Vermont, but only Henry heard him. "What's he need a second T.V. for?"

"*To plug in,*" Henry mumbled.

Angus did not hear him.

Even Vermont had a hard time hearing him.

SIXTY-ONE

"I NEED to get to Boucher's," Angus said watching the back of the storm head home.

The distant shape of Mr. Samuel and his TVs.

"The dairy farm?" Henry asked.

Angus nodded blankly.

"Why?"

"I don't know."

"What do you mean you don't know?" Henry raised his mousy voice ever so slightly.

"I just ... don't know. I need to see."

"See what?"

Angus put his fingers over his mouth. Stared through the earth. Saw nothing. "I ... just need to make sure."

"Angus, make sure of what?"

"What I heard last night, somewhere on the outskirts of sleep." Angus looked off towards the farm. He squinted his eyes. Then his ears. Tried to hear something vaguely remembered from some other time, in some other year.

Vermont didn't have shit to say.

The town, said even less.

The boys were listening to the ticking reel of this silent film.

"Look ..." Angus licked his lip, "I'll go alone. We can find someplace safe for you to hide, it won't take long."

"Safe?!" Henry exclaimed. "The Hell you talking about?"

The boys met eyes.

"Angus. Why wouldn't it be safe?"

Angus looked off to nowhere. Took an eyeful of nothing.

"This whole town is fucking dangerous. A kinda celestial bio-hazard or something."

"Yeah, but you're talking like Boucher's dairy farm is *more* dangerous."

"I think it is."

As if conducted on cue a small engine began torturing the air, broadcast by the wind. Not far away, not close. A distance the boys knew they could foot. Some *thing* singing on gasoline in the forest. Smaller than a car, eighty-nine times as deadly. Like a pistol kind of power tool. Henry knew it wasn't a generator. His bones told him it wasn't an air compressor. He looked to Angus.

Angus's eyes were wet with fright.

The juices of engine swam the town, deafened Vermont, blinded boys' ears, shot gasoline through fuel-lines. Browbeat building to building, menaced every tree, made them shiver like scared little shits.

"Is it a lawn mower?" Henry asked quietly, carefully.

Angus shook his head.

"A belt sander?"

Angus shook his head.

"A leaf blower?"

Angus shook his head.

"A hedge trimmer, a tile cutter, a jackhammer, a sewing machine?"

Angus shook his head.

"It's a floor sander. That's right, a floor sander. It's a floor sander, isn't it. Angus, tell me it's a floor sander."

"Henry, you know what it is."

And Henry did know what it was. Because every power tool has its own voice, but only one has the snarl of a serial killer. Only one was made famous for murder in West Texas.

Henry sat on the ground.

"... oh, no, no, no, no, no," someone murmured.

Angus touched Henry's shoulder.

Henry stopped saying, "Oh, no, no, no."

Far off, the chain machine beat the shit out of quiet, milquetoast day.

"Oh, God, why go there, Angus?"

"I have to see."

Henry noticed the forest. *Out of the woods*, that was the old saying, wasn't it? When you were safe. *Out of the woods*. That was the problem with Vermont, wasn't it? It was all woods.

"God damnit, Angus, let's just get in a car and go. Drive! Leave the town! Flee the state. Go someplace without trees. Detroit! Pittsburgh! Someplace that has twelve churches in the city. Twenty. Forty!"

"And what about my dad? Your dad? Leave them here to starve to death while watching TV static? Run away and always know my dad's body will be in his arm chair, turning into a skeleton, holding onto a magazine flipped open to a cigarette ad?"

Henry didn't have an answer.

"We can't just run Henry. This thing is you and me. You understand that? Me and you. We are the only ones that can fix the problem. Because we're the only ones that can see the problem. And we can't fix the problem 'til we understand the problem. And I don't get it. I don't understand. But something in my gut says there's some kind of answer in what I know I heard coming from the Boucher's dairy farm while I was dead asleep last night. I just gotta see. For some reason, I just gotta see."

"Why? Why not just stay here? Listen. Huh, Angus? Why isn't listening enough? We can hear it now. Do you have to see every sin? We sit, we listen, we learn. Why can't we listen?"

"I wish we could just listen." Angus blew clean air to the state.

Vermont and its apple-pie-order air made him sick. All tree-breath and leaf musk. He fished his pockets for a cigarette. Just to know it was there. Sat down next to Henry. "There's only one problem with listening."

"What?"

In his pocket, away in secret, Angus fingered the cigarette.

"I can't tell *what* he's cutting."

"Trees! Woods! He's trying to cut his way out of the woods, get out of the woods, we saw that, we know, we get it, we understand!" Henry exclaimed.

Angus drew the cigarette.

Sliced a match.

Opened the throttle. Flooded his lungs with fuel.

He took in Vermont. Breathed out Detroit.

"Don't you remember how your dad started watching *Dallas* for the swearing, horror films for blood, commercials for reasons I don't understand, and finally just static?"

Henry didn't respond.

"We can sit here and wait, and listen to Mr. Boucher rev that thing, and know that he is cutting, cutting, cutting ... but from here I can't see *what*." Angus sanded thirty-three seconds off his lungs. "... and I need to know, *we* need to know if it's still trees, or..."

"... or what?" Henry asked.

Angus took a drag of Pittsburgh. "*... something else.*"

Far off the chain machine growled.

Blew the grit of gasoline across town.

A sick kinda soundtrack for a bad kinda film.

"We need to know, but it'll only take one of us to see. We find a safe place for you to hide and—"

"There's no safe place left," Henry interrupted.

"Huh?"

"Where? There's no safe place left, you said it yourself, the town's a bio-hazard. Suffering from some kinda sin fallout. My bedroom's not safe, your bedroom's not safe, there is no church, the preacher's house is empty and open, but didn't feel safe. Hide out in the woods? We're not out of the woods yet, why would we go into the woods? If the woods are scary when the town is good, they can't be safe when the town is bad. And the school? Locked up tight. No kids anywhere, where did they go? I don't know. Why haven't we seen them? We can only guess. But the school, I can't go there, you said Mr. Van Grohl's got the building locked up. He's in there alone, I bet, lost in the labels. All alone, under the hum of one light bulb, in the janitor's closet, reading the names of chemicals man made-up, isopropano-whatever and blah-blah oxide-hydroxide. As long as that bulb holds out, he'll be there.

"And the cops?

"Sheriff Vault? Probably in there lost in the phone wires. Probably started three days ago, picking up the phone, listening to the dial tone. Hanging up the phone, listening to the dial tone, again and again and again, not calling anyone. Then he became obsessed with busy signals, and now he's probably sitting in a dark room somewhere, locked up alone in the police station listening to the ring tone forever. And somewhere in town is Mr. Johnson, or old widow Plumline watching their phone ring, and ring and ring and ring, and never picking it up. Never connecting. He's content to call. They're content to listen. Neither have interest in voices anymore." Henry took a breath.

Angus took a drag. Goddamn, the big city tasted good.

"Angus, you're the only safe place left in town."

Angus watched his cigarette melt away.

"Never thought of myself as safe," he said.

And two boys heard the machine motioning. Gliding. Around and around and around ...

It was the machine of a merry-go-round wasn't it?

Around and around and around ...

A proprietor of some small part of eternity. Music box mechanisms on steroids. A little toy ballerina spinning. A shrunk down merry-go-round.

That was a chainsaw.

SIXTY-TWO

The boys knew where the farm was.

But they followed the gasoline howl. It was damn near impossible to walk towards. Like the pitch disagreed with the bones of boys. But they followed it. Like Dorothy waking up in a colorful world and seeing that yellow brick road, and knowing she didn't have a choice, she was going to follow it; follow it until it ended, wherever that was. The boys were living *The Wizard of Oz*, in reverse. Directed by Hitchcock. They'd left the world of color, and were headed for the world of black and white. But Vermont wasn't quite there yet. Not yet. It was the 3rd of November, and October had blown away in the wind. There was no more red, or orange, or yellow in the maples. But there was still brown. Everything going brown. November brown. The shit-part of autumn. A place of pissed-away color. Soggy. Headed to a world of black and white. The place of noir films and monster movies.

The farm was a long ways from summer. From July heat and un-barned dairy cows. The farmhouse had grown top heavy. The barn leaning. The fences crooked. And nothing had changed but the lighting. The sun sliding by like a lazy piece of shit. Showing up after breakfast. Leaving before dinner. Doing as little as possible to not get fired. Tired from hard summer work.

The boys hadn't said a word. Didn't need to. Couldn't if they'd wanted. They had the word *Run!* primed on their lips, front loaded in their throats, ready to fire, fingers on the trigger, safety off. But for now they crept. Deeper into the silence of an abandoned farm, because, yes, the second they had stepped foot on Mr. Boucher's property, the machinery of the merry-go-round had stopped.

Silence made things worse.

They no longer knew where Mr. Boucher was.

They could not talk. They did not dare. Their legs carried them forward.

They saw the trees.

How many had he killed?

Three hundred and twenty-eight. Twenty-nine. Thirty.

Henry's eyes floated.

Three hundred and thirty-one. Thirty-two. Thirty-three.

Three hundred and thirty-three. He said it out loud.

Angus looked to the forest. The lazy son-of-a-bitch sun slanted down at shit angles. His hand itched for a cigarette. The boy needed his own sun. Something he could count on. Believe in. He woke up a match. Stoked a cigarette, his own private sun. Henry did not stop him.

The shadows of two boys surveyed the forest.

How many were left?

Six hundred and fifty. Fifty-one. Fifty-two.

Their eyes stirred.

Six hundred and fifty-three. Fifty-four. They lost count.

... less than a million ... Angus whispered into his cigarette.

The boys looked to the barn.

It rose above them like a preacher at the pulpit. Leaning into

November. The boys felt small. Angus dragged his cigarette. It needed to be tapped.

Vermont was as quiet.

Angus fueled his own private sun with his lungs. It cost a fistful of seconds from his life. He was glad to give 'em.

"I don't hear the cows," Angus said.

"Maybe they're sleeping?"

"Probably haven't been milked in days. Should be upset. Groaning."

"Stamping," Henry added.

Angus nodded towards the barn. He took the cigarette off his lips, held it out for Henry. "Do you need a cigarette?"

"I don't smoke," Henry said.

"Just in case."

"In case of what?"

"You want to start."

Henry looked at the fool thing drifting away like dandelion blowballs. His hand took it. Held it between fingers. It felt raw. Powerful. Almost like holding a gun.

Angus fired up another.

Took a step forward. The barn swallowed him whole.

Henry was next.

The barn dark—something made up from the corner of bedrooms, the back of closets, the nothing beneath beds. The boys' cigarettes played piss-poor understudies to flashlights, but at least they felt real. Grounded. Flashlights could not be trusted. It's true they weren't plugged in, but they were power all the same. Light bulbs running off a couple cans of Detroit's best.

Streaks of sunlight seeped between planks. Showing off the odd feed bag. Feeding troughs. There was enough light to see exactly nothing, but a little of something.

"Where are the cows?" Henry whispered.

The barn was silent.

The sound of low-slung noon leaking between planks.

And some tiny, thimble-sized scratch of static; a radio left on low volume.

Angus kept walking. And walking meant deeper. And deeper meant passing through the slants of light. Weak sun exhaust, from November, filtered into slanted little lines. Sunlight. Parted off. Put in lines. On the barn floor. Then there was his own private little sun burning between his fingers. They were the same thing, weren't they; cigarettes and lines of raw sun. Like the barn had become a giant cigarette rolling machine. Making cigarettes out of pure sunlight, which of course, is what cigarettes really were anyways, since tobacco was a crop, grown on sunlight. Dark as dirt, and then a fuck-ton of sunlight. That was how a man made tobacco, and tobacco is how you made cigarettes, and now this barn was following the same formula. Dark as dirt. And the planks were being beat by time and forty Vermont winters and most of all sun, and sunlight was starting to break through. No ... wait. It was the opposite. The sun wasn't breaking into the barn, something was breaking out. A tobacco crop pushing past the dirt, and the wind picks up loose gold like this and...

Angus saw *the pile* on the barn floor.

A big pile in between planked pieces of the wandering sun. Sitting in the dark. Radio waves sprinkling the boy like a Catholic baptism.

His foot moved.

What ...? he thought.

He stepped forward.

Could it be ...?

His heart went into 8/4 timing.

One more step.

And then he'd gotten too close. Smelled too much. Seen so very little, and yet too much.

There was no radio.

Only flies.

Feasting flies. Fanning their wings to broadcast the rot to the barn. Orbiting around a new earth.

Angus's stomach turned. His throat held back vomit, held back voice.

The boy stepped back, one single step, *any* distance away. And then froze. Because not far off stood a man.

Mostly a man ...

A box on his head.

A machine for his hand.

Barn-filtered sun slatted the shape; standing there and somehow hollow; this deep cavern where a man *used* to be. Cardboard head looking at the boy. Magnavox box tilted curiously. Two eyeholes black as cold TV's. Man standing mannequin still. Clutched in his fist night-beasts hung in mid-gallop on a carousel. Food stuck in the horse's teeth.

Some kind of liquid dripped from the merry-go-round in his fist.

The man shifted.

The carousel caught a glint of sun.

It was waiting for the pull-start. The defibrillator that would jolt this Frankenstein-thing from the dead. The jerk that would jam gasoline through its veins. Shoot it with August heat. Make it gnash teeth. The chainsaw waited like a puppet, for the hand that held it to pull its strings, make it dance, put on a play.

All these things waited in the chainsaw. Hid in the gasoline.

Angus blinked.

The man's grip on the circling machine was so tight, his hand was lost. He stood in the barn filtered by slants of light. The miniature merry-go-round waiting to ride round and around and around. Waiting to play Vermont a calliope song.

Angus's cigarette burned in the dark.

It fell from his lips.

Landed on the barn floor.

Smoke fled north, looking for The Rapture.

The cardboard box didn't turn. The body attached didn't rouse. Stood in the fat dark and thin sunlight. The music box mechanism waiting to dance round and around and around, waiting to soothe hungry flies with its cylinder pins and comb-teeth tune.

Angus took a step back.

The man did not move.

The boy took another step back.

The box head stared.

Back, and back, and back. Boy eyes watching cut-out holes.

A couple kids backing out of the barn, backing out of this 1987 gunslinger's duel. Backing away from high noon, in November, Vermont, where noon was worn low on the hip of the horizon.

SIXTY-THREE

S OMEWHERE, across town, in a house that hadn't had the curtains pulled back in four days, a man stood looking over everything he'd done.

A song that had been on for some time went on forever;

It was part white.

Part black.

All storm.

Shortly to be magnified by six, amplified by five.

Yes, math was fun again. The man smiled. Muttered something about *'length times width.'*

Thirty televisions made a wall of glass. Covering the front room window. The man no longer had need of anything the world had to offer. Vermont was shit compared to this. He'd spent the morning collecting. Running extension chords, and now it was ready. One box, his own, stormed on in the corner of this electrical version of the Berlin Wall. The rest were gassed up and waiting a godlike hand to command their weather patterns.

He turned on the *second.*

It joined the storm.

He turned on a *third.*

Snowfall.
A *fourth*.
Another nor'easter.
Fifth.
A blizzard.
Sixth.
Whiteout.

The man slumped in his chair. A cigarette fastened to his lips. Ash falling on his shirt. Snow falling all over him.

"Thirty." A pair of lips mumbled.

Thirty boxes combined their weather patterns. All the grit of Mother Earth. Electrical boxes vomiting their guts. Trying to say something, but no signal to say it.

   "thirty.
  thirty.
   thirty. "

SIXTY-FOUR

IN THE BARN, the shape stirred.

One of the boys had dropped a cigarette. It glowed on the floor.

The shape stepped on it.

Ground its boot.

Sniffed. Smelt burnt boy in the air.

Tar, and burnt boy.

The shape turned. Stood over the pile of meat.

The flies buzzed. Swarmed him. Unsure if he was alive or dead. Uncertain if this was a meal.

A hand steadied the circling machine.

Another pulled the rip-chord.

A merry-go-round exploded. Cogs and flywheels stampeded like horses and lions.

The machine sputtered.

Took big gasps of gasoline. Huge drags of barn air.

The shape revved a music box. The ballerina squealed through pirouettes.

The shape let it simmer.

Smoke.

The flies were not scared. They buzzed around the man.

He stood over the pile of meat. Machine idling. There was so much left to cut. And the machine was hungry to chew.

A finger teased the carousel. The horses nickered.

The shape lifted the chainsaw.

Jammed the throttle.

The flies liked the howl.

It reminded them of their wings.

SIXTY-FIVE

No matter where the boys went, they could not escape the sound.

The town was not big enough.

Vermont was too quiet.

The wind, too meaty.

All day, from pillar to post, two boys were haunted by a gasoline-wreck of a howl. Something cutting into cattle. Dismembering dead things. Cutting past kill. Wherever they ran, the machinery of a merry-go-round found them. Wherever they sat to catch their breath the teeth of a music box caught up. The boys ran without a purpose. Without a place. And two boys can run a lot of town between noon and sunset, think a lot of thoughts. They'd ended up out on the old rail lines, in the abandoned train car that kids of the town had once used to commit their bush-league sins. Kids like Angus Fitzroy.

Angus slid the grand door shut, and for the first time the boys could hear their own thoughts again. They sat in the fresh dark. And perhaps it was too much dark, because Angus lit a cigarette. It gave a dying carnival glow to the freight car.

Up went the cigarette.

Down went the cigarette.

Every time Angus dragged, their little world felt sane and lit. Steadied by this shit-rate sun.

Up went the cigarette.

Down went the cigarette.

The boys didn't need to say—*he'd slaughtered all his cows.* The flies had told them. The silence had told them. The chainsaw had told them. The boys didn't need to ask, *why was he wearing a cardboard box on his head.* Somehow it just made sense. Horror film kind of sense. The boys didn't know it, but their coming of age novel had turned. Their bones understood it. Sent the message, like Morse Code, through the beat of their blood.

Outside the wind ran around. Pissed that this boxcar was in its way.

The boys strained ears. Listening for bad news.

They might have heard an echo of it all. Something far off and vague. Like a fly somewhere deep in a house. But the steel of the freight car was bullish. All Henry could hear was the static of the cigarette. The signal coming in, going out. The clear grind of a drag, the simmer of dying coals, the unknowable husk of a boy sanding seconds off the end of his life.

This was their safe room. As long as Angus smoked.

"How many cigarettes you got?" Henry whispered.

Up with the cigarette.

Angus's face showed up in orange. Disappeared. Illustrated in smoke, then vanished.

Henry heard him fishing his pockets.

"Three."

"Three?"

"*Three,*" Angus said.

"We need more. We need a carton. Two cartons. A hundred packs. How many are in a pack?"

"Henry—"

"Thirty? Thirty times one hundred, that's, what? 3,000 cigarettes? Yeah, I think so, and how long does it take to smoke a cigarette? Like five minutes? Ten minutes? Let's assume five."

"Henry—"

"So, let's see 3,000 cigarettes, at five minutes a piece, that's 15,000 minutes, and you divide that by twenty-four, that's let's see … hell, I need a calculator."

"Henry—"

"Let's see, 150 divided by twenty is seven and a half, so add a few zeroes, and … ah fuck, there's gotta be an easier way to do this, maybe—"

"Henry!"

"What?"

Angus's cigarette simmered on his lips. He'd finally said Henry's name *through* the fire attached to his face. Like a microphone.

"We can't just wait out here for thirty, or forty, or fifty days smoking cigarettes."

"You're right," Henry said. "We'll need food!"

"Damnit!" Angus took a full metal drag. "No. Henry. We can't let your dad watch TV static to death. We can't let my dad die trying to escape to Cattle Country. And do we just leave Mr. Villanelle alone, trying to listen that record into food for his belly? Or Mr. Revelli radio static himself to starvation? What about Mr. Van Grohl? Leave him vacuuming till he falls over dead? And Sheriff Vault? Let the busy signal play over his corpse forever?"

The cigarette did the talking.

"You didn't say Mr. Boucher."

"What do you mean?"

"How come you left out Mr. Boucher?"

"I just forgot, ok." Angus blew smoke out his nose.

"Did you forget, or do you think he can't be saved?"

Angus stirred his own wind.

"You don't think he can't be saved," Henry said. "He's too far gone. Picked up too much sin. And with no church to drop it off, no holding pen to contain it, no Pastor to corral it, he's like a barnacled ship, no fresh water port in sight, dragging through his own ocean, slower, and slower, soon to be stuck at sea, unable to move.

"Right?

"That's what you think, isn't it?

"He's snorted too much gasoline. Poured too much chainsaw-growl into his ears. Slaughtered too many things. That maybe we could have saved him when it was just him and the axe. Maybe we could have saved him when it was him and his chainsaw and the trees. But now that the cows ... he's too far gone, picked up too much sin, and where's God? God knows."

Henry breathed.

"And maybe you don't even call him *he* anymore, but *it*, 'cause that thing he had on his head, what was it, a cardboard box, with two eye holes cut out?"

The cigarette wasted away beautifully. Giving the carriage its own set of clouds.

"Henry." Angus tapped a little, lost piece of autumn off the end of his cigarette. "It's getting worse. How many days has it been? Four? Five? I can't keep track anymore. The hungrier they get, the more desperate they get. All that fallout from the church's blinded the whole goddamn town, well those that are left. Don't you see? They're hungry. Do you know why your dad got a second TV? Because he's hungry. How much you wanna bet my dad's got thirteen magazine ads open right now? Mr. Revelli? Bet he's sitting between two radios, one for each ear, smack in the middle of some fine country radio static. And Mr. Boucher, he's hungry too, and something inside him is twisted, and creepy, and it's telling him, *this is how you feed yourself*, and he started chewing the toothpick that was already in his mouth the night the church burnt down, but it wasn't enough, so he picked up an axe, and chopped down a tree, and felt kinda fed, except it didn't last, its like something that he can taste in his mouth, but never makes it to his belly. So he chopped down a second tree, and a third, and a fourth, and he can taste the goddamn food, but he's not getting full, and so he tries harder, and he gets out the chainsaw, and three hundred trees later, it still isn't working, and he's starving, and growing desperate, and something tells him *the cows*, cutting into the cows will fill his belly, and he does, but of course it doesn't work, and don't you see Henry where this is going? The hungrier he gets, the more desperate he gets ..."

In the dark of the freight car, only Angus's cigarette lit their way.

A little, lost firefly.

"He's going to try to feed himself, until he dies." Angus itched his lip. "And when the trees didn't work, he went to the cows, and when the cows don't work he'll go to something else ..."

"... Something else?" Henry whispered.

"Henry, cows are more alive than trees, and what's more alive than cows?"

Henry blinked.

"*People.*"

"I don't know if the rest of the town counts anymore," Angus paused. "But you and I do."

SIXTY-SIX

"Teach me how to pray," Angus said, cigarette hanging off his lip.

"What?!"

"Teach me how to pray."

"Why?"

"Because I'm scared."

"*You're* scared?"

"Fuck yes I'm scared. This town's going to shit and no one is here to fix it except me and you, and we have no idea what the fuck we're doing. And now we got Mr. Boucher out there with a chainsaw and who knows when his belly will whisper '*not the cows, but the boys, the boys,*' and he'll come for us. You know it's true, and your dad won't hear it, because of the TV static, and Mr. Revelli won't tune into it, and my dad is lost in Cattle Country, so far away, it'll sound like a fly in the countryside, and what do we do Henry? We're at ground zero of this fucking celestial Chernobyl and this is something we can't fix and we need help, big help."

"We call the police!"

"Sheriff Vault? He'll be like the others, if he's still here. You already said so yourself."

"Maybe I was wrong?"

"Maybe you were right!"

"But you and I aren't like the others, Angus. Maybe we're not the only two in town that are normal. Maybe we don't have to do it alone? Maybe Sheriff Vault is sitting in his office right now trying to figure this out?"

"Oh sure, Henry, I can see him right now, sitting in the police stations, surrounded by four phones. The day after the church burnt to shit, he picked up his phone and suddenly liked the dial tone, never noticed it before, but yeah, it wasn't that bad, kinda soothing, and he listened to it, until it clicked off, then he blinked his eyes and hung up the phone. And the next day when he tried to call someone, he got the busy signal, and realized, *'hey, that's not so bad a sound, kinda nice actually'* and spent half the day funneling it in his ear. And the third day he called someone in town and it rang, and rang, and rang, and rang, and why? Because there was someone on the other end of town in love with the sound, lost in the ring, and Sheriff Vault smiled, leaned back in his chair. You know it's true, Henry, you said all this yourself. And where is he today? How much you want to bet he's hunched over four different phones, picking them up, waiting for them to have heart attacks, you know, that flatlined *off-the-hook beep.beep.beep.beep.beep.beep.beep.beep.* Picking up one phone, letting it die, a second, killing it off, a third, putting it down, a fourth, pulling the trigger, resurrecting the first just to listen to its heart thrash dead again. Like a God of telephones. Making them live, watching them die, resurrecting just to kill."

"We don't know that!" Henry said.

"We've been over this, Henry. We're different. I don't know why, but something about all this shit leaking out of that burnt-down church doesn't stick to us the same way. But we still didn't make the cut. God's pulled up stakes and The Rapture's rattled down the road to the next town somewhere deep in America, but it left us behind, and why? Why are we immune to the fallout of the church but didn't make the cut to go to Heaven? And you know what, it's two questions but the more I've been thinking about it, the more I feel like they got the same answer. So you, because you died. Maybe that's camouflage? Maybe this sin doesn't cling to you because it already thinks you're dead, so what's the point? But dying confuses Heaven too, because they came to pick you up that day at the swimming hole, and then you weren't there, back alive. And maybe they messed up the paperwork, maybe Heaven makes mistakes, thinks you're already up there so why would The Rapture rolling through town pick you up?"

"And what about you? Why doesn't the sin stick to you?"

"My name."

"Bullshit. It's more than your name."

"Angus is a shit name for a kid. A garbage name for an adult. I told you. I'm in limbo. Sin doesn't care about people in limbo, it cares about the living."

"Don't lie to me."

"What?"

"You're full of shit, it's not your name. Well, maybe a little, but there's something else. Something else about you that you understand why ..." Henry's voice fell into the dark of the freight car.

"What?" Angus asked.

Angus's cigarette smoldered between them.

"It's your mom."

"Huh?"

"You said she died, giving birth. You think you murdered her."

"What?"

"That's it. That's why the sin doesn't care about you. It's job is done. You're guilty of murder, there's nothing more it can do. What's it gonna do? Make you have sex with eighty different women? Smoke cigarettes, drink beer? All three at once? Play with Ouija boards? Murder's the worst sin. There's nothing badder. It doesn't give a shit about me because it thinks I'm already dead. It doesn't give a shit about you because it thinks you're already got."

Angus took a drag of his cigarette.

Torched his lungs with small-potatoes sin.

"Fine," he nodded. "Ok, bullshit boy, how about I call you on your own BS."

"What BS?"

"You don't believe in God."

"What?" Henry said. "Yeah I do."

"Bullshit."

"I went to church."

"Doesn't mean you believe in God."

Henry was silent.

"Then teach me how to pray," Angus said.

"What?"

"Teach me how to pray."

"What's that got to do with anything?"

"If you believed in God, you'd teach me how to pray."

Henry blinked.

The cigarette cast Angus in low contrast orange and black.

"You don't believe in God anymore, do you? Ever since that day at the swimming hole. That's what changed, you died, and God wasn't there and you came back from the dead an atheist."

Henry blinked.

Sat painted by the cigarette.

And freight car night.

"I don't know," he said.

"Or you do know, and you don't want to say."

Henry did not respond.

"God, Fuck. Maybe we all deserve to be here. You said it earlier Henry, it's like everybody's gone to The Rapture. Everyone except us. You fell through the cracks, the boy Heaven forgot because he died last summer and Heaven thinks he's already there. And me, the boy who killed his mom on the way out, some kinda small assassin, so we know why I'm not there, and if that weren't enough there's cigarettes and taking Cindy out to this old rail car. Your dad? Maybe God meant it when he said '*Thou Shall Not Kill*' and it doesn't matter if you're a boy sent by a nation and it's Viet Cong, it's still murder? My dad? Too many cigarettes? Sold too much gasoline? Too good at making a god-damn fist? Mr. Villanelle? Saw too many album covers with naked ladies? Mr. Revelli? I could only guess. Mr. Boucher? God knows. And why are we still here, you and I, with the rest of 'em? Maybe you and I aren't so different, maybe we have just enough sin to stay but not enough to stray? You tell me, I dunno how God works."

"I don't know how he works," Henry said low.

"You went to church."

"They teach you how he's supposed to work ..."

The train car was still.

Angus's cigarette buzzing like a baby fly.

Angus nodded, like he'd known it all along. "Look, Henry, just ... teach me how to pray," he asked.

"Why?"

"Because I don't know how."

"No one ever taught you?" Henry asked.

Angus shook his head.

"It won't work," Henry said.

"Teach me anyways."

Henry took a breath. "Not much to teach, actually. You address God, you thank him for what you have, you ask him for what you need, and you close it in Jesus's name."

"God's like the envelope, Jesus is like the stamp?"

"I guess you could say that."

"Ok. Let me try."

"Wait," Henry pointed to Angus's cigarette.

"Right."

Angus set down the cigarette.

"You should put it out."

"Yeah." Angus pinched off the tip beneath his sneaker.

"Close your eyes," Henry said.

"Right."

"Begin when you're ready."

"Hey God—"

"A little more formal." Henry interrupted.

"Hello God?"

"Try *Dear God.*"

Angus nodded. "Dear God, this is Angus Fitzroy, I know we've never talked before, but I live in January, Vermont. 34 Church Street, above the gas station, second floor—"

"He knows all that."

"Oh, ok. Well, I'm thankful for ... well, I'm thankful that ... *what if I'm not thankful for anything, can I skip this part?*"

"Try to think of something."

"Hi, God, Angus, still here, sorry, this is my first prayer ... I'm thankful for Metallica, and records, and the Sony Walkman, I think you did a good job on that. Thanks for letting me take Metallica to school, like that, portable, you know. Um ... and I'm thankful for cigarettes. I mean I know I'm not supposed to smoke, but um, it's relaxing, and er, thanks for um, math class ... I mean I didn't really like learning but I got to stare at Cindy's—"

"That's probably good enough," Henry said.

"Oh, ok."

"Ask him for what you need."

Angus licked his lips. "God, we need your help. Really need your help. The church burnt down a few days ago. You know the church; it's yours; it was the only one in town. It's the Old Parish Church on, oh wait, I guess you know where it was?"

Angus opened one eye.

Henry nodded.

"Right. Well, ever since it burnt down, bad stuff has been happening in town. To the people. You have Mr. Samuel who's watching TV static, and Mr. Revelli who's tuning his radio *to* static, and my dad, Vern Fitzroy is lost in cigarette advertisements, and Mr. Villanelle is listening to this old strange, creepy record over and over and over ... and Mr. Boucher started chewing toothpicks then cutting down trees, not for firewood, but like, just to kill 'em. First with an axe, and then with a chainsaw, and now he's butchered all his own cows, and shit—"

"Don't swear."

"Sorry, I meant to say *stuff* is getting really scary, and no one is eating anymore, and we're afraid our dads are going to starve to death, and when Henry tried to unplug the TV his dad burnt him with a cigarette. And we don't know what would happen if I tried to take my dad's magazines away. And I just can't shake this feeling that Mr. Boucher won't stop at the cows. That he's going to come for us, and we're afraid the police station will be the same way, because no one in town can help us anymore, there's no one left, only you, and we're really scared, please help us. We're all alone, our pastor burnt down our church, and they took him to jail, and the sin is leaking out all over town, and things are getting worse. Please help us. Please. Please don't leave us alone. Please don't let our dads die ..." Angus got quiet.

"End it in Jesus's name," Henry said.

"This is the end of the prayer, Jesus Christ."

"Try, *in Christ's name, Amen.*"

"In Christ's name, Amen."

Angus opened his eyes. He looked around the dark freight car. His half-smoked cigarette sat cold on the floor.

"What happens now?"

"You wait," Henry explained.

"Wait?"

"Yeah, wait for God to answer your prayer."

"What? It's like 'take a number' bullshit?"

"Yes."

"But we need help now!"

"God works in his own time table."

Angus snorted. "That's bullshit!"

"That's God."

Angus looked around the dark again.

"I don't feel anything, aren't I supposed to feel something?"

"In theory," Henry said.

"I thought praying was supposed to make you feel peace, or comfort?"

"It is."

"I don't feel that. I'm still scared. We're still alone. Nothing has changed!"

Angus stood and cracked the steel door on the freight car. He threw an ear to Vermont. Far, far off, buzzing like a little fly in a quiet house he heard the gasoline engine haunting Boucher's barn.

"It didn't work! What the fuck?" Angus slammed the door. Kicked the steel.

Henry was quiet.

Angus saw him sitting quiet. "What? Henry?"

"I told you."

"Told me what?"

"It wouldn't work."

"Yeah," Angus bent his lip angrily. "What a bunch of horseshit." He grabbed his cigarette off the ground. Struck a match. Took a drag to piss God away.

Hummed to warm his lungs.

Buzzed to fry his years.

SIXTY-SEVEN

ABOVE THE GAS STATION, a shape slumped in an armchair.

A pair of eyes darted to the north wall. It was now Cattle Country. The south wall. Cattle Country. East. West. It was all Cattle Country.

The windows were now Cattle Country.

The ceiling.

The floor.

His chair floated on a sea of advertisements.

Horses, and bulls, and mountains, and prairies, and above all, one man in a hat smoking a fine cigarette.

Come to Cattle Country said the ads.

Follow the flavor.

A thousand dead magazines lay in the corner like plucked birds.

There was no wind to stir their wings.

A country of flavor is calling.

Flavor. Two eyes focused on the word.

Flavor.
Flavor.
Flavor.

A pair of lips licked themselves. His tongue could taste something.

His belly groaned from hunger.

254

SIXTY-EIGHT

T HE BOYS LOOKED into the police station.

Mrs. Weaver was not at her desk.

The lights were off.

The door was not locked.

Standing in the doorway they could hear the sound of the country they'd fled this morning; the circling machine at the far end of town, the rolling in carnival of teeth and gasoline chewing on the meat and bone of slaughtered cow.

"Where is Mrs. Weaver?" Henry asked.

"I could guess," Angus replied.

The door closed behind them.

The merry-go-round song of chainsaw muffled by building.

"You think Sheriff Vault is here?" Henry asked.

"This is your idea, go find out," Angus replied.

"His truck was out front."

"His office is in the back."

Henry took a step into the station. To the hall. Looked down the long stretch. Some other sound had replaced the dull murmur of the teeth machine outside. Something *inside* the police station.

"Someone's in the back office," Henry whispered.

Angus waited in the lobby.

Henry crept down the hall. He stopped halfway down the hall. The sheriff's door hung open. He couldn't quite see in.

He heard a droning.

The colloquial drawl of a machine.

a dial tone.

The little machine hummed its one-note tune.

click

The sound stopped.

An old lady, half machine, on the way to a funeral, spoke on the resurrective power of Thomas Edison. Once upon a time they'd called her Operator, and she'd been a person.

"if you'd like to make a call, please hang up and try again
if you need help, hang up and then dial your operator"

.

.

.

.

.

"if you'd like to make a call, please hang up and try again
if you need help, hang up and then dial your operator"

Eleven seconds passed.

The phone went into cardiac arrest.

Then it was buried. Picked up again. Like the Sheriff was bringing it back to life, just to hear it die.

SIXTY-NINE

The bell rang.

Two boys stepped inside.

The gas station was dark. Unattended.

One boy went for the cigarettes. He reached for Cattlemans. His hand hung in the air, not moving, not deciding.

He'd filched every cigarette he'd ever smoked from his old man.

Like a dog under the table he'd only tasted scraps. His hand understood he was family now. The kitchen was his.

Cattleman
Prairie Creek
Old Gold
Lucky Strike
Newport
American Spirit
Pall Mall
Camel
Parliament

His hand floated.

Virginia Slims
Kool
Capri
Winston
Salem
Chesterfield

It couldn't decide.

Du Maurier
Seneca
Viceroy
Ashford
L&M

He saw an ad on the wall. *Lariat. Where Men Belong.*
He'd always wanted to be a man.
He'd always wanted to belong.
His hand decided he would smoke *Lariats* from now on.
He dumped out his school books.
He no longer needed them.

A second boy had also dumped his books. Filled his bag with a boy's idea of food. *Just in case*, they had said. *Just in case* they need to run. Hide. Stay safe. A boy scout was always prepared. One boy was a 'Scout,' the rank you get for showing up once. The other a First Class dropout. But they could still *'Be Prepared.'*

"You got it all?" Angus asked.

"It's full," Henry said as he slung his backpack on.

"Just in case," Angus said.

Henry nodded.

Henry's eyes darted to Vermont. *Outside.* Where Vermont had changed into something more comfortable for the evening. Tired of the business-attire sunshine required. Vermont was comfortable slipping into dark. Angus's eyes darted to the back of the convenience store. *Inside.* To the stairs. And his mind to the second level. Dad. The reading room. And what was it now? What had it become since this morning.

"What is it?" The boys said at the same time, to each other.

Eyes stirred.

Outside.

Inside.

Outside.

Inside.

One boy looking to where the other had looked.

Back to his own glance.

Back to the other's.

Inside, outside, inside, outside.

"You first," Henry said.

Angus looked back at the stairs. Murmured, "I just need to take a peek. It'll just take a second."

"But ..." Henry bleated.

"But what?"

Henry pointed vaguely outside.

"What, Henry?"

"Listen."

"I don't hear anything," Angus said.

"I know. I can't hear Mr. Boucher's chainsaw."

Angus looked inside.

"He's been running it all day," Henry said.

"It'll just take a second."

"A second? With the saw screaming down the town, we knew where he was. Now he could be anywhere!"

Angus looked at the stairs.

"Let's go!" Henry begged.

Angus looked at the stairs.

"Find someplace safe," Henry begged. "Develop a plan. Smoke, like Sherlock Holmes. Figure things out."

Angus looked outside.

Vermont's hands were fly-paper-fastened to the color of flies.

The boy looked inside.

The stairs' spine was crooked with scoliosis.

"I gotta see what my dad's done," Angus whispered.

The boy with the bad name took a step forward, or was it backwards?

"Angus!" Henry hissed.

Angus held up a finger that said one second. "... since this morning." He muttered, "I gotta see what he's done ... since this morning."

"What if Mr. Boucher's out of gas?!" Henry wheezed.

But Angus was at the stairs. Looking up. Taking them one by one.

Gone.

And Henry was alone downstairs. In a gas station. Watching the street, the trees, the buildings lose their color as the day went away, thumbing the strap on his backpack like an idiot with nothing to do, waiting for a silhouette half between machine and man to haunt him. He would not see it coming, he knew, no matter how hard he looked. The firm shape of a man. A box for a head. A case and guide bar for a hand. Because that chainsaw was a pig. Hungry. And on the other side of the window was the feeding trough. The pump machine, standing like a squatty mother, waiting to feed the chainsaw with her pistol-shaped baby bottle. Jam her gunslinger nipple down its throat and dare to feed so many fine chainsawing years.

Henry wouldn't see him coming.

Mr. Boucher would blow in with the leaves.

Come in on a lamp swing.

SEVENTY

January, Vermont was going gone. Like water down a drain. Those left caught in their own whirlpools. Somewhere, on the edge of town, a storm of TVs fell fresh snow. Somewhere, above a gas station, a cigarette ad was torn from a magazine like another puzzle piece. Somewhere, in the old record store, vinyl spun with the earth. Somewhere, walking distance from it all, a dial was finely tuned to radio static. Somewhere, in the center of town, a black and white character hoisted his automatic knuckles over a phone having a heart attack. Somewhere, in a library, another book was pulled from the shelves, the words burnt for warmth. Somewhere else, deep in a janitor's closet, a vacuum had run so long it peeled at the edges of town. And somewhere, in a barn, a chainsaw waited like a shut down carousel. Whispering of free rides. Itching for children.

SEVENTY-ONE

A BOVE, Angus took a step forward.

And another.

He'd never moved so slow in his own house.

One step.

And another. Laborious things, steps, when paid attention to.

The hall was long, dark, except for the spill of light coming out of his dad's reading room. All the reckless slop of run aground oil tankers, somehow reversed. Like if Heaven tanked light through the highest northern seas between stars, and cracked a ship open here; planet Earth, Vermont, Dad's reading room.

One step.

And another. Harder work than math.

The boy kept an ear out.

He only dared look with one eye. Dad's chair was in the center of the room. A little skiff, adrift in a sea of advertisements. The magazine pages splashed and surfed at Dad's feet as he rocked.

The lampshade was tilted.

Dad's tall body soaked in this reverse oil spill. His head lost in shadow. The wall painted in canned-sunlight. Normally light came from Heaven, but Mr. Edison had figured out how to bottle the goddamn stuff. Sell it. Cut God outta the deal. And for the first time man just didn't need God as much as he used too. Didn't have to pray through the night to get a sunrise, or pile stones in December to bring back the carousing sun. Edison had factories that manufactured daylight, and sold it in convenient little jars. And here was dad, basking in the spit-shine of factory-made day, sun-tanning in the fake sun bottled by the big city. Looking at the one lit wall of his very own four wall prison. Listening to it tell lies about where he was.

Cattle Country.

Back and forth went the chair.

Splish-splash went the pages at his feet.

The room was no longer dad's, but something that belonged to the ad men. Tall tales printed on Madison Ave. It wasn't about horses, but horseshit. Wasn't about lassos, but tying men up. Not about clean open skies, but shutting down lungs. Not about mountains, but burying a man. *Come to Cattle Country.* The wall was full of cigarettes saying they were the country, the open air, the wild, the space between places, but cigarettes weren't the American garden. Cigarettes were the machine in the garden.

They were full of shit.

Every last smoke.

Angus could not see any piece of the wallpaper. No corner of the ceiling. Not an inch of hardwood. And dad sat, taking it all in.

A Country of flavor is calling . . .

Angus dropped his backpack.

Suddenly, the boy didn't want to smoke ever again.

SEVENTY-TWO

Downstairs Henry blinked.

His eyes read over the calligraphies of the wind. The smoky lighting that sketched, that coiled, and crouched and ran throughout the town from light bulbs and lost daylight.

Outside dead leaves scurried like cockroaches.

He blinked.

His eyes breathing night like second-hand smoke. His eyes *click-snapped* like a camera lenses.

Taking pictures.

blink.

Fuel pump standing at attention like a tin soldier

click-snap.

The red brick building.

click.

The streetlight.

blink

The lamp swung out.

The street was empty.

click.

The lamp swung in.

There. On the corner of Church and Main stood Halloween, three days late.

SEVENTY-THREE

HALLOWEEN. Henry's bones said. Halloween his camera eyes recorded.

No longer Mr. Boucher.

No longer Mister.

The hollow black shape across the street.

Halloween.

The silhouette of a once-upon-a-time man. Hand tucked into a box of machinery with a guide-bar arm. Cardboard box head. Mr. Boucher was gone. Halloween had come, three days late. Not this kid-shit and candy fare. Not this horseshit holiday. Real Halloween. Raw and unfiltered. A cigarette taken straight. Meat served pink.

The shape did not stir.

Moths ticked off the high yellow-amber light-bulb which swung abandoned above the corner of Church and Main.

Back and forth.

Back and forth.

The street grew long the street grew short in the swinging light.

The Canadian wind had come to town. It couldn't boss around the buildings, but it could push the bulb, and with light swinging back and forth, the buildings were bullied into dancing.

Back and forth.

Back and forth.

All the scene moved. Except the shape.

The anchor to the town. A static object on the ocean floor. The iron piece of sanity in a fluxing seabed. All of Vermont was being pushed around by Canada. Treated like birthday cake candles. Abandoned by the sun, condemned to the breakneck angles of coming winter. The town tilted to low slung days. Black and white nights. And there stood the shape. Stark. Steep. Tall. A shape that meant something. Something like the church. Fine, firm, high. The man did not move.

Moths fluttered.

Bulbs swung.

Buildings moved about between.

Trees bent to soften the blow of Canada.

Dead leaves scurried.

The street grew long, grew short.

Long.

Short.

The barren shape stood.

The long bladed arm, the box head, stood in the color of old, burnt films. The black of *black and white.*

Across the street, in a deserted gas station in the midst of a country wilderness there was another shape. Holding still. A third the size. Similarly wrapped in shadow, in a garage-sized room, loose words bubbling on his lips, speaking to yet another boy lost somewhere upstairs, the boy left alone, holding onto himself at every slide of leaf, each flit of wind.

The boy was afraid to blink.

Watching the crude shape of Halloween in the moth-flicked light.

Afraid to lose sight of it.

The boy's eyes were dry.

He did not blink.

The boy gripped his backpack strap stupidly.

Back and forth swung the lightbulb.

Back and forth.

A flock of leaves passed.

Buildings showed up, disappeared,

showed up, disappeared.

The street grew long, grew short.

Grew long.

Grew short.

Moths fell in love again and again.

The bulb did not love them back. Only swung in the wind.

The projector above gave Halloween size, shape, depth, husk ... everything but color. The shape stood, like a hole in the town. Something cut out from the pages of the world. A book with a paper doll missing. A sheet of dough that'd met a cookie cutter. Something you'd only noticed because it was gone.

A chunk of the world had been cut out.

The space where Mr. Boucher used to be.

It reeked of Halloween.

The moths flicked the light.

PART 3
RED

SEVENTY-FOUR

Upstairs.
Angus stood next to a man,
vaguely remembered from some other time,
some other year.
Dad.
Tall, even sitting.
The man's stomach thundered hunger.
His eyes fed him another line,
The boy heard it go down the man's throat—*Come to Cattle Country,*
Follow the Flavor."

SEVENTY-FIVE

Downstairs.

The shape went for the pump.

It did not put $5 dollars on four.

Did not come inside to pay.

It stuck the mechanical teat in the sleeping machine. Started pumping milk.

Henry locked the door.

Somehow, he knew it wouldn't matter.

SEVENTY-SIX

ANGUS SHIFTED HIS WEIGHT LEFT, beneath his feet the advertisements splashed.

Shifted right, the propaganda surfed.

Dad did not move. Did not look. Did not say. Only listened to the incoming tide.

> *Here men meet flavor.*
> *Velvety and smooth through our discriminating filter.*
> *Treat your tongue to top-grade tobaccos*
> *The filtered cigarette, the unfiltered flavor*

Angus stood in the center of the room. Next to Dad's chair. He couldn't see dad's face in the dark. The lamp spilled lightbulb on his body.

"Dad?"

No answer.

Dad was watching the walls of ads like a movie screen.

"Dad?"

Nothing.

"Are you still there?"

No response.

Angus listened to the tide come in.

Don't you deserve smooth smoking?
Guard against throat-scuff.

Listened to the tide go out.

There's plenty to love ... a country full of flavor from Cattleman
The Cattleman blend is rich with burley and rough-cut Virginia.
Taste America in this cigarette.

'America?' Angus's lips mumbled loosely.

The cigarettes said they were America. Pretended to be Americans.

'Horseshit,' said a boy's eyes.

Angus's fists balled. His right, then his left.

He stormed the wall, tearing down paper white pigeons, blasting them from the sky with his bare hands. *Smokes smooth!* Boom! *Low tar!* Bang! Pages bombarded his shoulder, his arms, his upturned face. A dozen dead birds ripped from the air, wings fluttering, falling to earth. And Angus stood below, each hand a shotgun.

SMACK!

Angus dropped to the ground. Dad loomed above, the lightbulb behind his frame. A lean, lurking figure, all shadow and shape and fists and heaving lungs. Threatening over Angus. Breathing in, breathing out. Fists clenched. All the while shovelfuls of buckshot birds fell around them.

Angus nursed his jaw.

Dad's tall, tall shape crushing diamonds in his fists.

Hanging over the boy.

Breathing in.

Breathing out.

The same mechanical motion of all cigarette smokers.

"*... hang those back up ...*" The shape orbited above the boy, daring him to get up, breathing in, breathing out, stoking fists, left and right.

Angus looked at all the dead birds around him.

He started gathering up the bodies.

They'd never fly again, but that didn't matter. He'd pin them to the sky anyways.

The shape dropped a dispenser of Scotch tape. Returned to its chair. Sat down in the Edisonian-fallout of the lamp. Back to where Dad'd begun; face in shadow, body in lamplight.

Slurring himself quiet,

"… quitting smoking now greatly reduces serious risks to your health …"

SEVENTY-SEVEN

Outside the gas station.

The shape did not replace the nozzle.

It stood.

Steeping in Vermont night.

It drop-started the saw.

Chain shivered and flew around and around and around.

Around and around, this pint sized merry-go-round, with chain and teeth instead of horses and lions, pumping up and down, circus machinery, playing like a calliope its own sick song. Steam and air, that's all calliope music was. And a chainsaw; gas and air. It was the same song, so sickly wrong. It was the *same* goddamn song, Henry thought. But one makes a boy smile and run towards. The other makes a boy cry and run away. Shit his pants.

The shape stood off under the flat roof of the gas station, just outside the window, next to the pump with its arm dangling loose on the ground. Taking a drag from the throttle. Treating the chainsaw like a cigarette.

Revving the engine.

Letting it idle.

Opening the throttle.

Letting out the clutch.

The same motion as a smoker.

Vermont took the noise like secondhand smoke.

The shape ran the carousel. Let the horses gallop. Paced them down. Opened the music box. Snapped it shut.

Two matchstick lights in the boy's frightened eyes were ready to blow out.

He dare not look away.

Lose sight.

But he wanted to look at the stairs. See a friend. Feel safe. He wanted to shut his eyes, make his mind paint another picture, something besides the shape of a man with a cardboard-box head and a fistful of carousel.

Outside.

A drag of fuel.

A gasp of air.

Just like a cigarette.

The boy's ears bruised by the bark of gasoline.

The window between boy and man just a filter on a cigarette. Wasn't going to save him.

'*Angus!*' thought the boy, '*where are you?!*'

And the shape outside was content to casually stoke this fire in its fist. Like an arsonist on smoke break; playing with a pea-sized fire, knowing it was shades of the long night's work. He was hungry. Henry could tell. Angus was right. The shape was trying to feed himself the only way he knew how, and when the trees weren't enough, when the cows weren't enough, something on his shoulder had said '*the boys*.' Give the boys a ride on the carousel. Put them to sleep with the music box.

'the boys.

the boys.

the boys.'

The chainsaw idled.

I have to keep looking, Henry thought. Just like the westerns. Like the gunslingers. Like high noon. No one can shoot until someone moves. If no one moved, no one would ever die.

And Henry stood very still.

Sure, you can squint your eyes. Eyes are allowed to narrow. Fix. Watch. But they can't close. And heads cannot turn, hands cannot stir, fingers can hardly flutter. Legs cannot step, necks cannot itch, knuckles cannot crack. No. It's the gunslinger's code. Here, tonight, Vermont is both wild west and horror film. And he'd never thought of it before, how the genres of film were actually the same. Every western was a horror film. Every horror film a western. Something that could only take place on the fringe of society. Someplace like Vermont. Something that required the strange enginery of the modern world to work. There was no western without guns. No horror film without machinery. Chainsaws, axes, masks, werewolves, ghosts; they were all different types of unknowable machinery.

Still, thought Henry. *Very still.*

Off beneath the flat roof, next to the pump, the shape stood.

The chainsaw muttering to itself.

Coughing in the cold.

Still. Thought Henry. He can't shoot if I don't move. It's the code of the west. I'll stand here forever, until he starves to death, if I have to. I'll pretend I'm a statue. He's a gunslinger. The chainsaw his revolver. He can't pull the trigger until I move, so I will stand here. *Still.* I'll let high noon pass. I'll stand the night through. I won't blink. I'll lock him up by following the code of the west. That is the secret to beating a horror film, figuring out that it's a western.

Still, thought Henry.

His breath came in.

His breath went out.

Outside, the shape held the idling machine. It whimpered to be off leash.

Still, thought Henry.

Very still.

I can win the duel by being still.

My eyelash won't stir,

my hand won't blink,

I'll breathe slow enough he'll think I'm dead.

Still.

Still.

Still.

"Henry!" Angus was at the bottom of the stairs. Henry jerked to see.

The shape lifted his revolver.

The cry of gas filled the town.

SEVENTY-EIGHT

THE SHAPE CAME at the window. Chainsaw striking, window holding. Striking. Holding. Glass too smooth to catch teeth. The man stepped back. Machine idling in his hands, darkness dancing wildly in the two holes cut out of the cardboard box, no stupid little flat mouth on the box husking air from inside, Vermont coloring his breath the color of cigarette smoke coming out the bottom.

Eyes met, for one freak-show second.

Two boys saw a glint of yellow circus. Something wild and hungry in the box.

Loose flywheels.

Un-tightened cogs.

The shape saw the tremble of halos, the replacement of every hand-me-down shit-rate nightmare the boys had ever had.

The chainsaw sputtering.

Coughing like a smoker.

The box looked to the door. The lock.

"Oh shit." Henry backed up.

The boys were against the far wall.

"Can a chainsaw cut through a deadbolt?" Henry asked.

"I don't—"

The chopping machine squealed. It was every awful sound they'd ever heard—bicycle brakes, fingernails and chalkboards, dentist drills, first violin lessons, knives on glass bottles, microphone feedback, shopping cart wheels, crying babies—beaten together, like cake batter splattering the room, both boys, the ceiling and walls, a mixer on high speed.

Like a bulk of Vermont Northern Hardwood sliced, like the marrow of a cow's skull slivered, the deadbolt portioned, sliced and served.

"Shit!" said a boy.

"Shit! Shit! Shit!" said a second.

The door kicked open.

The shape cut a black and mortuary silhouette their way. A fistful of engine raised above head exploding with dust, ablaze with lumberjack anger, growling, roaring, like Buick City at full production, teeth wheeling and shivering.

A puppet hung over them.

Mr. Boucher screamed with his saw.

Henry shut his eyes.

Felt a push.

Debris rained on him. Chunks of sheetrock and wood spat from the teeth of carousel-horses. Angus had pushed him out of the way. Henry was on the ground. Listening to the pig squeal stuck in a wall above him. The Butcher's burnt-voice, *"fuel degrades over time, remember to use stabilizer."*

"Henry!" Angus pointed to the stairs.

Above Henry, the stuck machine was all drive shafts, flywheels and smoke stacks. Pissed-off steam, and gun-powder fuming. A silvery mouth opened to let cigarette smoke out. It burnt his face. The boy cried out. Covered his skin. Scurried away blindly.

A hand found his. He trusted it, it pulled him upstairs. A door shut. The boy blinked. Looked around Angus's bedroom. Blinked again.

"Are you ok?"

One boy felt the other's head. "Ouch." Henry recoiled.

Downstairs the boys heard the radio static of a chainsaw idling.

The creak of the stairs.

"Your dad!" Henry whispered.

The boys looked to the shut bedroom door. Imagined the hallway on the other side.

"What about your dad?"

"Shhh, shhh, he'll be fine. I don't think they can see each other."

Henry hunched himself. Angus trembled. Henry wanted to ask, but he had no whisper small enough. He looked in Angus's eyes. What did he fear? The carnival rushing in like an automobile in full stampede? His dad trampled beneath the horses of the hand-held merry-go-round? Drown in rains of gasoline?

They heard the sound of fly wings buzzing up the stairs.

A third stair.

The fourth.

They heard a merry-go-round waiting to spin.

The fifth stair.

The sixth.

Seventh.

Eighth.

A music box waiting to be opened.

Nine.

Ten.

Eleven.

A lit cigarette waiting to be dragged.

Twelve.

Thirteen.

Fourteen.

And the boys could see the shape, in their minds, at the long end of the hall, on the other side of this locked bedroom door. This shitshow of a thing; a boy's plywood bedroom door with a little click-lock that Angus had locked for whatever damn fool reason, because he'd already seen the shape slice through worse, knew this Butcher could cut down more. There, at the top of the stairs, at the deep end of the hall stood this shadow collected from funeral parlors across the country. This tall shape of a man, rounded beer gut, square head, black-box hand, guide-bar arm. The sounds of the Motor City leaking from its talking hand, telling stories about radio static, fly wings, gasoline, cigarettes, house-fires.

The boys looked at each other.

They'd never been so silent.

Angus looked to the window. They'd have to climb out.

Henry looked to the door. It'd have to hold.

The concrete weight of a man stepped in the hall. Big, meaty, boot-wearing man steps. Heavy steps only a man weighted by fifty-four years of collecting gravity can make. The kind of heft a boy can only grasp at.

The chainsaw idling.

The man stepped again.

Creak.

The machine muttering.

Whine.

Creak.

The boys could hear the shape now, standing in the middle of the hallway, with Cattle Country tucked away behind a closed door to its left. Angus had shut the door. Shut the door to Cattle Country. Didn't know what would happen if this Butcher saw his dad gone to the Country, fled to where the Flavor was. So Angus had shut the door. With the idiot-rambling machine telling everything about where the Butcher was *and* where it was looking.

At the door to Cattle Country.

A cardboard-box looking down a door.

The chainsaw sucked hallway through its nose, leaked moonlight out its mouth.

"I smell gas," Angus mumbled to no one. Gas, in his own house. Henry could see it in his eyes—the boy'd never smelt it before. Here was his house, set politely on the top of a service station, his dad the only peddler of gas in 12 miles, and he had never smelt gas in his own bedroom.

The shape stood looking at the door to Cattle Country.

The chainsaw burning low in the hall.

"Flavor," a voice said.

The boys listened, cold and growing colder, scared to be in with a roof above, floor below, wall and door between too much gasoline, too much noise, too much shape.

"Flavor . . ."

Mr. Fitzroy's voice, home sweet home, leaking through the hall, speaking to itself, and yet being heard by two boys and a county chainsaw killer.

"Flavor . . ."

".. rr.rr.rr...rr.rr..rr...rr.rr.rr..rr.." the idling chainsaw replied. It was now talking for the man formerly known as Mr. Boucher. Muttering like a lunatic. Trying to repeat the word. Speak English. But from a metal throat, with a two-stroke voice, slurring the vowels, jumbling the sound.

"Flavor . . ."

"..rr.rr.r.rr...rr...r.." the chainsaw said.

Flavor, thought Henry Samuel, seated on the edge of the bed. Do cigarettes have taste at all? Flavor. Thought Henry. Yes. Flavor, not sustenance. Not nourishment. Flavor. Taste. Chewing food and spitting it out. That was smoking cigarettes. Reading magazines for the ads. Watching TV without a signal. Tuning into radio static. Dialing for the dial tone, calling for the busy signal. Digging an earworm of a record out just to let it crawl into your brain. Chopping trees down just for the sake of killing. Parting bone just for the sake of cutting. Burning a church just to keep warm. It was all 'Flavor.'

"Why don't you take a seat," a voice said. It'd once belong to Mr. Fitzroy. *"Have a full-flavored cigarette?"*

" ... *flavor,*" Mr. Fitzroy's voice repeated.

"*..rr.rr.rr...rr.r.r..*" the chainsaw echoed.

SEVENTY-NINE

SOMEWHERE, across town, a man turned on his 88th television.

The storm got worse.

89.

More sleet and slush.

90.

Thunder threw sparks in the little front room of the house.

A mouth smiled. Muttered something about math being fun. Something about *'length times width times height.'*

The man'd spent the morning bricking the first wall.

The afternoon bricking the second.

The evening on the third.

He was walling himself in.

Bricking himself into a tomb made out of the space between stations. Using televisions as cinderblocks. Gravity as mortar.

He breathed deep. His lungs ached. He was tired. Slumped in his chair. He would rest. Build the fourth wall tomorrow. A pair of hands fumbled for a pack of smokes. A pair of lips went bobbing for a cigarette. A thumbnail struck a match.

His chair in the center of it all.

Thirty snowstorms ahead.

Thirty to the left.

Thirty to the right.

"thirty." A pair of teeth mumbled through a cigarette. *"thirty."* *"thirty."*

He dragged.

A pair of lips licked themselves, tasting the flavor of the storm.

A shape sunk into the chair. Cigarette clenched in his teeth. Ash falling on his shirt. Snow burying him alive.

He shivered.

He dragged—his only way to keep warm.

"Henry . . . ?"

His hand moved to his cigarette.

"You . . . *all* right . . . Henry?"

He dragged.

His son did not answer.

He could not tell him how he was.

EIGHTY

THE MAN who had been Boucher stood for a long while, breathing deep, lungs aching, looking down at the door. The chainsaw idling in the hall.

"*Flavor . . .*" said a voice.

The chainsaw tried to sound it out. "*..r.rr.rr....rr.r.r..rrr.*"

"*Flavor . . .*"

The merry-go-round blathered stupidly. "*..rr.rrr...r..r...r.rrr.*"

"*Flavor . . .*"

Downstairs, the chainsaw had been all growls, roars, like timberlands felled, bundled, rolled and crashed, lumberjacks exploding like atom bombs, gas cans jangling, cutting-chains shivering while engines neighed and trembled like brass-pole impaled horses, but here, in that hallway, holding still, looking at the door to Cattle Country, the chainsaw flickered like an old movie projector.

Spitting exhaust like a projector's beam.

"*Why don't you take a seat?*" Mr. Fitzroy's voice, on the other side of his door, muttered inanely.

The chainsaw muttered like a cigarette.

"*Have a full-flavoried cigarette?*"

Idling had filled the hall with smoke; pushed it to the corners, piled it to the ceiling.

The chainsaw simmered the hall.

Henry hugged himself.

Angus rested his knuckles on his mouth.

"Follow," said a voice. *"Follow ...*

Follow the Flavor."

The chainsaw stuttered in the drywall alley.

"have a full . . .

. . . . . . flavored . . .

. . . . cigarette . . .

. . . cigarette

. . cigarette

. cigarette"

The chainsaw chugged gasoline. Blew smoke down the hall.

The boys heard the man who once was Mr. Boucher drag. Stretch his lungs. Breathe in. Out. In. Out. Like a smoker. Exhaust down the throat, burnt fuel out the nose. His cigarette idling in the hallway. Something a man pull-started instead of lit up, but still a cigarette.

The shape breathed in.

Breathed out.

In with the smog.

Out with the soot.

"A full . . .

. . . flavored . . .

. . . . . . cigarette . . ."

The chainsaw making the wind of a giant cigarette.

". . . cigarette," said a voice.

The chainsaw spitting carcinogens.

The shape standing in the hall dragging gasoline, pushing it down his throat, shoving it out his nose.

In.

Out.

The carousel machinery gargling gasoline.

"a country . . .

. . . full . . .

. . . . . . of flavor . . ."

The boys knew, on the other side of their door, out in the hallway, behind that cardboard box head, the man once upon a time called Boucher licked his lips.

". . . flavor

. . flavor

. flavor"

Somehow, impossibly, the boys heard his stomach growl.

The hallway groaned, the cement weight of a man turned their way.

The motor in his hand shivered.

The hallway winced left, groused right.

A left foot fell.

A right foot landed.

Darkening the foot of their little plywood door with 237 pounds of shape.

The inbred rattle and pule of machinery clutched in his fist.

EIGHTY-ONE

THE FOOT of Angus's bedroom door was 3 a.m.

Boucher's boot-bending light-stomping center of gravity could be felt beyond the door.

His carousel rattling like dying grandmas.

Angus had his thumb fixed on a finger, waiting to crack a knuckle.

Henry had both hands on his face.

It was a duel.

The idiot machine chugged on the other side of the door.

c-h-u-g-g-
  c-h-u-g-g-
c-h-u-g-g-

Angus's eyes circled the room. The door. The dresser. The window. Henry's eyes looked to the door. The lock. The door.

c-h-u-g-g-
 c-h-u-g-g-
  c-h-u-g-g-

A thumb waited on a knuckle.
A pair of hands crept up a boy's face.

> *c-h-u-g-g-*
>   *c-h-u-g-g-*
> *c-h-u-g-g-*

'*As soon as it moves,*' thought a boy.
'*We'll wait forever, hold still, run him out of gas,*' thought another.

>   *c-h-u-g-g-*
> *c-h-u-g-g-*
> *c-h-u-g-g-*

Two fingers waited.
Inside the bedroom, a boy's on a knuckle.
Outside the bedroom, a man's on the throttle.
The chainsaw coughed itself low.

> *c-h-u-g-g-*
>   *c-h-u-g-g-*
>   *c-h-u-g-g-*

Inside, two boys on the floor looked up to the door.
Outside, a cardboard box stared down an understudy of a door.

>   *c-h-u-g-g-*
>   *c-h-u-g-g-*
>   *c-h-u-g-g-*

Inside, two boys held their breath.
Outside, a carousel hacked like lung disease.

c-h-u-g-g-
  c-h-u-g-g-
    c-h-u-g-g-

A cigarette fell, cherry-bombed the foot of the door.

A knuckle cracked.

The chainsaw screamed.

"Get to the window!" A boy yelled.

A door split. A cyclone of chain spun into the room. Spitting wind stolen from trees. Stinking of meat. Screaming of bone.

The dresser slammed against the door, pushed by Angus.

Angus looked back, yelled, "Out the window!"

Henry went.

Angus screamed, grabbed his hand. Could not see, there was too much blood. The teeth machine whining about having to eat more wood, smiling about having tasted boy. Half of Angus's finger lying on the floor. The machine squealing like a loose pig, bucking like a boar.

The door parted like the Red Sea.

The dresser fell apart like golden calves.

The machine barked like Moses.

EIGHTY-TWO

A PIECE OF WOOD FELL. The last gasp of the slaughtered door.

A finger eased off the throttle.

The handheld carousel paced down. Its calliope muttering a soft, tuneless tune.

A cardboard box head turned left, turned right.

Two round eye-holes dark as the space beneath a boy's bed.

No flat, slit-mouth to make expression.

Red flannel. Red overalls. Red boots.

The shape stood. Hulking over a boy's toy country. Chain machine sputtering. Window open. Curtains flapping in a Canadian séance.

Mr. Boucher stepped to the window.

Below, two boys, running for their lives.

The shape turned, surveyed this pissant little corner. A boy's life. Wood paneling. Crummy little twin bed. Fist marks in the wall. The chainsaw narrated the scene. Colloquial drawl. Plain as mud.

The box looked down.

There was half a boy's finger.

A hand picked it up. A couple black holes took it in. Behind cardboard a tongue tasted lips.

Down the hall a voice was saying, "*... Flavor ... Flavor ... Flavor ...*"
The hand twisted the finger, looked at it from another angle.
A stomach rumbled.
There was a trail of blood going out the window. Going out the
town.
"*. . . the filter won't get between a man and his flavor . . .*"
The fistful of merry-go-round was all tired steam,
cigarette ash blowing away.
The shape shut it off.
Vermont went to dead air.

EIGHTY-THREE

.01

   .02

   .03

   .04

A shape loomed over the pump.

Gasoline feeding the small carousel.

   .05

   .06

   .07

Tonight could be a long night.

   .08

   .09

   .10

Might as well top off the merry-go-round.

   .11

The machine spilled over. The shape took its box of horses and left.

The nozzle pumped on the ground.

   .12

.13
.14
.15
.16

EIGHTY-FOUR

HENRY HEAVED THE DOOR SHUT.

It was darker than blind in the train car.

"Light a match, lemme see it," Henry said.

"You don't need to see," Angus winced.

"I gotta see it."

"You a doctor? Gonna sew it shut?"

Henry didn't respond.

"Look, *ouch*, thanks Henry, *ahh*, but it's not bad."

"He just cut off your finger for Christ's sake!"

"Not the whole finger. *fuck*, It'll be fine ... once it stops bleeding."

"What if it doesn't?"

"Whaddya mean?"

"God, Angus, you think I didn't see it, gushing blood, all the way here, what if you bleed to death?"

"You can't bleed to death from losing, *ow*, part of a finger."

"Doesn't look like it."

"Hands bleed a lot. I read it somewhere."

Henry didn't respond.

The boys had no eyes in the dark, but somehow Henry's silence told Angus the look on his face.

"What?" Angus asked.

"*. . . Gushing blood, all the way here . . .*" Henry muttered liturgically.

"Huh?"

"*Gushing blood.*" Henry said softly, the words muted by something in the way, Angus could tell he had his hands over his mouth. " *. . . all the way here . . .*"

Angus heard Henry blink.

"Oh, God, Angus, we gotta stop that bleeding. Stop it now. Soon. Fast. And we gotta run, find someplace safe."

"Henry, *ouch*, slow down, why?"

Henry was standing now.

"Oh, God, Angus, we gotta go. Go now. Wait." Henry walked to the door, he put his ear to Vermont.

"What are you doing?"

"Fuck, Angus, we gotta fix that bleeding, then get the Hell outta here!"

"Where? This is the last safe place."

"Don't you see, he's just gonna follow the blood, by the moonlight, like a trail of breadcrumbs, like Hansel and Gretel. We're not safe. We gotta go. But we gotta fix your finger. Stop it from bleeding, stop it fast, so he can't follow us." Henry put his ear to the freight train door again.

"I think I hear him."

"I don't hear anything."

"He's gonna come. And it won't be a for finger. It'll be a foot, then a second, then when we're trying to crawl away it'll be hands, then when we're using stumps to try to thrash to safety he'll cut those off one by one, until we're just a torso sitting, bleeding, listening to him carve our arms and legs into a thousand pieces, lick his lips, listening to his stomach growl, until that voice on his shoulder says, '*not the limbs, but the body.*' And then he'll start carving us up from bottom to top, slicing us like deli meat, oh God, Angus he's gonna find us, and kill us, and not just kill us, but torture us because he's trying to feed himself something that can't fill a stomach! And if we don't stop that finger of yours from bleeding—"

"It'll stop."

"God! No! It won't. You think it'll stop when your heart starts pumping? You think it'll shut down and won't blow open again as soon as the chainsaw starts screaming through the woods?"

Henry was pacing now.

"How is the bleeding?"

Henry heard Angus peel back his blood-soaked shirt. He winced and didn't answer.

"Fuck. Fuck. Fuck!"

"Henry calm down."

"Calm down? Fuck. Calm down?! Fucking Mr. Boucher is out there wearing a cardboard box for a head and trying to butcher us like cows with a fucking chainsaw and all he's gotta do is follow the trail of blood! What are we gonna do?"

"Stop pacing."

"Stop bleeding!"

"Fuck you! I lost half my fucking finger pushing that dresser in front of the door trying to save us, don't tell me to stop bleeding."

Henry stopped pacing.

"Angus, I'm sorry. I'm just. I'm freaking out. God. What are we gonna do? We gotta call 911. Why didn't I think about this before?!"

"Because it won't work."

"What the hell are you talking about, it's 911."

"It's routed to the local authorities."

"Then we have to figure out how to reroute it."

"Henry, we can't call for help."

"Then we go for help. You know how to drive a car, right?"

"No."

"How hard can it be. Gas. Brake. Steering."

"Henry."

"Yeah, turn the ignition. Just need the keys."

"Henry."

"Keys in, turn ignition, umm ... shift from park to drive, I think. Then gas is forward, break is stop, and the wheel is simple, left is left, right is right. It's only 12 miles to Whitechapel and—

"Henry!!"

"What?"

"It's been, what? Four days, five days? I've lost count. And no one's eating. Everyone's starving. If we don't fix this tonight ... I'm not sure there will be a tomorrow. Besides ..."

"Besides what?"

"Besides ... you think the adults in town are any different from the adults across the county line? Across the state line? What do you think will happen when anyone comes here? With no church to contain it, they'll all get infected. You said it yourself. The town is drowning. This town is the swimming hole that killed you. Any adult who knows how to swim forgets once they jump in after you, after me. They get to town, they start drowning."

The train car was blank and quiet. Angus's finger dripping like a leaky pipe.

"Henry, anyone we bring here is gonna die.

And it'll be our fault.

You and I.

Murderers."

Vermont was awful quiet outside.

Henry sat down.

"What do we do?" Henry mumbled.

"I don't know," Angus said. Henry heard him shift his hand to his armpit. He groaned. A trickle of blood echoed through the train car.

"How is your hand?"

"Bloody."

"Is it slowing?"

"Not really."

Henry stood up again. Put his ear to the train car. Listened for the approaching carnival. Put an ear out for the marching music box.

"Nothing. Yet." He sat back down.

"How long does it take blood to clot?"

In the dark, Henry heard Angus shrug. "I dunno."

Henry stood up again. Pressed his ear to the train car.

Vermont didn't have much to say, as usual.

He paced around.

"Would you stop pacing?"

"I'm trying to think."

"Well you're making my heart beat. Just calm down."

"I am calm."

"*Sit* down."

Henry sat.

The small rust-holes of the boxcar catching the wind. Small whistles. Penny whistles. Dog whistles.

"How come it's different?" Henry asked.

"What?"

"TV, magazine ads, the record, radio static, ... chainsaw."

"Maybe they're all the same," Angus said. "Maybe it's all static."

"But ... it's like," Henry fished for the words. "Like, they're all going the same place, but on different roads."

Angus was listening.

"Why?" Henry asked.

Angus's hand itched for a cigarette. He didn't give it one.

"Their last names," Angus said quietly.

"Huh?"

"Their last names. Because what are they, really? Sinners that've traveled so long they've taken on the shape of their ancestral sins? Blood's just the motor oil of the body, dirty motor oil pumping through valves and atriums, oil that's got the scent of the road, the memory of the journey here. Grimy pieces of their ancestors scuttling through their veins, that's what. So why's a last name matter? It tells you what kind of dirt you got in your veins. So, your blood is half sludge and the church's cracked open like a walnut and you missed the last train to The Rapture, where you gonna go? Where your blood always knew it was meant to go. Take Fitzroy? That's easy. Fitz means bastard, a kid born on the wrong side of the bed sheets. And you got a kid what's bad news for his kingly dad, you got no choice to hide. Dirt like that in your veins, where you gonna go? Away, into the country. Muffled away in prairie land. You run, hide, forget your name or bury it in country. In this case, *Cattle Country*. Samuel, what were they once? If I can guess, Samuel, isn't that a figure from the Bible? Someone who heard the voice of God, clear and direct, you tell me, Henry, you've read the book. So now you got your old man pouring television static in his ear—the *opposite* of God's voice. Mr. Villanelle, isn't that a type of poem, do you know? So, rattling in his blood is the voice of poets and poetesses, people who took borrowed words and stretched them like animal hides over leather racks men were pleased to call form. And where is he now? Stretching himself over one simple, half-poem of a song, over and over and over. Mr. Revelli, probably means something in French, or Italian, but you don't have to speak either to put your thumb on it, probably came from the same place as reveler, so what were they once? Folks drinking today, letting tomorrow slide? Folks too concerned with having a good time to leave a footprint on the planet? Always in between celebrations. So where is he now, stuck between two places on a radio dial. Neither here nor there. Sheriff Vault? Was he descended from people who kept everything behind lock and key, buried in three-inches of steel? And maybe you get used to the safety from slamming safe doors, wake up one day and find your mind or heart or eyes in there for safe keeping. And where is he now? Locked away in his office tapping on his telephone like its a steel plate and combination lock he has to crack. Mr. Boucher, what was it? The long line of legitimate killers? Butchers of the French stockyards? An instinct that cutting things apart was how you fed your family? You tell me, you've seen him close. Ms. Hewett? Mr. Van Grohl? Pastor Phillips? God, what was it? We'll never know. They'll never tell. I've guessed, and probably guessed wrong on all of it."

The train car was quiet as forgotten steel.

The wind blowing one thousand tiny rust-holes at the same time.

"I wish I was driving a truck," Angus said suddenly. "Out there in the country. Somewhere on the roads. Not here, not there. Just always on the move. Going someplace, even if it were nowhere. Anywhere but here."

"Always being somewhere new is kinda like being nowhere, isn't it?" Henry asked.

"Maybe that's why it sounds good. Maybe we stayed here too long?"

The train car was stuffed full of silence.

"I wish I had my own house," Henry said. "Something I could buy myself. Pay for in cash. Enough money I could pay taxes 'til I die. Extra for utilities."

"You gonna hide in there?"

"No. Yes. Kinda. I mean, I'll come out. Go places. I just want to have my own place. For the end of the day. End of the week."

Angus nodded.

It was awful quiet.

Two boys. Nothing more to say. Lost deep in a state that was its own country. A state that had always been somewhere between a vow of silence and the public library hush. One boy fingering the cigarette burn his dad had given him. Another fingering the half of a finger he'd lost in chainsaw country.

"Wait, where are the cigarettes?" Henry asked.

"I dropped the backpack."

"What? We gotta go back, we gotta—"

"No, Henry, I dropped them on purpose."

"Wait, what?"

"I'm not a smoker anymore."

"Not a smoker?"

"I quit."

"Huh?"

"Cold turkey."

"No, I get it, but I don't understand."

"I don't want to smoke anymore."

"Why?"

"Because."

"Because why?"

"Because I don't."

"Why don't you?"

"Because I quit."

Henry breathed out. "What about your pockets?"

"Huh?"

"How many you got in your pocket?"

"Why does—"

"Just check."

Henry heard Angus shift in the dark. "Two."

"Gimme one."

"Why?"

"Just give it to me. And a match, you got matches?"

"Yes."

The boys bumbled hands in the dark.

Henry sliced a match.

Henry was lit up for the first time in ten minutes. Matchlight. With a cigarette hanging off his lips, muttering through the obstacle, "How do I do it?"

"Do what?"

"Light the cigarette."

"Henry, what—"

"Match is running low."

"You just light and suck."

"*Light and suck*," Henry mumbled.

The cigarette woke up angry. Henry hacked like a cold engine. The cigarette took it easy between his fingers. He held it naturally. Like smoking was always something his hand knew he must do.

The boy's lungs settled down.

He dragged again.

Coughed low.

Blew smoke.

"Henry, What are you doing?"

The freight car went dim, glowed warm, went dim, all the while ghosts wafted off the cigarette, tried to beeline for Heaven, got stuck on the ceiling.

In.

Out.

Up with the cigarette.

Down with the cigarette.

The motion understood somewhere in the boy's bones. Seared in his DNA. All his dad's practice had altered the boy's genes. Passed on to his son. He smoked his first cigarette like The Cattleman.

The cigarette lit the room.

Dimmed it down.

Up with the light.

Down with the glow.

Angus could hear the sizzle of a boy's tongue. Fire in a boy's lungs.

So *that's* what it sounds like.

"Hang on," Henry said. His voice was different. It had a kernel of sand stuck in it. A mite of grit. The boy stood, slipped out the door, came back with a piece of Vermont. Sat down.

"Put this between your teeth." He shoved a stick towards Angus.

"What? *Why?*"

Henry didn't say. He just ashed his cigarette. Held out the stick for Angus to bite.

"Henry?"

"Do it. Good. Ok, gimme your hand."

Henry stuck his cigarette on his lips. Held out his own hand to hold Angus's.

Waited patiently.

"No, your other hand."

The boys' hands met. One bled all over the others.

"Bite down."

Angus made a muffled noise.

Henry sucked his cigarette angry. "This is gonna hurt."

EIGHTY-FIVE

THE TRAIN CAR still echoed the grind and simmer of a boy's knuckle.

Smelt burnt.

Henry had taken in the smell once. Once was enough.

"How's your finger?" Henry asked for no good reason. He knew the answer.

"It stopped bleeding," Angus said.

"That's not what I meant, exactly."

"You know how it feels."

"Kinda. I'm not your dad," Henry said.

"Whaddya mean? A burn's a burn."

"It's different if your dad does it."

"A cigarette's a cigarette."

"Trust me," Henry replied.

They were in the dark.

Henry smelled again. Past the singed skin. A pea-sized pinch of humidity was in the air. He remembered that from when his dad had used him to stop his cigarette.

"You crying?" Henry asked.

"No."

Henry heard the boy wipe at his face. He didn't know a boy like Angus could cry.

"Figured you couldn't cry over anything."

"Everyone cries. Some people just don't let nobody see."

Henry's first cigarette was dead. Not ground out. Not fully smoked out. He'd done the deed then set it down where it died alone.

They were in the dark again.

"Let's go," Henry said.

"Go where?"

"Anywhere, now that you're not bleeding."

"But *where?*"

"We'll figure it out, I wanna get outta here before ..." Henry shut down his voice, put an ear out. There was only Vermont being quiet. Canada whispering to the trees. No chainsaw, not even miles away. "Come on, let's go."

The boys stood.

Henry heaved back the train door.

Shape filled the space. Square head. Machine hand. Henry didn't know it was possible to be so tall. It looked like he would never end.

It pull-started the merry-go-round.

EIGHTY-SIX

The shape filled the doorway.
    Chainsaw smoking like a cigarette.
    Blistering like TV static.
    Invading like a cigarette ad.
    Sizzling like the space between radio stations.
    Flat-lining like a dial-tone.
    Spinning like a record.

Burning, like the church.

The shape hung in the doorway like a screen door, stoking a gasoline-haunted wreck of a howl.
    The boys backed into the railcar.
      The boys stepped back.
        The boys stepped back.
          The boys felt river-cold wall against their spines.
    The merry-go-round spun wild.
    The music box ballerina pirouetted.

The shape torturing them with the private hymns of a
slaughterhouse.
The Butcher stepped in,
stepped forward,
stepped forward,
sticking his motor-pig, making it squeal.

S-Q-U-E-A-L!!!

Henry closed his eyes.
The sour breath of the pig machine lapping his face.
Stirring his hair.
Parting his eye lashes.

S-Q-U-E-A-L!!!!!!!

"Henry . . . ?" Mr. Samuel stood in the doorway.
The merry-go-round slowed.
A hand moved to a cigarette.
"You . . . all right . . . Henry?"
Mr. Samuel dragged.
The bottom half of his face lit low.
His son tried to answer.
His voice failed.
He could not tell his father how he was.
Mr. Samuel took a draw.
Stepped in.
His cigarette moving like a firefly.

And then he was a reservoir broken. A busted dam. Every second
of his life gushing loose. No longer human, Old Faithful dyed red,
Niagara run red, as The Butcher throttled one continuous run of
horses into him. There was a scream like a great mob of impaled
horses banging their lungs against a tin roof, their hooves against
steel floor, a pitch and whine as if a ballerina had broken all ten toes.
Henry shut his eyes, shouted, screamed against the scream, Angus
clapped a hand over the boy's mouth, but Henry shouted again, and
fought to get his hands at his ears to cut away the sound. The
chainsaw, like the Earth spinning, whipped away air, sunlight,

seasons and spirit, leaving only dark, cold, and meat. Dad flopped over and over and over, and at last twisted back on himself like a paper doll and lay there on the floor, an empty hand-puppet, trickling the sound of rain-gutters on rainy days.

The boys did not move.

Could not.

The moon spilling in the door, sketching out this husky, weighted shape. Square head. Machine hand. Carousel horses pacing themselves down, galloping, cantering, trotting, walking, idling in the pasture. Smoking cigarettes. Sleeping standing up.

The Butcher cut the engine. The carousel rocked to a halt like a roulette wheel.

Stood over the body.

Staring.

Listening to the sound of rain-gutters.

Staring down, licking lips, tasting flavor, trying to get fed.

His stomach growled.

It growled again.

It growled a third time. Or maybe it was all one long growl.

Mr. Samuel's body was just a colander now. All the liquid running off. Leaving only meat behind.

The Butcher's stomach growled one last time.

He jerked the chainsaw back to life.

Began carving meat.

Angus took Henry by the hand. The boys slipped out behind, while the shape was bent over carving what must have been a Thanksgiving turkey in his head.

On the floor of the freight train

Mr. Samuel's last cigarette burned itself out.

EIGHTY-SEVEN

Vermont started crying for the boy. Never meant for him to lose his dad. Vermont had done everything it could to make the world safe for a boy. But sometimes bad shit happens to good people in great places. Vermont understood that, it'd been around. Vermont knew it wasn't guilty. Had done all it could. But still felt like shit. If Vermont got a choice, it would have given the boys a sunrise. At 2 a.m. But, while Vermont may be bigger than the rest of us, it's just as helpless as any of us. They say God can do a 2 a.m. sunrise. But he didn't.

Angus had taken Henry home.

Why home?

He didn't know. But probably because every boy needs a home worse than he needs a girl. And his own had been invaded by chainsaws. Advertisements. Was balanced over a gas station.

Henry's house may have been the last home left in town.

Dad or not.

Henry sat on his bed.

Angus was out in the front room, shutting down the TVs.

... *86*

Another microburst died.

87.
The storm let up.
88.
The clouds parted.
89.
The wind carried it away.
90 ...

The last picture had shrunk to a tiny white dot. Shutting down the last T.V. was like burying Mr. Samuel.
The room didn't know what to do.
Without noise.

Angus stood in the living room, starting at ninety dead T.V.s.
Somewhere off in the house, shadows of rain moved on far windowpanes.
A boy listened to the downpour.
Angus walked through the dark, silent house. Down the hall to Henry's room. Henry did not look up. Sat on his bed, alone and broken.
"You're not crying?"
Henry didn't respond.
"You can cry, you know."
Henry didn't stir.
Angus sat down on the bed, next to Henry.
"I don't remember the day my mom died, but I cry about it sometimes."
He took Henry's hand. The boy didn't stop him.
"I cry about it a lot. I don't know what else you do with a broken heart. All you can do is cry. Crying is the best thing you can do sometimes."

The bedroom was quiet.

The rain did drum rolls on the roof.

"Vermont is crying for you, Henry." Angus pointed to the window. "I'm ..." Angus wiped at his eyes. "I'm crying with you. I was there once, when I was the chainsaw that killed my mom, and yeah, my mind doesn't remember it, but my body does, and I'm sorry Henry. I know what it's like to have this big fucking hole and I don't know what you do with it, but I've been trying to fucking fill it with tears all my life and I don't know if it works or not, but it's all you can do. You don't like life? You cry. Life shits on you? You cry. Crying is the best revenge. No one will admit that. No. Fuck life. Life serves you a big fucking bullet to your heart and wants to see you become numb, stale ... static. Stop showing emotion, stop caring, stop getting excited because you might come down, stop feeling sad because you're afraid you can't get up. Fuck that. Life throws all this shit at us because it's trying to turn you into a fucking accountant that can't feel anything good or bad and just runs the numbers because they are safe. You know what I say to that? Fuck you. You serve me shit, life? I'll cry. I'll prove I'm not afraid to feel what you got to offer. The more bullets you fire at my heart, the more tears I'll shed. Carve a grand canyon out of my chest, I'll turn it into a lake. I'll cry it full. You hear, Henry? Crying is how you win at life. Crying is how you beat the fucking game."

Angus squeezed Henry's hand.

Put his arm around the boy.

Tucked him into himself.

"Come on, Henry. Cry with me. You cry for your dad. I'll cry for my mom. Life serves us shit, we wipe our mouths and ask for seconds. Life breaks our hearts, we make a mobile out of the pieces. Have it ready before we even meet the women who will have our kids."

Tears were running free down Angus's face.

"She died because of me. My mom isn't here *because of* me. I killed her. She didn't want to be here with me. Couldn't stand to be in the same world at the same time with *me*, and that fucking hurts and I'm not gonna bottle that shit up and put it in jail behind my ribcage. I'm gonna let it all out and let it stream down my fucking cheeks and I don't care, because crying is how I know I'm alive. Crying is how we get revenge, Henry."

And Henry started sobbing into Angus's lap. Sobbing like Vermont outside, and Angus knew the only thing he could do anymore was to rub the boy's back. Somehow, he knew. In spite of not having a mother. Maybe, for *not* having a mother, he understood touch by never being touched. Knowing what he missed. He rubbed the boy's back like a mother would.

And the boy sobbed for ten minutes. Fifteen. Twenty. Thirty. Couldn't say anything. Could only break open, like a dam. And he cried, and cried. And cried. Until he was dry.

And then, shuddering in Angus's lap he muttered.

"I'm a fucking orphan."

And a boy's hand went over the other's back. Back and forth, like a mother's. Not understanding what to say. Not knowing the words to fix. Sensing touch was all he had. The wrong tool, to fix a big thing. But the only tool he had. Sensing it was the only way to patch something that couldn't be fixed.

"And you will be too. Your dad ..." Henry sobbed, fingering the cigarette burn his dad had given him. "We can't fix this!"

And Vermont cried with them.

Angus sat silently on the bed, Henry's tears falling on his legs, his hand rubbing the boy's back, staring out the window, watching the rain bead down the window, feeling the rain on his legs, inside, under roof, feeling his own weather pattern on his cheeks, his hand going up the boy's back, down the boy's back, listening to the boy cry, knowing the boy was getting his revenge with each tear shed, understanding revenge never made shit smell good.

He watched the rain,

waited till the boy had his fill of revenge.

Henry sat up.

Angus stood up. "I'll be right back."

Angus went in the next room. Mr. Samuel's bedroom.

Rummaged through a dresser. Came back with a photo. Thrust it in Henry's hands. Pointed.

"You're not an orphan."

Henry stared at the photo.

"You got a mom. Somewhere, out there. We'll find her."

"Find my mom?" Henry mumbled.

Angus nodded.

"We save my dad. We find your mom. We're not gonna be orphans."

EIGHTY-EIGHT

T HERE WAS one light on in town.

The 30-watt sunshine of Cattle Country.

The boys hid down the street, behind a building. Watching the gas station quietly cup a whole country.

The electric sun warmed the far room above the gas station.

Henry had an ear out, for the carousel.

Angus had an eye out, for the small sunshine of Cattle Country.

Otherwise the gas station was dark. Doing nothing by night. Rotting by millimeters.

Like Vermont was slowly getting its way.

"What are we gonna do?" Henry whispered.

"Get him out of there," Angus replied.

"How?!"

"I don't know ..." Angus's voice trailed off.

"Angus? Where are you going?"

But Angus was walking down the street. Like the boy was a moth, going where he always knew he must go.

Henry caught up with him. Angus was standing beneath the carport of the gas station, looking at a large pond of gasoline. Pumping machine carrying on—

$1,079.84

.85

.86

.87

"How much gas do you guys have?" Henry whispered.

"Twelve thousand gallons."

The nozzle pumped on the ground.

.88

.89

.90

The state wouldn't take it.

.91

.92

.93

The gasoline pooled up; a lake.

.94

The boys had never seen so much raw gasoline. Never smelt so much city. They could get high if they sniffed too freely.

.95

.96

.97

.98

.99

Angus hit the shut-off switch.

"He left it running?" Henry asked.

"I guess so."

Angus looked at the lake of urine from Detroit.

To the gas station.

To the power lines.

To the gas station.

To the puddle of Motor City piss.

"We need to blow it all up," he said.

"Wait, what?!"

"The gasoline. The electricity. We need to kill it all. People don't have power, don't have gas, maybe they'll wake up."

"Whoa, whoa, did you already forget what you said? '*You cut power temporarily, he hurts you temporarily. You cut power permanently ...*'"

"Kill or cure," Angus said.

"Kill or cure? What's that even mean?"

"Sometimes a doctor does a surgery that's dangerous because the patient is gonna die anyways."

"Yeah but ... what if *the kill* is us?"

Angus stared at the stuck meter.

$1,079.99

Angus flipped the switch back on. Vermont's newest lake began filling again.

$1,080.00

.01

.02

.03

"See that power pole?" Angus pointed.

.05

.06

"Yeah."

"You go get Mr. Boucher's axe from his farm. Cut this down like a tree. You know how to direct its fall? So it falls here." Angus pointed.

"In the puddle of gas?!"

Angus nodded.

"Electricity meets gasoline. We marry the two, they'll kill each other."

"What are you gonna do?"

Angus looked up at the dim high-noon of Cattle Country.

"Get my dad out."

.10

.11

.12

.13

EIGHTY-NINE

Henry stood in Boucher's field.

Wind blowing his footprints out of the grass.

At his feet was the axe.

Somehow he'd known he'd find it amongst the slaughter of trees.

It lay there, glinting moonlight. Like an overturned film projector, ready to be righted.

Ready for one more showing.

One last film.

NINETY

Angus stood in the doorway.
Cattle Country lit by its own petty sun.
Mr. Fitzroy didn't notice the boy on his border.

"there's plenty here to like," a tall voice muttered. It once belonged to Mr. Fitzroy *"flavor-filter-flip-open pack."*

Angus looked over the vast panoramic view.
Mountains.
Barns.
Open ranges.
Horses.

"the filter won't get between you and Cattle Country."

Men in cowboy hats.
Lassos.
Handsome faces pinned to cigarettes.

"Why don't you take a seat."

Red shirts.
Moustaches.
Denim.

"Have a full-flavored cigarette?"

Cupped hands.
First drags.
One cowboy, all alone, lost in no-man's land.

"Follow the flavor."

Angus tightened his right hand. It held a shovel.
Tightened his left. It held a rope.

"Come to Cattle Country."

NINETY-ONE

T-H-U-N-K

T-H-U-N-K

T-H-U-N-K

HENRY STOPPED CHOPPING.
Looked to the second floor of the gas station.
To the window.
The junk bond sun of Cattle Country.
It was quiet upstairs.
He put an ear out. Listening for the sound of incoming carnivals.
Merry-go-rounds. Calliopes. Ballerinas. Music boxes.
There was only the sound of the pumping station pissing in the street and the tick of the gasoline tab.

.33
.34

.35
.36

    T-H-U-N-K

     T-H-U-N-K

      T-H-U-N-K

NINETY-TWO

ANGUS STOOD in front of Mr. Fitzroy.

Once called dad.

He could not see a face. The lightbulb spill wouldn't let him.

The boy's left hand opened.

A rope fell to the ground. Cracked the paper soil of Cattle Country.

The silhouette in the chair stirred.

"Surgeon General's Warning."

Angus's right hand tightened on the shovel.

His left went up to the country sky of Cattle Country. He clutched a bird.

"Quitting Smoking Now Greatly Reduces Serious Risks To Your Health."

Bang!

The bird fell to the high-gloss ground of Cattle Country
Mr. Fitzroy rose,
the tall dark man,
towering above boy,

like a church pouring over a doll.
Angus holstered his left hand on the shovel.
Gripped it like a baseball bat.

NINETY-THREE

T-H-U-N-K
  T-H-U-N-K
    T-H-U-N-K

Henry stopped chopping.

Had he heard a noise?

The thud of a body?

He looked up to the window spilling Cattle Country sun.

It was quiet upstairs.

Henry looked out to Vermont. There was only his chopping walking back towards him.

He put an ear out.

Listening for the sound of radio static. Fly wings idling his way.

There was only the lapping of the gasoline lake.

The pumping station counting money.

.80

.81

.82

.83

Something was wrong.

Henry looked to the high window. He could not see in. The cloud-cover of Cattle Country had long ago drifted across it. A shadow stirred, projected on the papered window by the shit-rate lightbulb, some kind of bush-league film projector. There was a break in the clouds, patched quickly by an ad from a magazine ...

Henry looked to the street light.

He was close.

He didn't know how many more chops it would take, but less than when he'd started. Less than one hundred. Somehow, he knew that. Less than fifty. Somehow, he knew that too ... somewhere between one and thirty-three. Strangely, he knew that. The streetlight told him. The axe told him. The night told him. Vermont whispered it in his ear.

Behind him the gasoline pump marched to its logical conclusion...

.33
.34
.35
.36
.37
.38

The youngest lake in Vermont swelled. Pulled into tides by the moon.

The boy looked to the high window.

Something was wrong.

NINETY-FOUR

THE AXE RESTED against the mostly-hacked streetlight.

All alone.

Because the boy had crossed over to the convenience store. Passed through the store. Approached the stairs. Gone up the stairs, one by one. Looked down the hall. Approached the light-spill room. Peered around the corner.

There he stood in the doorway.

Catching a raw eyeful of Cattle Country.

Mr. Fitzroy sat. Shoved half in, and half out of the light. Comfortably lost in his armchair, the kind of coffin a man got in these parts. Cattle Country. There Mr. Fitzroy sat, dying by degrees. Taking in the eternal daylight of a country lit by matches, lightbulbs and lighters.

And there was Angus. Tied up. Lying in the processed, printed dirt.

Groggy.

Waking up.

Catching Henry's eyes. Flooding full of worry.

"You can breathe easy in Cattle Country," a voice said.

Angus's eyes went to the shovel. Henry's followed. There it lay in the brown Cattlemanian loam halfway between Henry and Mr. Fitzroy.

Henry shook his head.

Angus nodded yes.

Henry could not fail here. One boy was down. Tied up. Waiting for the mercy of a starvation death. Waiting for his own strange dad to rot of hunger in that chair, and then die himself like-father-like-son. But that would be the merciful death, the hoped-for death. Because the real death would be the trampling of merry-go-round horses. Licked by painted lions. When the man with the cardboard-box head found two boys lying and tied up in the dirt of Cattle Country, he would open his music box and the ballerina would dance. The machine would smoke a cigarette, and Mr. Fitzroy would breath in, lungfuls of pure Cattle Country air, muttering something about *'flavor,' 'flavor,' 'flavor,'* listening to the soundtrack of a chainsaw glide in a great and greedy horror-film motion. If Henry ended up tied up too ... who would stop this?

Angus's eyes shot to the shovel.

Henry shook his head.

Angus nodded fiercely.

Henry breathed the dark.

Angus's eyes striking fire on the metal shovel.

Henry shaking his head.

Yes said Angus's eyes.

No said Henry's.

Do it said Angus's.

I can't.

Henry looked around the country. Saw a thousand different mustached men and their burnt lungs just over a hill. A thousand different burdened lips off in the prairie.

Cattle Country.

Vermont Country.

They hated each other.

Standing on the border, Henry had a foot in both. In Cattleman, the electric sun simmered on low, and a thousand men lived and died alone. In Vermont, thunder turned, sleeping in the clouds. The wind played house-cracks like a harmonica.

This town wasn't big enough for the both of them.

Had cleared out.

It was only the two left.

Cattleman held its breath.

Vermont blew air.

"No other country breathes so rich, smokes as smooth."

Angus slammed his gaze on the shovel.

Henry nodded reluctantly.

Cattleman was a stalled landscape.

Vermont big-bad-wolfing the house.

Angus bit at the dirt of Cattle Country. Pulled at the seams with his teeth. Ripped a hole in the country. The shadow hulked into silhouette. Stood. Tall, lean, lank. All shape and fists and heaving lungs. Billowing in, billowing out. Fists clenched. A boot landed on Angus's throat. Pressing down like a gas pedal. Angus choked and gasped.

The boy's windpipe pinched off.

Mr. Fitzroy's black shape urging boot on.

The shape of a man hung over the boy. Breathing in. Breathing out. The same mechanical motion of all citizens of Cattle Country. *"... inhale 'til your heart's full ..."*

NINETY-FIVE

Behind the man, the Cattle Country soil made a soft, muffled noise.

There was the rustle of dry leaves.
The turning of library book pages.
The extraction of a fortune from a cookie.
The crackling of a campfire.

The shape orbiting above Angus turned. A boy stood in the middle of the room. Lost in the Country.

"... most low tar cigarettes taste like dirt ..."

The boy did not respond.

Cattle Country held its breath.
Vermont howled outside.

The shape took a step forward.
The boy blinked.

The shape sniffed.
The boy swallowed.

The shape took another step. Stirring up the paper-dust. A pair of lips licked themselves.
The boy's eyes darted to the shovel, halfway between them.
The shape looked.
Both knew where they would meet.

The shape breathed in.
Breathed out.
Like a citizen of Cattleman.
The boy stirred. The Country rustled.
The shape grew taller.

A small foot stepped forward.
The shape growled.
The foot stepped back.

The two stared each other down.
If the boy'd had a hat, he would have adjusted it.

The boy licked his lips.
Fluttered fingers.
Eyes on the shovel.
Halfway between them. In the dirt of Cattle Country.

The shape cracked a knuckle.
The boy ground a foot into the paper dirt.
The shape grew taller.

There might have been the sound of a whip-crack, and the shape was already there. Looking up, with a fistful of shovel. Gripping it like a gun, ready to sling. But there was no boy within range.
The boy had not moved. Except for one arm. Raised.

The shape could not see what he was holding.
The boy pulled his hand.

click.

The room felt the minute stirrings of moth wings.

In the dark, the man's eyes widened.
The boy had the chain of the ceiling fan.
He pulled it two more times

click.
click.

NINETY-SIX

The three clicks echoed through Cattle Country.
Like gunshots running over the hills.
Echoing through the valley.
Above, the ceiling fan turned, like clouds shifting suddenly.

A breeze picked up.

The shape stood, a defeated gunslinger, clutching the shovel, this stupid, useless thing. A shovel could bury a boy, but couldn't do shit to the wind.

The wind came down.

The boy stood still, pull-chain in hand. On his third pull he'd broken it off.
It fell from his hand.
Rustled in the paper-soil of Cattle Country.

A storm was coming. It could no longer be stopped.

Above, in the clouds of this fake country, thunder turned in the circling machine.

The first citizen of Cattle Country shuddered in the wind.

The second let out a paper-flap murmur.

A twister was coming.

The storm rolled over the hills.

The citizenry began to wheel about, wanted to run for storm cellars, wished to take cover, but could only stand still, lighting cigarettes.

Men stood stoking cigarettes.

Horses bucked wildly.

Barns waited to be destroyed.

This was the end of the world.

The chorus of freaks; models and Cattlemen, citizens of this cigarette country, trapped in their mid and late century mass-market-oil-paintings began to twist and turn.

The shape dropped the shovel. Jolted to a flapping page.

Thrust left hand to a loosening corner.

But it was too late. He only had two hands.

Suddenly this cyclone touched down in the dead center of Cattle Country. A twister with the spin of a chainsaw, meant to cut the world in two. The nicotine freaks flapped, flipped, flitted. Bent in half. Were ripped into the storm. Circled boy and man. The tornado circling round and round the room, again and again, chainsawing each page and citizen loose. Tossing their two dimensional bodies into the storm, spinning around boy, man, disintegrating country.

Citizen spiraling.

Pages flapping.

Birds pulled into weather patterns.

Screaming like radio static, fly wings, the sound of plastic grocery sacks.

The boy flung open a window.

The bucolic pastures broke like a nest of snakes.

The boy let fly a pane of glass.

The pastoral vistas spilled like a bag of sugar.

Soil torn loose.

Sky cracked.

The horizon came to an end.

With a hiss of cigarettes, swirl of smoke, the staked-out country unraveled, slithered, snapped, whipped boy and man with frictional paper-cuts.

Paper circling the room.

Round and round.

Around boy.

Around man.

The whole made-up citizenry convulsed, parted bones, stampeded north, south, east, west, loosed of wall, floor, ceiling, the law of scotch tape, loosed above all of Cattle Country.

Citizens fell into the cracked soil.

Were carried away by tornados.

Flung to far countries.

The boy's eyes shadowed this way, then that, pulled by the cave-in of country, the flap of paper, echoes of old and always meaningless earthquakes. The going gone of make-believe souls. Red shirt, firm moustache, matchbook fishers, rope wranglers, horse riders, mustang tamers, lung arsonists. Going, carried away all. Red barns, chap-wearing men, bucking broncos. Never coming back. Chiseled jaw, going, smooth smoker, gone. Over. Quiet. Gone. All gone. Never coming back.

There should have been the sound of a mountain range slid to ruin,

as a whole country collapsed,

but there was only the sound of magazine paper rustling in the crosswinds.

The wind blowing footprints out of the room.

NINETY-SEVEN

MR. FITZROY FELL to the floor. Caught by his once upon a time carpet that had been forgotten beneath the soil of Cattle Country.

The sound of metal reverberating like a tuning fork.

Henry dropped the shovel.

Stray cigarette ads ran around him. He looked around the room. Watched the chunks of old country running loose like plastic sacks in big cities. He'd never witnessed the death of a country. Even a made-up one. The boy's eye caught one single page, in a storm of paper going out the window. Red shirt. Cigarette itching a man's lip. And the wind took the man away and Henry saw the hatted man and his burnt religion go over a hill.

There was only the sound of the ceiling fan.

A few dead citizens flapping in the wind.

The light bulb simmering.

A single magazine ad fell, an abandoned toy in a room.

"Henry!"

The boys met eyes.

"Untie me!"

'Yes,' Henry thought. *'I'm still in Vermont.'* He'd almost forgotten.

"God. Henry, how'd you know to do that?" Angus rubbed his free wrists.

"Do what?"

"*That*," Angus said, as he started tying up his father.

"What ... did I do?" Henry asked.

"Something." Angus finished the knot.

"*Something?*"

"Something good," Angus nodded. "You were like a gunslinger."

"... is he ok?"

Angus put his ear to dad's breath. "I think so." The boy stood up. Suddenly he realized he was standing over his father. He'd never stood here before. The roles had always been reversed. But here he was, high above, dad off far below. He understood if he made a fist, he'd know what it felt like. He made a fist. So this is what it felt like to be his dad. Stoking a fist, orbiting above, way off far below him dad looked very, very ... different. And Angus, above, gazing down, eyes dry, fist clenched, thought, Oh my god, why didn't I see it before? Dad's small. Dad's very small indeed.

Henry sensing the shift of the world called out, "Angus?"

No answer.

"Are *you* ok?"

The boy swallowed once. His face burnt by unbelief.

"I feel ... tall."

Henry nodded, like he'd known it all along.

The ceiling fan stirred above.

"Angus?"

"Yeah."

"How do we get out of here?"

Angus walked to the open window. Looked down at the old '71 Cutlass.

"We drive."

"Drive? Do you have your license?"

"No." Angus fished the keys out of his dad's pockets.

"Do you know how to drive?"

"Two pedals, and a wheel. Not much to know. You said it yourself."

"What about your dad?"

"We'll throw him in the trunk with some food and a flashlight 'til we get clear."

Henry looked out the window. Somehow he knew he would be saying goodbye to Vermont tonight. Goodbye to Vermont forever.

"You realize once we go, there's no coming back."

"I don't wanna come back," Angus said.

"Even if you wanted to," Henry replied.

"What do you mean?"

"I have a feeling January Vermont's a town that won't be on any map come tomorrow."

Angus nodded, like he'd known it all along.

"Angus?"

"Yeah."

"What about the rest of the town? We just can't leave them ..."

Angus looked down at the power pole Henry'd been chopping.

"That thing's got phone lines on it too."

"Huh?"

"Phone. Power." Angus's eyes went to the lake of gasoline. "Gas." He licked his lips. "We blow it all up, people won't have any choice but to wake up."

Henry nodded.

"It's all we can do for 'em. It's more than God's done." Angus breathed out. "We get my dad in the trunk. We get the car down the road. We finish chopping down that power pole, then we get the Hell outta here. Drive and never look back."

"Where are we gonna go?"

Angus looked to the trees. Like he was saying goodbye to Vermont too.

"Someplace with a lot of churches."

"Texas?"

Angus shrugged.

"Nashville?"

"Who knows."

"I saw once on TV Nashville is the largest producer of Bibles."

"France," Angus said. "The whole goddamn country's Catholic."

"You can't drive to France," Henry said.

"I know that."

"Besides," Henry said.

"Besides what?"

"Old churches ..."

"Have more time to collect sin, yeah, you're right. We need a place with young churches, and a lot of 'em," Angus said.

"Somewhere in the Bible Belt."

"No." Angus walked to the far window, looked west. "Utah."

"Sure, The Mormons," Henry said. "They love churches. Got one on every street corner they say."

"And they're just about the youngest churches you can find on the planet. And they don't just got churches. They got temples."

"What are those?"

"Who knows, but it's a second line of defense."

"And Joseph Smith was born here," Henry said.

"What?"

"In Vermont."

Angus nodded, looking west. "Maybe that's why."

"Why what?"

"He built a lot of churches."

NINETY-EIGHT

.62

.63

.64

.65

.66

The gasoline pump shut off.

$1,534.66

Fifteen hundred dollars worth of the modern world lapped behind them. Vermont's newest, quietest, smallest lake. The wind caught the surface. Made it ripple. Brought the smell to the boys. Tried to get them high. Angus snorted it out. Henry pushed it clear. The boys looked to the silent pumping machine. Listened to the lake. Somehow knew, in the back of their minds, this smell is where it had all began. *This* was the scent ripping the nostrils of Pastor Phillips when he sliced a match and set his church on fire. Gasoline is where it all began.

"Smells like gas," Henry said.

"It *is* gas," Angus explained.

"Why did it shut off?"

"No more gas to pump."

"Where's it come from?"

"Tanks in the ground."

Vermont was still. The lake rippled in the breeze.

Henry looked at his watch.

3:33

"What do you think he did in between?" Henry asked.

"Huh?"

"The night he burnt down the church. He buys the gas at dinnertime but doesn't torch the church 'til 3 in the morning."

"I don't know."

"He must have done *something* …" Henry whispered.

Vermont was awful quiet. Like it knew.

Angus didn't reply.

The car sat in an abandoned, empty gas station.

A father lay, tied up in the trunk.

And two boys watched this tiny lake, sniffing the wet air, understanding this was the tide come to drown their town, and their only hope was to try to use it to baptize the town instead.

"How many people you think went to get baptized, and drown instead?" Henry asked.

"In town?"

"Ever."

"In the country?" Angus asked.

"In the world."

Angus scrunched his lips "Couple hundred. Maybe a thousand."

Vermont threw a breeze.

"You ready to go?" Angus asked.

Henry pulled the picture from his pocket. "So this is what a mother looked like."

"Do you think she's there?"

"Where?"

"In Utah?"

"Who knows, but Utah is safe a place as any to start. Besides, they got genealogists there."

"What's that?"

"Like a cross between a bloodhound and a private detective. They'll sniff her out."

Angus put another six pack of Coke in the trunk. The trunk was all gas station food and dad. Chips, candy, beef jerky and cans of Coke. And dad.

"How's he gonna eat?" Henry asked.

"We untie him."

Angus cut the knots free. Mr. Fitzroy groaned. Angus turned on his flashlight, threw it in, shut the trunk.

"How do we know when it'll be safe to let him out?"

"We're in a church parking lot, in Utah."

Angus handed Henry the axe. "I'll move the car down the street." Then the car was turn-keyed like some kind of grown-up toy, and Angus drove it slowly off into 3 a.m. and Henry stood there axe in hand looking at the job he had to finish, this power pole chewed by the doggish-teeth of the axe, waiting to be broken in two, to fall, to light a fire that would cause gasoline to kill power and power to kill electricity, so the whole town of people wouldn't be able to slumber to the big city lullaby anymore.

The gasoline lake lapped.

Power stirred above on the crucifix.

The gas station light hummed blue electricity.

An axe rested beside a boy's leg.

The moon suddenly filled itself full. Like it knew it was time to be a projector again. Its favorite silver screen had come to catch the film.

Henry made fists along the haft.

Hefted the axe.

It caught the moon above his head.

He swung once.

T-H-U-N-K

He swung again.

T-H-U-N-K

He raised the axe.
Swung again.
But there was no *thunk*, at least not to his ears. It was muscled out by another bigger, badder sound. The drop-start of a music box. The ripping of a merry-go-round.
Horses spooked to life.
The ballerina woke-up dancing.

NINETY-NINE

The chainsaw cried like a newborn.

Dr. Boucher the delivery surgeon.

Knocked its lungs.

Slapped its butt.

Henry's spine didn't need to turn to see the chainsaw smoking. Did not need to twist to see a tall dark man printed on dewy gasoline air.

But Henry did turn.

His ears made him do it.

There! Standing across the street *in the dead center of the murdered church,* framed between the tallest alley of trees, all cardboard box head and silhouette, the man once upon a time called Mr. Boucher. Chainsaw in fist. Breathing in, breathing out, dragging carousel-exhaust through his lungs. His merry-go-round choking on clean Vermont air. Spitting out ghosts. Hacking like an end-of-life emphysemiac. Spurting like it was struggling to stay alive. A horse with a punctured lung. A ballerina having a seizure.

The handheld corral of carnival horses snorted.

Rustled in their carousel.

The shape did not whip the stallions. The horses did not run around the track, neighing wildly. They hung impaled by brass poles, flashing panic-colored teeth parading fright-colored eyes. Wafting the scent of Mr. Samuel. Dripping pared down years. Waiting to splatter Vermont red. The wind carried the odor. Shoved it up Henry's nostrils.

The horses still in their spines.

The ballerina taking five.

The horses nickered to themselves.

The ballerina rummaged for a cigarette.

Over the distance Henry couldn't hear it, over the sputtering of the handheld cough-factory Henry couldn't *possibly* have heard it, but somehow he knew Boucher's stomach was growling. Screaming in starvation. Eating itself.

Some kind of liquid trickling from the horses' teeth.

Henry understood it was the last broth of his dad.

The tall dark man.

Bronchitis-machine crouping at Vermont.

Vermont silence was a type of church service. A sacramental meeting. Something that can't be interrupted. Except with a chainsaw.

This was any American town run to its logical conclusion—

A chainsaw.

Screaming stories about leveled forests, dead American myths, slaughtered Americana. Butchered iconography. The chainsaw was the dead-end of the American experience. *Feed a country a steady diet of gasoline, this is what you get. Pour static in your ears, this is where we go.* Barns of slivered cow skulls, abandoned gasoline stations, human slaughterhouses in freight cars, merry-go-rounds throwing scraps of dead dads. Cracked spines of little churches in northeast Vermont. It was all there. In that handheld machine. On the rise. Coughing at Henry Samuel.

The tall dark man stood,

stomach growling,
Carousel smoking ...

... Vermont too afraid to say shit

The man threw back his merry-go-round to buck at the moon.
The horses ran 'round.
The ballerina spun in circles.
Down the street Angus turned his head
Beneath the power pole Henry Samuel winced.
Speared horses screamed.
The ballerina forced to sing.
Angus ran towards.
Henry's hands tighten on the axe.
And Mr. Boucher ran their way, carousel high above his cardboard head exploding with music.

Angus. Henry. Mr. Boucher. The only three people in chainsaw country.

ONE HUNDRED

Henry struck the power pole.
  Angus's right foot landed.
  Mr. Boucher throttled.

Another swing. Wood-chips flew.
  A boy's left foot landed.
  A throttle was fingered again. Screamed in delight.

Again axe sunk into wood. Again pole spat teeth.
  A right foot stretched.
  The ballerina cried out.

Axe sliced cold Vermont air.
  A left foot strained.
  The merry-go-round squealed.

The power pole groaned, but did not break.
  A boy's right foot touched down.
  A roar of horses spun Henry's way.

Henry spun.
Stared.

All he saw was a run of teeth.

Angus's foot hit street. "Duck!" he screamed.

Henry dropped. Heard a whole string of American horses go over him. Saw, out of the corner of his shut eyes, a pair of wild eyes jerk around in holes cut out of cardboard box. The carousel chewed and spat. Henry covered his head. Wood flew like meteors. There was a buckle. A snap. The sound of some cyclopean back breaking in two. And then nothing but a sound like the soft crackle of a lit cigarette as the power pole began to listen to gravity.

Fell in love.

The severed power pole came down, with all the hate and noise and spark and sizzle and frying-ire of television static, of cigarette ads, of dying phone lines, of slowing record players. Kissed the lake of gasoline. Set off a chain reaction. Vermont had never seen so much daylight. Not even in July.

... Henry felt someone helping him up. The flames came into view. This is what it looked like, the night the church burnt down, something a lot like this. There was no light left in this corner of Vermont. Just the raw incandescence of fire, the gas station burning up, away. Going away. Gone. Soon to sleep, but right now on fire. Burning. Like a religion going up in smoke. Plenty to burn. Lots of fuel. It'd burn through the night. But not through the winter, no, Vermont wouldn't let it.

"On your feet!" Angus ordered.

"Huh?" Henry groaned.

"Let's go!" Angus said. Henry could hear the worry in his voice.

And then they were stumbling, remembering what it was like to be boys, on their feet, trying to run. Trying to remember how to run, how did it go? Left foot, right foot? That's right, left, right, left, right. Henry was beginning to remember. He looked back.

"Don't look back," Angus warned.

But it was too late.

Henry'd already seen a shape rise. Some kind of shadow puppet on the wall of flames.

> *It dropped chainsaw left,*
> *ripped chord right.*
>
> *Brass pole impaled horses*
> *screamed.*

It should have sounded familiar. The boys'd heard it come to life before. Like any other chainsaw. But it didn't. It understood its food supply had just been burnt to shit. It screamed like a starving baby. The machine cried like the newborn it was. There was no nipple or nozzle to keep it alive. No mother. Only a couple of boys and sweet meat.

> *Mr. Boucher ran, chainsaw overhead.*
> *A bent shape on a wall of fire.*

"Don't look back," Angus panted.

They didn't need to look. The machine would tell them where it was. Shrilling raw tunes off gasoline.

The boys ran.

> *The shape spurred the string of stallions.*
> *Beat the ballerina.*

"There's the car!" Angus pointed.

There was only Vermont, the merry-go-round and the boys.

The moon came out.

The boys let it tow them its way.

> *The teeth machine tilted in the tides of gasoline.*

"He's catching up," Henry panicked.

"Keep running!"

The machine swallowed spit.
Ran full tilt.

The car, closer, closer. And then the car went from being there, to here. And the boys pawing at handles, shutting doors, pushing locks, Angus fumbling keys, trying to stick them in the ignition, wrong key, wrong key, shaking and Henry watching the shape of a man with a box head and a chainsaw held high grow in the rear window against the backdrop of a burning gone gas station.

"Oh Shit!" Henry cringed.

"Shut up!" Angus sweated. Fumbled keys.

The silhouette growing tall behind. Mr. Boucher revving
merry-go-round.
Letting it idle.
Throttling it open.
Letting out the clutch.

Angus found the key. It slipped the ignition.

Henry gripped the seat, the cold leather squealed, but no one heard it.

The chainsaw; stallions in full stampede.

The car roared to life.

The driver's side window shattered.

A cyclone of chain spun into the car. Angus slid to the floor. The carousel reached for him. Sang about free rides on the merry-go-round. The run of horses trampled the leather. The machine remembered the taste of cow. Cushion and leather caught in its teeth.

"Shift it to drive!!" Angus yelled.

Henry reached. The chopping machine came for his hand. Spun

madly above Angus's head. The carousel, spun a hundred, two hundred, three hundred impossible times, the horses ran wild, tasting car seat, steering wheel, window, door, odometer, upholstery, anything they could get their teeth on. Swamping the night air to summer heat by friction of sun metal brass, carrying the scent of the spinning earth. The carousel tilted this way, lurched that way. The boys fled to the corners, hid in their spines. Horses running 'round. Snorting through their nose. Squealing through their teeth. The ballerina spinning herself to death, pushing opera through her teeth, the toothed smile on the shuddering dancer spun, spun, fast, fast, faster still, very fast, fastest of all, oh dear god fast! Henry tried again, the horses bit at his fingers. The merry-go-round pitched towards him. Spun down towards Angus. Leather and foam stormed inside the car like television static. Chainsaw smoking like a sauna. Dancing! Oil! Red! Smoke! Metal! Rrrrr! From the floor of the car, Angus pulled the door handle, the door popped open, he kicked it, the man stumbled back.

Angus threw his hand to the brake.

Henry slapped the gear shift to drive.

Angus slammed the gas.

The car squealed rubber.

The chainsaw lurched for them. The teeth machine chewed sparks all along the side of the car.

The car shot into the night.

Mr. Boucher left behind.

Angus did not let off the gas.

Neither did Mr. Boucher.
 Growing distant.
  Screaming, through his chainsaw.
   Swinging it in circles.
    Spinning like a music box ballerina.
     A horse on a carousel.

RRRRR!
RRRRR!
RRRRR!
RRRRR!
RRRRR!
RRRRR!

rrrrr!

rrrrr!

rrrrr!

rrrrr!

rrrrr!

rrrrr!

rrrrr!

rrrrr!

The chainsaw became a screw rattling in a tin can.

The car took the road.

Tires combine-harvesting the autumn leaves, spitting country road, spinning the boys away from Vermont.

The engine purred.

Angus came off the floor. Took over the remnants of the steering wheel.

Henry sat back in his seat.

Looked out the window at the lights-off country, the far country, the deep country, the straggling territory off in night country, nowhere country, out-country on the backside of nowhere, autumn country, bedtime country, shut-off in the night, shut-up in the sticks, the far flung place, the gone country, a place so dim they had to pipe in daylight.

The engine purred.

They were saying goodbye to Vermont with a gas pedal.

Vermont didn't say shit as they left.

No goodbye.

No farewell.

CLOSING

Angus Fitzroy, age sixteen, Henry Samuel, age 13. Two of three atheists left in January, Vermont. Two boys with a strong belief in The Rapture, but little faith in God. Soon to cross the county line and cart every last non-believer out of a town that won't be on any map come morning. Boys who will never try their hand at the one thing most men try at some point in their life—*going home.* Two boys who will someday grow into men and when asked the question of where they grew up will only ever say something like *'back east.'* And maybe, just maybe, in the slim shade of possibilities, if it's the right or wrong night, and if the man is too drunk or too sober, he might admit it was the state of Vermont. Two someday-future-men who will never say, no matter how hard they're pressed, even though for them it's literally true, the most common phrase the expats of the American small town are apt to say. *'It was a small town, you've probably never heard of it.'* And maybe, someday, like most men, sometime, on some quiet neighborhood street lined with elms and serviced by milkmen, Angus Fitzroy will hear his neighbor start up the appropriate power tool to take down a dead tree. And perhaps like most men, sometime, on some night, Henry Samuel will find himself in the wrong bar at the wrong time with the TV tuned to the wrong channel broadcasting any non-descript home improvement show. But unlike most men they'll look up from what they're doing and listen to the distant music of a chainsaw and hear the static of the people and places of their past—January, Vermont the little town that stopped broadcasting its signal to the world like a boarded-up radio station. A little town that lost its way after losing its church. Worn, weather-beaten and lived in as far as small towns go. A place neighbor still talked to neighbor and the pastor never lost count of his flock. Once upon a time, a place a man named Boucher treated his cows like family, a man named Samuel seldom turned on his TV, and a man named Fitzroy would never immigrate beyond his country's star-spangled borders. Where the leaves almost touched over the streets, fresh milk was just down the road, the sweet smell of tobacco let you know the mail had arrived, and a white picket fence existed on Sam Samuel's to-do list somewhere in the years to come.

ACKNOWLEDGMENTS

If you've gotten this far, you have one person to thank. Michael Dolan. Without him, this book would not be in your hands. Thank you, Michael, for believing in this book, plucking it from the dusty corners of my hard drive, and understanding it on levels I didn't.

To my mother who showed me how to fall in love with books, words, the arts in all forms. How to work. How to focus. How to aim high.

My father who taught me how to laugh, how to have a soft heart, and how to be a boy.

Linda Q for always caring for me as one of her own, showing me how big a heart can be, and to both of them for taking me to Vermont many times. More Vermont trips to come.

Annette W. for being a friend when I needed a friend, a second mother when I needed a second mother, and a poet when I needed a poet.

Annette E. for holding my hand while I figure out who I am.

Chris Chambers, official mayor of October Town, for his friendship, poetry, guidance, pats on the back, cheerleading, arcane horrors, encouragements, imagination, tolerance of the cigarette smoke I bring into the room, neverminding the carousel grease in the carpet, for starting a cigarette company, and most of all for never losing faith in my writing.

Justin and Jarin for being patrons of my art, my best friends, and sitting on my bedroom floor when I am low.

Nate for always believing in me as long as I can remember, and making me feel less alone in the world just by talking.

Mike Snow for being an Ancho, Ancho, Anch.

To my bestie for being so brave. So strong. So sun-shiny. You inspire me. I believe in you, I love you.

Boopy for being my best buddy, wellspring of laughter, letting me be part of her family, and engaging cinchmode on occasion. Rally B. Luv U 4 Ever.

Bog for always reminding me when I forget that I am lovable, handsome, talented, and to believe in myself.

The twins for letting me be a kid one more time. Dudes, game on.

Makenna, Keilani – I love you.

Jamestown and Kelsey for always attending readings, friends in tow, and bringing Stray Country to the old country.

The King's English Writing Group for putting up with the horror in hopes there might be some poetry. You've always made me feel like a writer. Rebecca. Brian. Maggie. Mugoux. Christine (Audrey). Sarah. Holly. Peggy. Karen. Celeste. Diane. Pete. Steve. Another Rebecca.

Meggie for telling me 'the world deserves your stories' when I'd lost hope.

C.M. Heidicker for showing me how to edit. How to stand up. How to share stories. And for believing I have a voice somewhere in the back of my throat.

To Margo, who always made space in her heart for my books.

Wayne Herring, my oldest fan.

Michon Vanderpoel for helping a stranger, twice over.

Victoria Straus who made the path forward less scary.

Alex Nader for setting my heart at ease.

Summer Mull for being on this journey since the beginning.

Tiffany Mull for eating the candy.

Johnny Kats for believing.

Linda Taylor – I hope you're smiling wherever you are.

Jamie Chambliss whose advice helped hemstitch this book to the good earth.

Christopher Steffan for believing I meant business, even when I didn't know the business of words.

Jessy Poole for not letting me disappear.

LBK & Michelle for always being in the audience, even if you're the only ones.

To Jeff Adams for bragging about this book to everyone he knows and carrying the excitement for me when I am afraid to.

Everyone at PWS & Jasmine and Meglet.

Cody Allen for putting a box on his head.

Jonny Lawless for being a reader.

Keith McMillan for being the first to make it out of January, VT.

Turkey for explaining my stories to my sister.

Joshy – love you brother.

K Collings you said you'd find it on the shelf someday, and the way you said it, I knew you believed it.

Davey Davis for encouraging me to layer my voice on top of my voice.

Marti J, you know what you did.

John Day for the years.

Ben A. for trudging through a whole book.

Missy for her excitement and Kali for her marshmallow paws.

Meatball and Mud for somewhat loving me.

Nat in the Hat for reminding me "it's ok to feel."

Walt Hunter for being Walt. For giving me a school bus. For making a thoroughbred.

And to KC January, poet laureate of my heart, patron saint of Vermont.

STRAY COUNTRY PODCAST

There is a country beyond that which is known to humankind. A stray country. A country that exists west of October. Whose borders are somewhere between midnight train whistles and the distant howl of a dog. A country that lies somewhere in the stitched and jittering static between radio stations. A country that drifts through America like a travelling salesman, but every now and then stops to nest on a small town. A small church. A single street.

And maybe, just maybe, some kind of delayed radio broadcast you've stuffed in your ears.

Look for STRAY COUNTRY on all major and minor podcast platforms.

ABOUT THE AUTHOR

C.K. Turner is an inkslinger from the Salt Engine. C.K. writes about cigarettes, carousel grease and factories, the prayers of the manufacturing class, ghosts, and the piggish machinery that is the modern world.

Social Media

Instagram: @c.k._turner
Twitter: @CKTurnerAuthor
Facebook: C.K.TurnerAuthor
www.ckturner.com